THE
NIGHT WIND'S PROMISE

THE
NIGHT WIND'S PROMISE

THE NIGHT WIND SAGA, VOLUME III

BY

VARICK VANARDY

Edited and with a Foreword by Christopher R. Yates

The Borgo Press
An Imprint of Wildside Press

MMVII

CONTENTS

A NOTE ON THE TEXT

The text of this novel was reproduced from the 1914 bound edition of *The Night Wind's Promise* published by G. W. Dillingham Company, New York, through The Frank A. Munsey Co., 1914. Other than correcting for obvious, unintentional grammatical or typographical errors, this reproduction remains true to the letter and spirit of the 1914 G. W. Dillingham bound text.

ACKNOWLEDGMENTS

This project would not be possible without the cooperation of the Old Worthington Library, Worthington, Ohio and the interlibrary loan service that put the original text of *The Night Wind's Promise* in my hands. Thanks, also, to the Quarles Library at Spelman College, Atlanta, Georgia whose wonderfully preserved copy of *The Night Wind's Promise* was the source of this edition. My sincere thanks go to Steve Miller for the original cover scan that graces this book and to Bill Thom and Phil Stephenson-Payne for introductions to Mr. Miller. This cover is a digital copy of the cover of *All-Story Weekly* magazine, October 26, 1918, wherein one of the Night Wind installments originally appeared.

Special thanks to the following folks (with a plug for their websites) for their efforts to circulate my inquiries about this project among the pulp community and their kind words of support:

Michael Ward: www.magazineart.org,
Bill Thom: http://members.cox.net/comingattractions/,
Jack Suto: http://www.vintagelibrary.com/index.php,
Phil Stephensen-Payne: http://www.philsp.com/,
George A. Vanderburgh: http://www.batteredbox.com/,
Ed Hulse: http://www.geocities.com/poppub/,
John Pelan: http://www.darksidepress.com/,
Guy Gordon: http://24.131.35.146:8080/SFAuthors.htm,
Georges T. Dodds: http://www.erbzine.com/mag18/1802.html.

FOREWORD

Let's be brutally honest about Bingham Harvard, alias the Night Wind. While not as shallow as Superman, his stories are not the work of Shakespeare. He is a product of his time; that is, although virtuous and moral, a wee bit patronizing to the ladies and non-WASP males.

Bing has a "short fuse." In *Lady of the Night Wind*, his own wife had less fear of the villain; "It was Bingham Harvard's temper that she feared—the tremendous, the superhuman, the awful strength, and the uncontrollable temper when once roused, of the man who had once borne the *alias*, The Night Wind."

He did save his good friend's life once in *Alias "The Night Wind,"* but thereafter his feats of super-strength were reserved for saving himself from arrest or overtly baiting police officers to attack him.

Bingham Harvard's internal conflict is not particularly earth-shattering; it is his struggle not to use his power to kill people. His commitment not to literally tear apart Lieutenant Rodney Rushton is the major dramatic turning point of *Alias "The Night Wind."* The "promise" in this installment, *The Night Wind's Promise*, is that Bing vouches to his wife that he will not beat the villain to death with his own hands. We're not grappling here with the conflicts oft used in great literature: the search for personal fulfillment or identity.

The Night Wind stories are not psychologically weighty epics on the human condition. But neither are they four-color fantasies. "Internal conflict" in the average superhero comic-book only meant an upset stomach. This is true from the medium's birth (roughly 1938) to at least the early 1980s.

The Night Wind series is not for the very young, or immature, and likewise is not on the reading lists of the profoundly cerebral. But these are the extremes of the reading audience.

The rest of us—most of us—fall in between, and may really enjoy the world of Bingham Harvard, alias the Night Wind.

In fact, Bingham Harvard, the personally flawed man with grossly understated (or at least rarely resorted to) super-strength is the most popular heroic archetype today.

Even the characters catering to the imaginations of the very young and profoundly cerebral are being reintroduced as more like the Night Wind. Comic-book superheroes are being rapidly reinvented as less flashy, more fleshy—that is, more depth of character. Multi-dimensional protagonists of staid fiction are being reinvented as heroes, or at least persons of vastly, above-normal abilities.

Remember *The Adventures of Superman* television series, starring George Reeves (1952-1958)? This show was little more, and sometimes less than a cut and dried four-color comic-book episode done-up in live action. Since then, we have had *Lois & Clark* (1993-1997)—whose title alone makes it clear that this show is as much, or more, about the relationship of Lois Lane and Clark Kent than about Superman. How about *Smallville* (2001-ongoing)? Another Superman incarnation on the small screen minus the "man," (it's all about young Clark Kent), and sans much of the "super" (absolutely no costumes and even acts of super heroism are NOT guaranteed in every episode).

The long-underwear crowd are now the subject of lengthy works of prose. Literature—yes, I said "literature"—starring comic-book superheroes have exploded in the last decade. For example, the hardcover release of *It's Superman* (Chronicle Books, 2005) by Tom De Haven checks-in at 384 pages; most of which is dedicated to character development and setting than fisticuffs between über-dudes. *The Forensic Files of Batman* (I Books, Inc., 2004) by Doug Moench portrays a Batman in the vein of a mildly eccentric Sherlock Holmes with a focus more on practical crime-scene investigation and less on cowls and codpieces.

The move from pajamas to drama has been most successfully portrayed in the cinema. The Spider-Man series of movies (Sony Pictures, 2002, 2004, 2007) is as much about Peter Parker's relationship with Mary Jane and his own inner-demons than it is a duke-fest with supervillains. *Batman Begins* (Warner Brothers Pictures, 2005) didn't even give the audience a costume to ogle until late in the show, instead favoring an "origin" back story. The Blade (New Line Cinema, 1998, 2002, 2004) and X-Men films (20th Century Fox,

2000, 2003, 2006) didn't bother with costumes at all—instead favoring angst ridden protagonists bent on revenge (Blade) or the preservation of their species (X-Men) over saving humanity. All of these big screen features have been huge commercial successes.

Not only do the superhero screenplays have more depth than one might expect from a comic-book story, the actors and actresses cast for the roles of hero or villain are increasingly drawn from a pool of Academy Award winners—known, first, for their dramatic roles on the big screen, not necessarily for their ability to fit into a spandex bodysuit.

Jack Nicholson, Kevin Spacey, Gene Hackman, Geoffrey Rush, Nicholas Cage, Anna Paquin, Tommy Lee Jones, Faye Dunaway, Halle Berry, Sean Connery, George Clooney and Christopher Walken all have portrayed either the antagonist or protagonist in a variety of comic-books-to-film features. All likewise have an Oscar for Best Actor or Actress or Best Supporting Actor or Actress from some prior or subsequent dramatic film role.

Possibly lacking the physique for the lead role as a superhero or a supervillain, Academy Award winners have, and continue to take even supporting roles in superhero movies. These include the roles of the hero's love interest, mentor, parent, civilian assistant, etc. The list of supporting performers is at least as impressive as the role-call for the lead actors/actresses: Anthony Hopkins, Catherine Zeta Jones, Eva Marie Saint, Marlon Brando, Jennifer Connelly, Frances McDormand, Michael Caine, Morgan Freeman, Nicole Kidman, and Kim Basinger.

Strangely, fictional characters previously endowed with literary devices such as drama and depth are being re-invented as more like the comic-book's unitard clan.

Oscar Wilde's Dorian Gray, from 1890 (Figure 1), is now a superhero. His immortality is now a superpower (not merely a literary device) in the smashingly successful *League of Extraordinary Gentlemen* comic-book by Alan Moore and less-than-smashingly-successful *League of Extraordinary Gentlemen* motion picture (20th Century Fox, 2003).

Van Helsing; that old Dutch guy who got a sentence or two of description in Bram Stoker's *Dracula* is a leather clad, cross-bow slinging, loner saving the world from monsters in *Van Helsing* the movie (Universal Pictures, 2004). To be precise, for marketing purposes, Stoker's Abraham Van Helsing was changed to Gabriel Van Helsing.

Let's not forget Allan Quatermain (H. Rider Haggard, *King Solomon's Mines*, 1885), Nina Harker (Bram Stoker, *Dracula*, 1897), Professor Griffin (H.G. Wells, *The Invisible Man*, 1897), Dr. Jekyll and Mr. Hyde (Robert Lewis Stevenson, *The Strange Case of Dr. Jekyll and Mr. Hyde*, 1886), Captain Nemo (Jules Verne, *20,000 Leagues Under the Sea*, 1870, Figure 2) as a TEAM of world-saving crime-fighters. All from the comic-book turned movie *The League of Extraordinary Gentlemen*.

Not to be outdone, Sherlock Holmes (Arthur Conan Doyle, *A Study in Scarlet*, 1887) and Tarzan (in his more genteel guise as Lord Greystoke) (Edgar Rice Burroughs, *Tarzan of the Apes*, 1912) have formed their own "League of Heroes" in a series of novels begun in France in 1998 and slowly getting English adaptations in the United States (*The League of Heroes*, Xavier Maumejean, adapted by Manuella Chevalier, Black Coat Press, 2005).

Even Mary Shelley's *Frankenstein; or, The Modern Prometheus* (1818),—a warning to modern man not to tinker with nature— is taken down a few pegs from the rarified air of "classic literature" to comic-book superhero. In *Batman—Castle of the Bat* (DC Comics, 1995), by Jack C. Harris, Batman is portrayed as Victor Frankenstein. In *The Superman Monster* (DC Comics, 1999), by Dan Abnett, The Man of Steel *is* Frankenstein's monster.

Stoker's *Dracula* is, and has been, a supervillain in comic-books. He has had a blood-feud with Batman, (*Red Rain*, DC Comics, 1992; *Bloodstorm*, DC Comics, 1994) Spider-Man, (*Spider-Man v. Dracula*, Marvel Comics, 1993) and the X-Men, (*X-Men v. Dracula*, Marvel Comics, 1993, *X-Men: Apocalypse/Dracula*, Marvel Comics, 2006) among others. The Count even scored his own comic-book title: *Tomb of Dracula* (Marvel Comics, 1972—1979) wherein he tried to take a bite out of Spider-Man and the Silver Surfer. In fact, *Tomb of Dracula* spawned its own superhero, Blade, who went on to his own comic-book title, trilogy of movies and television series. (*Tomb of Dracula #10*, Marvel Comics, 1973).

Of course there are the heroic characters that hail neither from comic-books or aged literature but have their origins in the middle ground between the two. *The Wild Cards* series of novels spanned from 1986 to present day and portray deeply flawed personalities choosing a virtually infinite variety of paths (from the purely selfish to the altruistic) in the use of their super-human gifts. No costumes. No damsels in distress. The continued existence of humanity does not depend on them.

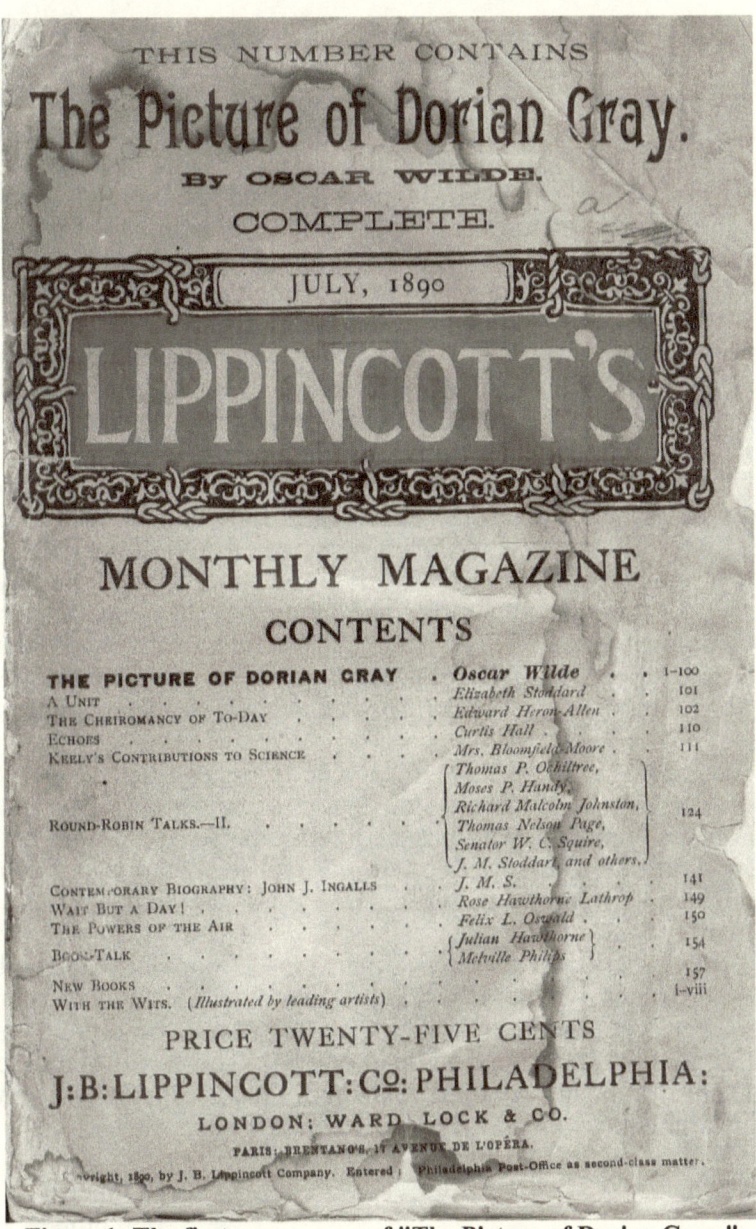

THIS NUMBER CONTAINS

The Picture of Dorian Gray.

By OSCAR WILDE.

COMPLETE.

JULY, 1890

LIPPINCOTT'S

MONTHLY MAGAZINE

CONTENTS

PRICE TWENTY-FIVE CENTS

J·B·LIPPINCOTT·CO·PHILADELPHIA·

LONDON: WARD LOCK & CO.

PARIS: BRENTANO'S, 17 AVENUE DE L'OPÉRA

Copyright, 1890, by J. B. Lippincott Company. Entered at Philadelphia Post-Office as second-class matter.

Figure 1: The first appearance of "The Picture of Dorian Gray."

The television series *Heroes*, although fashioned with input from comic-book superhero scribes, is merely a quilt of lives of otherwise average "Joes" and "Janes" dealing with new-found super abilities. "Daring-maybe" as opposed to "daring-do." Buffy the Vampire Slayer is likewise a supernaturally endowed girl (in the creepy house) next door, who just happens to feed the public's appetite through a motion picture, a long-running television series with successful spin-offs as well as an ongoing line of prose novels.

Why does everyone want to be Bingham Harvard, alias the Night Wind? Why the shift from extremely flashy or extremely dusty to mainstream? My best guess is simply commercial demographics—what sells. Who read *The Picture of Dorian Gray*? The older, more educated set. Who PRESENTLY reads *The Picture of Dorian Gray*? Few, if anyone. Who read *The League of Extraordinary Gentlemen* wherein Dorian Gray is re-invented? The vastly larger crowd of younger, school-aged folks. Who reads Superman comics? Young males. Who watches *Smallville*? Young males AND females. Media of all stripes—comic-books, novels, television, motion pictures—have run for the oh-so-lucrative and vast 18 to 35 male and female demographic market. To do so they are forced to "dumb down" some of their more intellectual products while simultaneously upping the maturity level of their once adolescent or teenaged-targeted media.

Maybe it is a bit on the cynical side to suggest that some mega-corporation's bottom line is the cause of metaphorically putting flesh on the bones of child-targeted comic-books or dusting off old fiction. Truth be told, I am certain the real explanation is far more complicated, far more nuanced. But does the explanation matter…really?

Superhero fiction in three dimensions is popular…again, both prose and other media. It's not just about action and adventure, scene after scene anymore—it is as much about the drama, inner-conflict as it is about head-to-head combat. The Night Wind series got it right…almost a hundred years ago. This is especially true with this installment, *The Night Wind's Promise*. Enjoy.

—Christopher R. Yates
September, 2006

Figure 2: Alphonse de Neuville's portrayal of the famous battle with the giant squid in "Vingt mille lieues sous les mers" ["20,000 Leagues Under the Sea"] (1866-1869)

CHAPTER I

THE BEGINNING OF A FELONY

When Eulogio Llorente, photographer, having his studio in the *calle* Plateros Secundo, in the city of Mexico, posed Anderson Van Cleve, the American contractor, mine-owner and speculator, for his picture that bright September day, and imparted certain apparently unimportant information to the man who accompanied Van Cleve, he little thought that he was assisting in the commission of a crime that was soon thereafter to be enacted in the city of New York, four thousand miles away. Yet it was so. Let the fact of it and the circumstances surrounding it be a warning to all who read these words against the giving of unnecessary professional information to chance acquaintances, no matter how well recommended or in whose company they may happen to be.

The circumstances happened in this way:

Two hours before the pictures were taken, Van Cleve, seated in his sumptuous office in the *calle* Gante, a few doors in from the *calle* San Francisco, near the Plazuela de Guardiola, turned quickly in his swivel-chair when the door opened.

"Hello, Chilton!" he exclaimed cordially, getting upon his feet and extending his hand to a tall, bearded, sun-and-wind-burned man of little more than half his own age, who came breezily and briskly forward and grasped the proffered hand of his employer.

"You are on time, I see," Van Cleve went on genially. "That is your long suit, Chilton. Sit down. Help yourself to a cigar. I have got a lot to say to you. Otherwise I would not have brought you in from Guerrero in such haste. But, first, how are my affairs going forward in Guerrero?"

16

"Badly, Mr. Van Cleve," was the reply. "The work is at a stand-still everywhere. The *peons* won't work. They sneak away or boldly walk out, by twos and tens and scores, to join their fortunes with the Federals, or the Constitutionalists, or the Zapatistas—it makes mighty small difference to them which so long as they feel assured of getting paid. But it leaves us in the hole just the same."

Van Cleve nodded understandingly. He was a tall, spare man, smooth-shaved, past sixty, rather handsome and distinguished-looking for one of his years, and with scarcely a gray hair to show among the almost black ones that crowned his fine head. He was dressed conventionally and immaculately; a polished silk hat rested upon the top of the desk at which he reseated himself after shaking hands with his superintendent and general manager.

Holbrook Chilton, in contrast, wore the *charo* costume of the Guerrero mountaineer, save for the American-made, laced, civil-engineer's boots, hobnailed and effective for use among the mountains. He made a picturesque figure when he came into the room attired in the tight-fitting leather trousers, decorated with silver coins down each outer seam, beginning at the waist with pesos, of which there were several, and growing smaller in groups of threes until they disappeared beneath his boot-tops in *realés* and *médios*. And his huge Mexican sombrero that he tossed to the top of the desk beside the silk hat of his employer was the real thing, and could not have cost less than sixty Mexican pesos.

One might well have mistaken him for a native of the Guerrean Mountains. It seemed impossible that the skin of a white man could be tanned to such a deep brown, even by the out-of-door life that Chilton had been living during the two and a half years he had been Anderson Van Cleve's general manager. And, as proved to be the case later on, the sun and wind and exposure to the elements *had not* done all of it. Art, dexterously applied, had been called upon to aid in the making of that leathery-brown complexion.

He was thirty-five, and he looked fifty-five in some ways; and yet if he had told you that he was fifty-five you would have doubted it. If you had sought to describe him to another you would have said that he was either a very old-looking young man or an equally young-looking old man. All of us have seen and known such characters.

As the two men were seated facing each other Van Cleve appeared scarcely older than his employee, save for the expression of the eyes and some shallow wrinkles here and there which age inevitably bestows.

"Bad, eh?" Van Cleve responded without a pause and nodded his head again. "I know it," he went on. "It was bad enough very soon after Don Porfirio, of *la mano dura*, left the country; it has been growing worse ever since. It is about the limit, now, Chilton."

"It sure is, Mr. Van Cleve," the manager replied with emphasis.

"That is why I sent for you to come in," the employer added.

Chilton nodded his head without replying.

"I have decided to get out of the country," Van Cleve continued after a short pause. "I am going to fly the coop, Chilton. America— little old New York, where I was born and where I lived until I was thirty-five—is good enough for me. I haven't been back there but twice in all that time since then."

"If you leave Mexico now, Mr. Van Cleve, the act will entail great sacrifices of money and property, will it not?" Chilton asked tritely.

"Naturally; more as to property than as to cash, however," was the reply. "For the last three years or more I have been sending all the money I could spare from my undertakings here out of the country."

"Indeed?" said Chilton, with a rising inflection.

Van Cleve nodded sagely.

"I have quite a substantial balance to my credit in the Centropolis Bank in New York," he said retrospectively; "quite a substantial balance. I have been sending large sums there as rapidly as I could do so. The president of that bank is an old friend of mine. We were boys together, schoolmates, and all that. Later, we were associated more or less intimately in business affairs. He went into his father's bank, and when the old man died succeeded him. I entered a broker's office in the 'Street.' Then, at thirty-five, I pulled up stakes and came here. I haven't seen Sterling Chester but twice in thirty years, and the last time was ten years ago."

"Who?"

"Chester—Sterling Chester, the president of the Centropolis Bank that I just now mentioned. Or rather he *was* the president of it until very recently. The last report I received, which the bank annually sends out to its depositors, stated that Bingham Harvard has succeeded to the presidency and that Chester had retired."

Chilton coughed spasmodically. He explained after a moment that the smoke from his cigar had strangled him when he inhaled it.

"I suppose, Mr. Van Cleve, that you are well acquainted with him also, this—er—Bingham Harvard?" he inquired.

"No. As a matter of fact, I am not," the contractor-miner replied. "I did not see him the last time I was back, ten years ago, although I heard enough about him. Chester is very fond of him. He is an adopted son."

"Then—you have never seen him? He has never seen you, Mr. Van Cleve?"

"Oh, yes! I saw him when I went back the first time. But that was more than twenty years ago. Bingham Harvard was only a child then."

"I see."

Chilton spoke half to his employer, half to himself, to judge by his manner and tone. He spoke as if he were weighing some possibilities that had occurred to him.

"Of course there are many others in the city who could readily identify you?" he inquired.

"Eh—what? I don't know about that, Chilton. Almost all of my old friends and acquaintances in New York are dead, or have gone to other parts of the world, the same as I have. My best friend, next to Chester, died three or four years ago."

"Who was that?"

"His name was Brian Clancy. He had a son, Tom, who succeeded him in business. But I have not seen *him* since he was five years old, although he has transacted some business for me lately. But he wouldn't remember me. But, good heavens! I won't have any trouble about the identification, Chilton. There is my signature for one thing. For another, there is my letter-file. It contains carbon copies of every letter I have sent to Chester and of every transaction I have had with his bank. I shall take all of those letters with me, of course. They recite the amounts I have sent to the bank from time to time, the dates when they were sent, and all that."

"Still, Mr. Van Cleve. By the way, when do you propose to start?"

"Within the week. To-day is Monday. I shall leave Mexico City by or before Saturday."

"Might I make a suggestion—er—relative to your proper identification when you do arrive in New York?" Chilton asked tentatively.

"Certainly. What is it?"

"More than likely you will regard it as an entirely unnecessary proceeding, but certainly it can do no harm; and it might turn out to your advantage, Mr. Van Cleve."

"Well, let's hear what it is."

"Just a matter of precaution and—er—preparation. Go to a photographer and have some pictures made of yourself. Enclose one or two of them with the letter you will write to the new president of the Centropolis Bank, informing him of your expected arrival there. Retain copies of the pictures you send in the letter and carry them with you when you leave here."

"Have them with you, as well as the letters you have mentioned, when you present yourself at the bank. It is only a suggestion, but you may find it advantageous to be well prepared. New York bankers are sticklers for identifications."

"It's a good idea, Chilton. I'll do it. Come along with me. I'll attend to it at once. Do you know of a photographer anywhere near here?"

"There is one on the Second Plateros, two squares down, whose sign I have seen frequently. Llorente is his name, I think. Shall we go there—now?"

"Yes. There is no time like the present, Chilton."

Eulogio Llorente received the two men effusively. Business had been miserably dull with him for many months. He was glad of a customer, and particularly of one so well known and respected in the city of Mexico as the Señor Van Cleve.

Several negatives were exposed, front face, profile, quarter-view, *et cetera*. Mr. Van Cleve was told that the proofs would be ready for his inspection the following morning, and he promised to send for them. Then he turned to Chilton as they were about to go out.

"Why don't you have *your* picture taken, too, now that we are here?" he asked smilingly.

"I? Oh, no!" Chilton exclaimed in mock dismay. "Looking as I do now? Not on your life! It's as much as I can stand to look at myself in a mirror when I have to. But a photograph? To perpetuate this travesty of myself? No, I thank you!"

"But, really, Chilton, you are quite picturesque in that *charo* costume."

"Huh! Do you suppose I'd wear it if it were not for the impression it makes upon the *peons* I have to boss? That reminds me: I'm out of a job, I suppose."

"I am afraid so, Chilton." They were on the street again. "It is rather short notice, isn't it? Come to me to-morrow morning early and I'll settle up with you—and I will add three months' salary to your account because of the short notice."

"Thank you, Mr. Van Cleve. Shall I stop at Llorente's on my way, and bring the proofs to you?"

"Yes; I wish you would."

They parted at the corner of Colegio Viego. Chilton remained standing where his employer left him for several moments. Then, turning abruptly, he sought a near-by store that dealt in all sorts of photographic supplies, where he parted with very nearly all the cash he possessed, exchanging it for the paraphernalia he required to carry out his plans. He was quite heavily laden when he came out again and sought the rooms where he lived when he was in the city—in the *calle* San Felipe Neri. But there was a smug smile of satisfaction in his countenance, nevertheless. Chilton had succeeded in purchasing the very things he wanted.

CHAPTER II

THE PLOTTING OF HOLBROOK CHILTON

An Irishman once explained that to make a cannon you take a hole and surround it with iron. In the city of Mexico residences are built in much the same way; they select a hole and build a house around it. There is one wide entrance from the street, big enough for horse and carriages to pass through. This leads into a *patio*, or court, from which, after mounting three or four steps to a narrow balcony which surrounds it, entrance is obtained to the various rooms. If the house is two stories high—they are rarely more than that—the stairs to the second one are nearly always from the balcony in the *patio*.

The house in San Felipi Neri Street, where Chilton had his two rooms that fronted on the thoroughfare, was two stories high. His rooms were in the upper story. It was there that he took the supplies he had purchased immediately after he parted with Van Cleve. Those supplies, when he had relieved himself of the burden of them, proved to consist of a very excellent camera, capable of producing four-and-a-half by five-and-a-half pictures; a tripod, all the paraphernalia and ingredients necessary for flash-lights, some carefully selected plates—and, in fact, everything that was necessary to carry out the designs that the schemer had in mind.

And it was an evidence of Chilton's quick wit and resourcefulness, of his ingenuity and his daring, that the present "scheme" had not occurred to him even remotely until during the conversation between him and his employer at the latter's office in *calle* Gante. In fact, not until the question of proper identification when Van Cleve should arrive in New York City came up. Then, with the brilliancy of one of the flash-lights he had just purchased, the idea took possession of him, and he did not lack anything of the necessary effrontery to carry it out, once it had taken tangible form in his mind. Nor did he lose any time after he had locked himself inside the larger of his two rooms in San Felipi Neri Street.

Sheets taken from a bureau drawer, tacked against the wall, created a background. The crex rug on the floor was sufficiently like a studio interior. The furniture in the room was carefully removed from the vision of the camera. One of his purchases was a sixteen-foot rubber tube, with a bulb at the end, for working the shutter, and that he laid along the floor from the camera and tripod to the point at which he intended to stand. Close beside the tripod he placed a small table, and upon that he arranged his flash-light, with which he connected a short fuse that would consume approximately half a minute in burning.

When everything was arranged to his entire satisfaction—the preparations consumed nearly an hour—he took his stand in front of the lens at the proper distance from it and directly facing the camera's eye. Chilton wore his sombrero, pushed slightly backward on his head, and his filled cartridge-belt and holsters; and a Mexican saddle rested upon the floor beside him. This last was included in the picture for the sake of offsetting any possibility that the rubber tube that connected with the shutter might appear upon the negative. He stood with his hands behind him, and one of them grasped the bulb of the tube. He watched the burning fuse narrowly, and at precisely the instant when the flash came he squeezed it. That process, with exactly the same view of himself, he repeated twice. Then he made three more exposures of himself in the same manner, with the difference that he removed the sombrero and turned his left profile toward the camera's eye.

Six exposures in all he made, and he had not a doubt that from the lot there would certainly be one out of each three that would fulfill his wishes; and because he had found opportunity to observe and measure while he was at the studio of Llorente that afternoon he knew that they would be of the requisite dimensions.

Simultaneously with the ignition of that last flash-light Chilton plainly heard the sound of carriage-wheels and hoof-beats on the pavement outside, and they stopped directly under his window. An inner sense—intuitiveness possibly—warned him instantly of the bare possibility that his employer, Van Cleve, might be seeking him again, and, without pausing to readjust anything in the room, he passed quickly outside of it upon the balcony that surrounded the *patio*, closing and locking the door after him and dropping the key into his pocket.

In all of the older Mexico City houses the rooms do not connect from one to another; access between them is had only by passing to the balcony, and thence to the room adjoining, as Chilton did then. He stepped quickly into the other one of his two rooms, threw his sombrero upon the bed, dropped his cartridge-belt and the two "forty-fours" beside it, seated himself upon a chair that faced the window—night had fallen before he began his flash-light experiences—and was busily engaged in rolling himself a cigarette when a quick, distinct rapping sounded against the panel of the door.

"¡*Venga aca*!" he called out without turning his head, as if he supposed the summons was made by the *mozo de la casa*, or the *portero*. He twisted the cigarette into proper shape and applied a *cerillo* to it just as the door opened and the voice of Van Cleve greeted him.

Chilton sprang instantly to his feet with a well-simulated exclamation of surprise.

"Hello!" he said in feigned astonishment. "You, Mr. Van Cleve? I was just wondering what to do with myself to-night. I am mighty glad you looked me up. Did you forget something that you wished to say to me this afternoon?"

"No. I came around to ask you to go to dinner with me, if you hadn't already gone—which, I perceive, you have not," was the smiling response. "Will you come?"

"Sure."

"We will go to the Concordia. I don't want anybody to get the idea that I am contemplating a sudden departure from the country. See?"

Chilton nodded.

"I have got some maps and blue-prints in my pocket," Van Cleve continued. "We will pretend to be examining them and discussing them while we wait for our order to be filled at the restaurant, Chilton. That will reassure anybody who happens to be watching us; for I suppose you know that all Americans are observed rather closely just now, particularly those who might take it into their heads to leave the country suddenly and carry a wad of money away with them. So, come along. Oh, by the way—"

"Yes?" Chilton replied.

"That next room there is yours also, isn't it?" and he jerked his head toward the room from whence the flash-light had shown for an instant as he stepped down from his carriage.

"It used to be," the manager replied indifferently. "I gave it up before I went away the last time. There was no use in keeping two rooms, you know."

"Certainly not. Who occupies it now?"

"I really don't know, Mr. Van Cleve. A young Mexican civil engineer came to look at it the day I gave it up, but I don't know whether he took it or not. Why?"

"Oh, nothing. There was a flash of light through the window just as I got down from my carriage at the door. I thought it was one of your rooms, and when I came in here and discovered you rolling a cigarette I thought the circumstance an odd one."

"Perhaps the young engineer is making blue-prints," Chilton suggested, donning his sombrero. And Van Cleve was entirely satisfied with that explanation, although it was destined that within a few weeks the circumstance was to be recalled to his mind very vividly indeed—after his arrival in the city of New York.

They drove together to the Concordia Restaurant. They dined together sumptuously. They pored over maps and blue-prints while waiting for their order to be filled. They came away from the restaurant together after eleven o'clock, having spent nearly three hours at table, and they parted at the door, Chilton having insisted upon walking home.

It was nearly dawn before he sought any rest, for with blankets and many large sheets of orange-colored paper he had to manufacture a "dark-room" in which to develop the negatives he had made, and it came out that one negative out of each three he had taken was very nearly perfect. Thus far Chilton's schemes had prospered. There remained the matter of a very small and easy theft to accomplish and some deft sleight-of-hand to be performed and a hint dropped wisely and well, and in the right place, for the purpose of detaining Van Cleve in the city of Mexico longer than he intended and all would be well. Van Cleve, however, was not one to be easily detained anywhere against his will.

CHAPTER III

THE INSIDE OF AN ENVELOPE

Chilton walked into the photographic studio of Eulogio Llorente shortly after nine o'clock the following morning and found that the proofs of Van Cleve's pictures were ready for inspection. He examined them attentively. Then he made a request of the photographer to see two of the negatives, and while Llorente was absent from the room to procure them Chilton deftly pulled out a drawer from a cabinet and extracted therefrom several blank, cabinet-size cards, which bore Llorente's name and address in letters of gold and which were used for mounting photographs that he had made. These Chilton quickly concealed about his person, and was quietly rolling a cigarette, over by one of the windows, when Llorente returned with the negatives.

Within a few moments thereafter Chilton arrived at Van Cleve's office and the two men put their heads together in an inspection of the photographic proofs, and it was the general manager who finally made the selection for his employer. That being done, Chilton took the selected proofs back to Llorente, after assuring Van Cleve of two things: That the mounted photographs would be ready for him by two o'clock of the following day (there is always bright sunshine in the city of Mexico, so one does not have to consider a possible cloudy day), and that he would return to Van Cleve's office himself late that afternoon to arrange the settlement of their mutual affairs and to prepare for Van Cleve's departure from Mexico.

From Llorente's studio, Chilton sought his own rooms in *calle* San Felipi Neri, and he made good use of the bright sunshine, too. It is sufficient to say that the product of his efforts was entirely satisfactory to himself, and that after his flash-light pictures were mounted on the cards he had stolen from the studio it is doubtful if the photographer himself could have sworn that they were not of his own make.

Later, Chilton kept his appointment with Van Cleve, and the settlement of their affairs was concluded. At the close of their conference Van Cleve asked:

"Why don't you go north with me, Chilton? I'll be glad if you will."

But Chilton shook his head.

"No," he replied. "I shall stay here; or, rather, I will hike back to the mountains of Guerrero. There is nothing in the North that calls me, and in the light of your generosity regarding the properties there is much to keep me here."

At half past four o'clock in the afternoon of the day following— Wednesday—Chilton carried the mounted photographs of Van Cleve to the office in *calle* Gante. The contractor-mine-owner was awaiting him and at once exhibited a letter that he had dictated and signed. It was addressed to Mr. Bingham Harvard, president of the Centropolis Bank, New York City, and we will quote only the closing paragraph. It said:

> "If all goes well, and I am not delayed by unforeseen circumstances, I will present myself to you at the Centropolis Bank on Thursday, or possibly Friday, of next week, shortly after noon. I am inclosing with this letter two photographs of myself that were taken the day before yesterday, and they are very good likenesses, so, if you study them, you will have no difficulty in recognizing me the moment we meet."

> "It is twenty years or more since I last saw you; you were a small boy then. But I heard much about you on the occasion of my last trip to New York ten years ago, from Mr. Chester. I need not say that he spoke of you with great affection. But, it has occurred to me that Chester, having retired, according to the last report I received from the bank, might be away from home, or something of the sort, and, therefore, the photographs which I inclose."

> "I would be glad if young Tom Clancy, the son and successor of another old friend, could manage to

be present at the bank when I call. I have had some business dealings with him, by letter, as you probably know. I have already written to him, asking that he meet me as stated, and have also requested him to prepare and take with him a statement of my account with his firm."

Chilton had brought with him from Llorente's studio one of the latter's cork-re-enforced envelopes, made expressly for mailing photographs, and he passed the envelope to Van Cleve, with the suggestion that he address it in his own handwriting. Then, while Van Cleve's back was turned, while he was bending over the envelope he was addressing, Chilton took two of his own pictures, that he had made himself, from one of his pockets and replaced them with the two that Van Cleve had selected to send to Bingham Harvard. The two pictures of himself he placed face to face, with Van Cleve's letter to Harvard between them, and he snapped two rubber bands, lengthwise and crosswise, around them—and the instant the envelope was addressed and blotted he reached out for it, slipped the whole arrangement into it, and sealed it.

Chilton took great chances in that act, for Van Cleve might naturally have desired one more glance at the photographs of himself that he was sending away. But Van Cleve only looked on smilingly, well pleased and satisfied and with no suspicion whatever that there had been an exchange. Nevertheless, the pictures of himself which he supposed to be safely enclosed inside of the envelope addressed to New York were at that moment in the inside pocket of Chilton's *charo* jacket, and the pictures that were really within the Llorente envelope were the photographs of Holbrook Chilton that he had made by flash-light Monday evening.

The two men walked to the city post office together to mail them. Afterward they sought the Concordia again, and while seated at the table Chilton remarked quite casually:

"I think, our business together being concluded, that I will hit the trial for Guerrero in the morning, Mr. Van Cleve. Particularly as I want to take a run down to Puebla first. So, when we part, presently, it will be good-by."

"I had hoped that you would wait and see me off," Van Cleve replied; but made no further remonstrance, and an hour later the two parted with each other, presumably forever.

Van Cleve went to his home, on the Paseo de la Reforma. Chilton sought a neighborhood that is well out toward the shrine of Guadalupe and disappeared for a long time within an unsavory-looking saloon. When he came out there was a satisfied smile on his face, and he seemed well pleased with the result of his call. Because of Chilton's visit to that saloon Van Cleve's departure from Mexico was quite certain to be delayed.

CHAPTER IV

THE VALUE OF TWO GOLD PIECES

The visit that Holbrook Chilton made to the saloon in the short and filthy street that was situated a goodly distance between the Zocolo and the Shrine of Guadalupe, called the *calle Amarillo* (which is the same as saying Yellow Street in English) was not without its definite object, and in some measure that object, despicable as it was in motive, was attained.

The saloon was in a mere hovel, built of *adobe* bricks of mud baked to hardness in the Mexican sun. It was innocent of a floor, the hard-trodden earth of *tepetate* texture and formation answered that purpose. Some rough tables were bestowed about the one room it contained, for the proprietor cooked his food over a charcoal fire that was contained in an earthen jar in one corner of that room, and at night rolled himself in a gaudy *serape* and stretched his body upon a woven grass *petate* across the doorway. And he had a numerous brood that accommodated themselves in like manner.

One customer alone patronized the place when Chilton entered it, and he was seated at a table sipping *pulque viejo* with the proprietor. But he got upon his feet instantly and saluted—as did also the other man—when Van Cleve's superintendent-manager appeared. Evidently he was expected.

"You have seen the *cargador de la esquina* I sent to find you?" Chilton demanded abruptly.

"*Sí, señor.*"

Chilton ostentatiously withdrew two gold pieces from one of his pockets and held them for a moment so that the man called Pancho could see them. They were American five-dollar coins, but they represented twice that amount in Mexican money and looked like a fortune in the eyes of the brutal-looking, ragged *charo*, whose gaze literally glittered at sight of them.

"These are yours, *amigo*, if you will do as I direct," he said. "I will give them to you now. Then, when the thing is done, there are two more like them which will also be yours. Well?"

"They are mine already, *señor*," was the quiet response.

"Good. I supposed as much."

(The conversation was, of course, entirely in Spanish.)

"It is to do—what, *señor*?" Pancho asked softly. "Somebody—a man, no?—is in the way of the *señor* and is to be removed? Yes? A *señorita* has attracted the *señor's* eye and is to be carried into the mountains? No? Yes? It is the same to Pancho. It is done."

"It is the Señor Van Cleve," Chilton replied shortly. "You know him. You worked for him. He caught you doing *ladrone's* work. You stole. He struck you and sent you away. You hate him. No?"

"*Sí, señor*; I hate him. ¿*Bien*?" Pancho's eyes glittered fiercely when he made that reply.

Chilton put the gold pieces upon the table between them. Pancho let them lie nor offered yet to take them up.

"He is to be killed?" he asked softly.

"Yes."

"When, *señor*? Where?" There was no hesitation in the question, no suggestion of negation.

"When you will, so that it be soon enough."

"*Bien*. Tell me more, *señor*."

"Van Cleve thinks to go away from Mexico. He must not go away. He must remain here and be buried."

"*Está bien, señor*," was the calm reply, which, being translated, means: "It is well, sir."

"He plans to go away by Friday or Saturday—or at the latest, Monday. He must not go."

"*Señor* Van Cleve will not go away from Mexico," Pancho stated immovably.

"Do you know where and how to find him so that it can be done, Pancho?"

"*Sí, señor*. I have watched. Some day it should have been done without the bestowal of these coins—for myself. You but hasten matters. *Bueno*."

"At his office in the *calle* Gante, or in the street at night, Pancho. It will be all the same to me. You throw the knife superbly, and see! I have brought you a new one, just purchased, so that when it is found in his body and plucked from it there will be no recognizing it as your property. *¿Intiende usted?*"

"*Sí, señor; y mil gracias, tambien.*"

"It is a good one, Pancho. I have seen you throw one like it as much as thirty feet and put the point through a piece of paper an inch square. Can you still do that?"

"As well as ever, *señor.*"

"Do you need further instruction, Pancho?"

"No."

"It must be done before he leaves Mexico City—I do not care when nor where nor how."

"I understand, *señor.*"

"Remember, he may start away next Friday morning; so before that, if possible."

"I have not forgotten. Now, *señor*, what of the remaining two gold pieces? Does the *señor* intend also to go away?"

"No. Not yet. Not for weeks to come," Chilton lied calmly. "The other two gold pieces—we will make it three—will be ready for you as soon as the work is done."

"*Está bien, señor; else—*" The pause was significant.

"Else there may be another knife of the same sort reserved for me, eh? Oh, I know you, Pancho. When have I failed in a promise to you?"

"Never, *señor.*"

"Not this time, either," Chilton answered, smiling, and rose from the table. But he threw a silver dollar upon it in front of the proprietor, who had listened to the conversation unmoved. "Drink that up to my good health," he said: and then, dropping another one beside it, he added: "And bestow that one upon the *señora* and the *niños.*"

Then, without another word or glance, he turned his back upon them and went out. Chilton being gone, Pancho bent forward half across the table, somber-eyed.

"You heard, Sus?" he asked quietly.

"*Sí.* I heard."

"Don Holá" (it was the name by which he spoke of Chilton) "lied to me."

The proprietor of the *cantina* nodded comprehendingly. It was apparent that he thought so, too.

"There will be no more pieces of gold."

"No."

"He will go away, also."

"Yes. That is evident."

"So there will be no killing. Why should there be? Why should I risk *Belem* and the bullets of the executioners?"

"Why, indeed?"

"But—I will earn these two gold pieces if not the others, *amigo*."

"But how, then, Pancho?"

"Señor Van Cleve shall be detained, not killed. He may go away Monday, perhaps, or Tuesday or afterward; but not Friday or Saturday. So will I keep my faith. But if Don Holá had given me the *four* pieces it would have been better, for then I would have done as he desired. I would have thrown the knife. Look!"

He picked up the knife which Chilton had left upon the table, poised it for an instant in one hand, and said:

"See! The letter 'O' in the sign over the bar."

Then he threw it from him, and exactly in the middle of that letter "O" it struck, point first, and held there, deeply imbedded, quivering like a live thing. There was more *pulque viejo* after that; many *copas*. Some *tequila*, which is stronger than absinthe and quite as deadly, followed. Other men entered the place and were invited to drink—but no mention was made again of the visit of Chilton to the *cantina*. And the knife he had given to Pancho was concealed in the clothing of that enterprising person.

So, hours later, he went outside and betook himself to the plaza of the Zocolo, and thence to the corner of San Francisco and Gante streets, and again thence to the curb opposite the windows across the street, through which the head and shoulders of Anderson Van Cleve could be seen as he bent over his desk. Pancho, the discharged employee and Holbrook Chilton's tool, was studying the ground and making ready to keep faith with Chilton—as far as the two gold pieces would go.

CHAPTER V

THE KNIFE-THROWER

Anderson Van Cleve, when he had finally arranged his affairs sufficiently to his own satisfaction so that he was prepared to leave Mexico never to return to it, strode through the main thoroughfare of that city from the bronze "*caballito*" at the entrance to the Paseo de la Reforma to the city palace just across the plaza at the Zocolo, looking in for a moment at places he had been wont to frequent during his long residence there, and pausing at times, undecided where to go next. For he was not leaving the city of Mexico, beautiful in many ways then, without deep regret. He had lived there too long a time for that, and many of the ties had become very strong indeed. But the prophetic eyes of the man could see, he believed, far into the future.

He believed that the tranquility of the moment was only on the surface in that country; that beneath it a volcano of strife was ready to burst into eruption at any moment, and that he would be better, far better, away from it. Once he would have elected to remain—but that was when he was younger. Now the years were beginning to suggest their weight to his energies, and he knew that it was better to go. If Porfirio Díaz had remained, he would have stayed also; but—Díaz was gone. True, Van Cleve sacrificed much in making such a hurried departure—a fortune, in fact. But, he argued, there was enough besides to serve him bountifully for the rest of his life.

The Centropolis Bank was not the only one in the North to which he had been forwarding funds during the latter years of his stay. There were others, and he owned property in various places; he had many investments; he owned U.S. government bonds to a considerable extent—and, in short, he had no fears for the future, notwithstanding his present sacrifice.

In the middle of the Zocolo, near the music-stand, he remained for a long time. Night had fallen, although it was still early; but lights gleamed out everywhere when he turned to retrace his steps. He stopped for a moment to chat with a friend in front of the Iturbide Hotel. He looked in at an office at the Plazuela de Guardiola, to take a last glance at another acquaintance—for he did not mean to say good-by to anybody. It was a part of his present policy to tell nobody of his going away.

He strode onward presently into the Avenida Juárez, and thence turned into the Alameda, where, being a bit tired by his long walk, he sat down upon one of the benches. The huge trees of cypress would have rendered it intensely dark in there but for the somewhat infrequent arc-lights that were along the paths. They dispelled a part of the gloom. Nevertheless, just where he had seated himself the trees hung downward all around him, and he noticed that few people were in sight—mostly *peons*, or *cargadores*. The Alameda was as deserted as it ever was. He was quite alone, in fact, but it suited him to be so.

He had no idea that he would experience such regret when the time came to go away. He was remembering that Mexico had been his home for a good many years. It was Friday night then. He was prepared to leave the city the following morning. Nobody would suspect his real destination, for he had been in the habit of making frequent excursions out of the city during all the years he had been there—and he had taken his ticket for only a part of the way to the border. He would purchase another when it was required. Holbrook Chilton, he supposed, had returned to Guerrero; to the properties that he had bestowed upon the man as a free gift—since he could no longer develop them. At all events, Chilton had left the city.

While he sat there on the bench, a *charo*—a mountaineer, in other words—paused in passing, and spoke to him deferentially in Spanish.

"You remember me, *señor*?" he asked, showing his teeth.

"Yes. You are Pancho, who worked for me. What do you want, *hombre*?"

"To speak to you, *señor*. To ask that you will employ me again."

"Never. You stole. You are a *ladrone*. Go away."

"But, *señor*—"

"Well?"

"I am poor—very poor. I have no money to buy food. I need work; and I will be honest."

Had Van Cleve but known it and consented to employ the man again, Pancho would have passed on, and nothing would have happened that night. Such was Pancho's intention, for he believed that the work of his former employer would still go ahead, even though the man himself should depart. And Pancho would have kept the two gold pieces and still not have kept even part faith with Chilton; for Pancho was wise, and had watched Chilton, and he knew that the man who had given the gold to him was already gone from Mexico. But the *señor* said no, again, with emphasis. Still, he took a handful of silver from one of his pockets and gave it to Pancho, saying:

"Take this, then, and buy food. But I cannot employ you again."

"But the *señor* will need me while he is gone away from Mexico," Pancho said placidly, accepting the money nevertheless, and with ten thousand thanks—in three words.

Van Cleve started to his feet, surprised. How could this man know of his intended departure? Nobody but Holbrook Chilton had been informed of it.

"Why do you say that?" he demanded sharply.

"Because the fact is known to me, *señor*. You go—to-morrow, perhaps? No?"

Van Cleve was impatient, and he was angry, too. He was accustomed to handling his *peons* and *charos* roughly. And this particular one he disliked intensely. So he did the natural thing to do under the circumstances—the thing that years of experience with such men in that country had forced him to do: he swept his right hand and arm around, not exactly in a blow, but in something very like one, and it would have fallen upon Pancho and shoved him roughly aside, had it touched him; but Pancho sprang backward out if its reach. And then he turned, but not until he had made several of those agile leaps to attain a greater distance. When he did turn, something gleamed brightly in his hand, and Van Cleve knew what it was, and exactly what Pancho intended to do with it. He knew, moreover, that he could not dodge the thrown knife in time to avoid it when it should be cast at him. So he leaped directly toward it. Another man would have been killed. Van Cleve was not, for he knew the expertness of knife-throwers.

Such weapons turn in the air while speeding toward a target. Had Van Cleve remained where he was the point of it would have found him. As it was, he met the missile several feet in advance of where he had stood when it left the hand of Pancho, even though he stumbled when he jumped. Falling forward as he did, his head was lowered to the level of his own breast had he been standing upright, and the thrown knife struck him, hilt foremost, squarely upon the forehead. It was a heavily-hilted weapon, made for throwing purposes, and Van Cleve fell face downward in the path, stunned, insensible.

And Pancho?

That faith-keeping assassin turned about and fled even as the knife left the grip of his finger-tips and before it had made the first turn in the air; and never having been in the habit of missing his mark, it is doubtful if Pancho believed he had done so then. No doubt, as he fled away, he thought of the knife-blade imbedded in the heart of his former employer, for he had not stayed to see whether it was the point or the hilt of the weapon that struck its intended victim.

Ten minutes later two gentlemen who were crossing the Alameda toward Buena Vista discovered Van Cleve and the knife beside him. They summoned a policeman from the Avenida Juarez, and the stricken American, still unconscious, was taken to the American Hospital. Van Cleve might still have begun his journey north the following morning if that policeman had not been summoned to the scene of the attack upon him, but the devious ways of some forms of Mexican justice are peculiar—and arbitrary. He was notified in due form that he must appear before a certain court on Monday, at noon, which was hours after train time, and—there was no help for it. He had to wait. To attempt to get away before Tuesday, under the circumstances, then, would have been fatal to his plans. So he waited. And Chilton had his way after all. Van Cleve was delayed considerably beyond the time he had appointed for his departure. Nevertheless, he was not buried in Mexico, as his general manager had planned. Pancho slept, that Monday night, in Belem prison.

CHAPTER VI

CHILTON'S UNSPEAKABLE CLEVERNESS

Bingham Harvard let his eyes dwell for a moment upon the card that had just been given to him before he raised them and directed that its owner be conducted to the private office at once. It was not an engraved card, but a written one. It bore the characteristic and unmistakable signature of Anderson Van Cleve. The man whom we know as Holbrook Chilton entered, halted just inside the doorway, and then stepped briskly forward with extended hand.

"You are Bingham Harvard," he said in his strangely mellow voice when the proffered hand-clasp was accepted. "My, my! You were a little boy when I last saw you; but, really, I almost believe that I would have known you at that. Some of us change very little with the passing years." Then he laughed aloud and added: "I am the exception that proves the rule, I reckon. Years of exposure to sun and wind have left their stamp—eh?"

"I am delighted to see you, Mr. Van Cleve," Harvard replied, indicating a chair, and relapsing upon his own at the desk. "You are certainly tanned and browned, and a bit grizzled, sir; but for all that you do not look your years. You see, I know your age. Mr. Chester has spoken of you to me very often indeed."

"Sixty-five my next birthday."

"Surely? One would never guess it, or even suppose it."

"Did you receive my last letter, with the photographs?" Chilton asked.

"Yes. In the first delivery, Tuesday morning. This is Thursday; the day you thought you might arrive. I was anticipating your coming, Mr. Van Cleve."

"Good. I am glad that I got here on time," the supposed Van Cleve replied as Harvard pressed a button beneath the edge of his desk. "How is Chester, and *where* is he?"

Harvard's secretary appeared in the doorway of an adjoining room.

"Telephone to Mr. Clancy that Mr. Van Cleve is here," he directed. Then: "Mr. Chester is in Egypt; somewhere on the Nile, I believe. He won't return to New York for six months, or more."

"To be sure. I remember, now, that I saw an announcement to that effect in a file of the New York papers at the Anglo-American Club in Mexico. In fact, that was one reason why I sent the photographs. I was afraid that I might have some difficulty in identifying myself."

"I don't think there would have been any difficulty about that, Mr. Van Cleve," Harvard replied smilingly. "Your signature—the ink is barely dry on the card you wrote to send in to me—would have sufficed, under the circumstances; and there must be many of your old friends in the city who would remember you. However, the photographs render that expedient unnecessary."

Harvard reached out his hand and took the Llorente envelope containing the pictures from a wide pigeon-hole of the desk. Then he smiled broadly and said:

"I have been wondering if you would appear here in that costume. It would have created quite a sensation among the clerks in the bank had you done so."

The pseudo Van Cleve laughed aloud and heartily.

"Hardly that," he said. "I had just come in from the mountains, and it struck my fancy to have the photographs made, just as I stood. You see, there are two reasons why I dress in that fashion down there. One is that it is very much more comfortable for mountain work than any other; the second is that it gives one a certain prestige over the *peons* one employs."

Harvard returned the photographs to the envelope and replaced them in the pigeon-hole from which he had taken it. Chilton, observing closely, noticed that the letter that had been sent with the pictures was still there.

"Is there anything that I can do for you before the bank closes, Mr. Van Cleve?" Harvard asked as he swung his chair around again. "Do you wish to draw any money to-day?"

"Well, yes, Mr. Harvard, I do. Oddly enough, as it happens, I wish to draw a considerable part of it. But I have no intention of withdrawing my account from the Centropolis Bank, understand. In fact, before the expiration of another thirty days I shall be carrying a much larger balance with you than now."

"Draw whatsoever you require, Mr. Van Cleve. Our charter is a very old one, granted in the days when New York City was young. It requires that only two hundred and fifty dollars shall be maintained as a balance."

"Oh, I shall leave much more than that with you. The fact is, I am investing nearly half a million in an enterprise which has interested me for more than a year. I already have a hundred and fifty thousand in it; and—well, my idea is to obtain the control. In fact, that is one of the reasons why I determined to pull up stakes in Mexico, even though I sustained a considerable loss in doing so."

Harvard nodded comprehendingly.

"I have brought with me," the pseudo Van Cleve continued, lying glibly, and with a winning smile of which he was a past master, "Chester's letter to me in Mexico, and also the carbon copies of my letters to him, in which the amounts of my various deposits, and the dates thereof, are clearly stated. I can show you those if you require any further identification."

"I don't think they are necessary, Mr. Van Cleve. However— have you brought them here with you?"

"No. They are with my baggage at the hotel; but"—rising and reaching for his hat—"I can easily get them and bring them to you."

As a matter of fact, Chilton did not have the letters and carbon copies with him. He had been afraid to filch them from Van Cleve's letter-files in Mexico lest the contractor should discover their loss and telegraph to the bank concerning it.

"That will be entirely unnecessary, Mr. Van Cleve," Harvard interposed—and the man from Mexico resumed his seat, greatly relieved.

It had been a dangerous bluff to play, but it had worked. "Did you bring one of the small checkbooks with you, or shall I—" Harvard inquired.

"Yes. I have one of the small ones that you forwarded, with my name printed on each check. Thank you."

He hitched his chair forward. Harvard pulled out the desk-slide, dipped a pen and handed it to his companion as the latter drew the small checkbook from an inner pocket. Then Chilton consulted a notebook which he took from his waistcoat pocket.

"Just what do you make my balance, Mr. Harvard?" he asked, pausing with the pen suspended over the checkbook.

Harvard consulted a memorandum on his desk which he had caused to be prepared in anticipation of that question.

"Three hundred and sixty-four thousand, one hundred and eighty-two dollars," he replied. "And here are the vouchers for the few drafts you have made upon us, from Mexico, from time to time since you opened the account."

"Correct. Thank you."

He wrote rapidly upon the check, finally affixing the signature of Anderson Van Cleve at the bottom of it with a freehand flourish that would have astonished Bingham Harvard beyond words had he suspected for an instant that the man was not Van Cleve at all.

"I have drawn the check for three hundred and fifty thousand, five hundred," he said, tearing it from the book and holding it up for Harvard's inspection. Then he laid a blotter upon it, remarking casually as he did so: "The three-fifty is for that investment—and for reasons of my own I prefer to use cash—and the five hundred is for pocket money. The amount will not inconvenience you, I hope, at this late hour in the day? It is after two, now."

"Not at all, Mr. Van Cleve." Harvard pressed a button beneath his desk. "How will you have it?" he asked.

"In one-hundred-dollar bills as far as they will go—that is, to the extent of as many of that denomination as you can spare. The balance in five hundreds and thousands—except that five hundred dollars for pocket money. I would like a few tens and twenties."

Harvard made some rapid memoranda on a pad and passed it to the man who had answered his summons. Then, as the man departed with the properly endorsed check upon which the president of the bank had placed his O. K. he remarked:

"That will make quite a bulky package, Mr. Van Cleve."

"Oh, no; not particularly. A package of a hundred bills is only five-sixteenths of an inch thick. They are a trifle less than seven and a half inches long, and a trifle more than three inches wide. So, you see, if they were *all* one-hundreds, and were stacked, three packages in a row, my bundle would be, approximately, five by eight by nine inches. That isn't very large."

"No; but it is a dangerous kind of a package to carry around the streets of New York."

"Oh, I won't carry it very long, nor far. I have an appointment with the men who are interested with me at six o'clock—after banking hours. That is why I wanted the cash. And I am accustomed to taking care of myself."

"I suppose so. I would like to have a good talk with you about Mexico, sometime. When could you dine with me? To-morrow evening, say?" Harvard produced a card which bore his address. "Mrs. Harvard will be glad to meet such an old friend of Mr. Chester's. Will you come?"

"Thank you. Certainly. I will call here and go home with you after banking hours if that is agreeable."

"Fine. Just the thing. Ah, here comes your cash. Mr. Blake"—to the man who brought in the money—"give Mr. Van Cleve the five hundred in smaller bills, then make a neat package of the rest of it." Then to Chilton: "You will still have a balance with us of $13,682, Mr. Van Cleve. Here is Tom Clancy, now. Hello Tom. How are you?"

"Bully, thank you, Bing. And this, I suppose, is the returned Mexican bandit. How do you do, Mr. Van Cleve? Harvard has showed me your photograph, so I recognized you at once, notwithstanding the change in costume. My dear old dad used to talk about you a great deal."

"That is pleasant to hear, Mr. Clancy. A man likes to be remembered by his old friends."

"Oh, call me Tom. Everybody does; and *you* knew me when I was a kid. By the way, I have brought that statement with me that your letter asked for. Here it is. My firm holds to your credit exactly thirty-six thousand dollars, as you will see. Shall I write you a check for it now?"

"Oh, no, thank you. I will call at your office in the morning and do the thing in proper business shape."

Blake entered and gave Van Cleve the packages of money at that moment, and he left his chair.

"I will look in on you some time in the forenoon to-morrow, Mr. Harvard," he said, reaching out his hand. "And I'll call upon you, Mr. Clancy, at ten in the morning. But I must be going now."

"I will ask Tom to dine with us to-morrow evening, Mr. Van Cleve," Harvard said, rising. "Now, step outside with me and I will introduce you to the cashier and to the tellers. They already know your signature."

Chilton, as the supposed Van Cleve, with the well-wrapped package of bills held tightly beneath his left arm, halted while his hand was outstretched to pull open the swing-gate in the brass rail that guarded the president's slightly elevated and outer office. Then he turned slowly around again. Harvard, noticing his hesitancy, paused also. The pseudo Van Cleve appeared to consider a question that had occurred to him. Then, as if he had satisfactorily determined the point, he crossed the enclosure again to Harvard's desk and put down the package of money upon it. And deliberately, still in utter silence, he began to remove the wrappings.

"Is anything wrong, Mr. Van Cleve?" Harvard inquired.

The man from Mexico did not reply until the paper-strapped packets of bills were exposed; and even then he counted out several of them and laid them aside before he spoke.

"On second thought," he announced slowly, "I think I will not require all of this cash to-day. Possibly I can make a dicker so that I will not need it at all—and I would very much prefer to maintain a larger balance with you than I have left just now."

He picked up the packets that he had laid aside and put them into Harvard's hands.

"There's a hundred thousand there," he said. "I wish you would restore it to my account. I can draw it later on if I should need it—but I hardly think I will; and he began at once to rewrap the remaining packets while Harvard busied himself in making out the necessary deposit-slip.

"We will pass the hundred thousand in at the window when I introduce you to the receiving teller, Mr. Van Cleve," Harvard said. A moment later, after again assuring Tom Clancy that he would call upon him in the morning, the imposter followed the young bank president down the few steps to the main floor of the institution. Then, when he had been properly presented to the cashier and to the receiving teller, with whom was left the hundred thousand dollars deposit, and to the paying tellers, he once more shook hands with Bingham Harvard and passed outside. He had drawn from the bank two hundred and fifty thousand five hundred dollars in cash, and there still remained one hundred and thirteen thousand six hundred and eighty-two dollars to the credit of Anderson Van Cleve.

* * * * * * *

At precisely ten o'clock the following morning the pseudo Van Cleve walked into the offices of Clancy & Co., and found Tom awaiting his arrival, with the check already made out and signed. The two men chatted amiably together for nearly half an hour, and then went across the street to Clancy's bank, where the supposed Van Cleve was properly identified, and drew the thirty-six thousand dollars that the check called for.

At eleven o'clock he entered the Centropolis Bank and stopped before the window of the paying teller.

"You remember me, of course, Mr. Mordaunt?" he inquired, and handed in two checks.

One was for an even hundred thousand dollars the other called for ten thousand five hundred; and there was a penciled slip with them which explained exactly how he wanted the money. He waited with exemplary patience while it was prepared for him thanked the teller when he received it, bestowed it in various places about his person, nodded again to Mordaunt, stepped away from the window and continued through the bank to the president's office. Bingham Harvard rose to receive him with a cordial greeting.

"I am afraid," the imposter announced after greetings had been exchanged, "that I must disappoint you about the dinner engagement for to-night, Mr. Harvard. The fact is, things did not go through as expeditiously as I anticipated yesterday. But we are to have another session to-night, and, possibly, still another one to-morrow. But, later—"

"Then why not come to us on Sunday, Mr. Van Cleve?" Harvard interposed. "To-day is Friday. Shall we say Sunday, at four?"

"I shall be delighted, of course—if Mrs. Harvard will overlook my remissness of this evening."

Harvard was assuring him that there could be no doubt on that point when one of the clerks entered and said something to him in a low tone.

"Excuse me just a moment, Mr. Van Cleve," he said, rising; and he passed outside to the floor of the bank to attend to some detail that required his personal supervision.

Chilton was, of course, left entirely alone in the president's office. He was seated quite close to Harvard's desk, near the end that was toward the bank, and Harvard's temporary absence gave the imposter the very opportunity he had wished for, which he had feared might not occur, but which he had been resolved to wait and watch for as long as it might be discreet on his part to do so.

The two photographs of himself were still contained in the Llorente envelope, in the wide pigeon-hole of Bingham Harvard's desk, he knew. Yesterday, late in the afternoon, he had seen the young bank president restore them to that receptacle. They were within reach of his hand when Harvard left him alone beside the desk, and he did not hesitate. He flashed a quick and comprehensive glance toward the bank floor, then reached out for the envelope and drew it quickly toward him. It required only an instant to make the change and substitution that he had determined upon if the opportunity should occur, and to restore the Llorente envelope, with its contents apparently undisturbed, to its place in the pigeon-hole of the desk. Then he leaned backward in his chair and was occupied in lighting a cigar when Harvard returned.

Chilton rose to depart a moment later.

"You are busy, and I will not occupy your time needlessly, Mr. Harvard," he said; "and probably I will not see you again until Sunday afternoon, at four. I came, in fact, merely to make another draft on my balance here, for I found that after all I needed some additional cash to carry through that deal properly. Shall I have the pleasure of meeting Mr. Clancy, too, on Sunday, as would have been the case to-night?"

"Assuredly Tom will be there," Harvard replied.

"Then I shall look forward to dining with you Sunday afternoon with additional pleasure. My only regret is that Mr. Chester is not to be present also. It is unfortunate that he should be abroad at just this time. Well, Mr. Harvard, until then—"

Holbrook Chilton, the imposter, passed deliberately through the bank to the street. Much that remained of the banking hours of that Friday Chilton employed in what appeared to be an aimless wandering through the streets of the city. But, in fact, there was nothing aimless about his conduct. Quite the contrary. He entered every bank he could find and sought the teller's window in each one; and there he inevitably changed a thousand-dollar bill—two of them, or three, in many places—into bills of smaller denominations.

Just before three o'clock that same afternoon he paid his bill at the hotel, engaged a taxi to take him to the Grand Central Station, purchased a ticket there for Chicago, secured a stateroom in a Pullman, and went aboard the train. People who saw him and noticed him—and it afterward developed that there were many such—recalled each of these incidents; and also the fact that he had carried two satchels, one of them being quite small. Neither the Pullman conductor nor the porter of the car could tell when or where he left the Chicago train, save only that he must have done so some time during the night.

In the stateroom he had occupied the larger of the two satchels he had carried remained. Inside of it was the suit of clothes he had worn when he boarded the train in New York, and also the hat, shirt, tie, collar, and even the tan shoes. The smaller of the two bags was *not* there. Neither was there the slightest clue of any kind. Not a shred of lint; not a hair, nor a button, nor the stump of a cigar, nor a cigarette-butt, nor a scrap of paper. Moreover, a heap of soiled towels demonstrated that he had carefully wiped off any possible finger-prints that might have been left upon the windows or the furniture of the stateroom. The berth had not been slept in. All that the porter could disclose was that the gentleman had retired as soon as he returned from the dining-car and was not seen afterward. But even that much information was not forthcoming until several days later.

* * * * * * *

Then at eleven o'clock of the day following—Saturday— Anderson Van Cleve himself, in proper person, walked in at the door of the Centropolis Bank and sent his card to the president.

CHAPTER VII

THE OTHER MAN FROM MEXICO

There are sensations, and sensations. The one experienced by Bingham Harvard when the real Anderson Van Cleve's card was put before him defies description. Intuitively he perceived at that instant, before he had so much as had a glance at the owner of the card, that he had been the victim of a malicious hoax. A sixth sense within him told him at once that the other man to whom he had paid the money had been an imposter. The card was not a written one, as the other had been, bearing the signature of the man who had sent it in; it was a properly engraved card, and Van Cleve's address in the city of Mexico was announced in smaller letters in one corner of it.

The clerk who took the card to Harvard stood waiting, but it was nearly half a minute before the young bank president recovered from the shock of the sudden revelation and directed that the gentleman be admitted to the private office. There was an interval of only a few seconds until Van Cleve appeared; but Bingham Harvard, even in his strenuous "Night Wind" days had never thought so rapidly nor so intensely as he did during that brief interval.

Then Anderson Van Cleve came into the room. Harvard rose from his chair to greet him—and wondered inwardly as he did so how he could have been deceived even for a moment, by that other man. Twenty years and more had elapsed since he had looked upon the face of Anderson Van Cleve, and he had been a mere boy when that happened; but as he looked upon it again, at the present moment, he recalled it distinctly and perfectly. The sight of it unlocked the door of the particular brain-cell of memory where it had been stored away since Harvard's childhood, and in that instant, as he

47

shook hands with his caller, he remembered even the circumstances of their last meeting.

"Do you remember me, Bingham?" Mr. Van Cleve inquired in his soft, quiet tones, and in a manner that was perfectly at ease.

"Perfectly—now—that you stand face to face with me. But I had forgotten you entirely until you crossed that threshold," Harvard replied, pulling forward a chair for his guest.

Van Cleve replied:

"I was afraid that you might have forgotten me—you were only a lad when I last saw you, you know—and I surmised, because you had become president of the bank and your foster father had retired from active participation in its affairs, that he might be absent when I arrived. Hence the photographs that I sent to you. You received them, of course?"

Harvard hesitated, then nodded his head. Then, as entire frankness and truthfulness was his rule of life, and because he realized that the whole truth must be told, he said:

"I received a letter and some photographs which arrived in the same package, contained in an envelope which bore the name Llorente. But the photographs were not of you, Mr. Van Cleve. Evidently there had been a substitution of others in the place of yours at the last moment. Do you recall who was with you at the time the envelope was sealed for mailing?"

"Perfectly. Why?"

"Bear with me a moment, Mr. Van Cleve. I will make it all clear to you presently. And, before we proceed, you of course understand that if there has been a loss it is not yours. The bank—or rather, I personally—must sustain that."

"Has there been a loss?" Van Cleve asked in his quiet tones. "Has some person succeeded in imposing upon you by representing himself to be Anderson Van Cleve?"

"Yes. I will come to that in a moment. Who was with you when the envelope that contained your letter and the photographs was sealed?"

"My superintendent and general manager—a man named Holbrook Chilton."

"Nobody else?"

"No."

"Is he a tall, bearded man, tanned and browned to the complexion of an Indian? Has he a heavy shock of rather long hair that was once black but is now quite gray; that is white, in fact, over the temples? Is his beard nearly white in front of the ears and grizzled where it is not white? And did he wear the *charo* costume of Mexico and a wide sombrero?" Harvard asked evenly and slowly.

"That is a very good mental picture of him, save for the description you give of his hair and beard. I don't remember that he had any gray hairs at all."

"Then he must have made them so with some preparation."

"Probably. How much did he succeed in getting away with?"

"A very considerable sum, Mr. Van Cleve; but, as I said before, the loss is not yours—it is ours. Wait. I will show you the pictures of himself that he sent in place of yours."

Harvard turned his chair and reached out for the envelope of the photographer, Llorente, in which, he still supposed, were contained the two photographs of the man in *charo* costume who had so successfully introduced and identified himself as Anderson Van Cleve.

"Here they are," he said, and drew the two pictures, with Van Cleve's letter between them, from the envelope.

For a moment afterward he sat quite motionless, staring at the objects he held in his hand, an expression of utter amazement depicted upon his countenance. Them amazement became anger—and anger faded slowly into chagrined amusement. There was a wry smile in his eyes and twitching at the corners of his mouth when, without further comment, he put the two photographs into the outstretched hand of Anderson Van Cleve. It was the latter's turn to manifest amazement then.

"Why," he exclaimed, raising his eyes quickly, "these are not pictures of Chilton! They are the photographs of myself; the very same two that I sent to you from Mexico City."

Harvard nodded.

"I know it—now," he said, still smiling that wry smile. "There has been another substitution; that is all. The other two pictures—those that I have described to you—were in this envelope at a late hour yesterday afternoon. Mr. Holbrook Chilton is an exceedingly clever person, Mr. Van Cleve."

"He is even more resourceful than I had supposed," was Van Cleve's dry comment. "But never mind the loss of those photographs of *him*. I have a small Kodak snapshot of him that I took myself less than a year ago—if it will be of any service later."

"He must have made this second substitution yesterday, when I left him alone near my desk for two or three minutes," Harvard said.

"Do I understand you, Harvard, that Chilton was here in this bank—in this very office—as late as yesterday?" Van Cleve asked.

"Yes. And he occupied that same chair upon which you are now seated. He was here at eleven o'clock. He went away about eleven-thirty. But I had better tell you the entire story, just as it happened, Mr. Van Cleve."

"Yes, of course. But wait a moment before you begin. I remember now that it was Chilton who put the photographs into the envelope and sealed it in Mexico. That was when he made the first substitution. Afterward we walked down to the Zocolo together and put it in the general post-office. But never mind that now. Let me hear the entire story."

Harvard told it. He began at the moment of Chilton's first appearance, and he omitted no detail with which he was familiar, up to the time when Chilton walked out of the Centropolis Bank at half past eleven the preceding day; and Mr. Van Cleve listened to the recital with close attention. In the beginning of it, however, Harvard paused long enough to use the telephone and to call up the detective agency that handled the bank's business. By the time he had finished, the chief of that agency, with two of his best operatives, sent in their cards. Then Harvard had to go entirely over the story a second time, to reply to innumerable questions and to describe as well as he could do so the man himself. Thus was developed, in a comparatively short time thereafter, the information described in the closing words of the preceding chapter.

Also, during that conversation was disclosed the exact amount that Chilton had succeeded in getting away with, as follows:

By the first check, O.K.'d by Bingham Harvard, $350,500—of which $100,000 was redeposited at once. By a second and third check, cashed at the teller's window (where the man had been introduced by Harvard), $10,500 and $100,000, respectively. And from Tom Clancy, $36,000. Total, $397,000. Chilton had left in the Centropolis Bank only $3,182 of the amount that Van Cleve had placed on deposit there.

"The only wonder is that, with his superb assurance and nerve, he did not take it *all*," Mr. Van Cleve remarked dryly.

"He might have done so," Bingham Harvard replied. "I had not a doubt concerning the identification; neither had Tom Clancy. Why, the fellow offered to show me the letters he had received from us here and carbon copies of your letters to us which, he said, were in his baggage at the hotel. It shows the extent of my gullibility, Mr. Van Cleve, that I waved the offer aside as unnecessary."

Harvard wheeled his chair around until he again faced the chief of the detective agency.

"What do you think about it, chief?" he asked with a half smile.

The chief shook his head.

"One cannot answer such a question offhand," he replied. "Chilton, as he called himself—and you can bank on it that it is *not* his right name—has had twenty-four hours for his get-away. He might be in Chicago, St. Louis, New Orleans, or any old place by this time. But I will get the wires busy at once, Mr. Harvard, and report to you as soon as there is anything to report."

As soon as Van Cleve and Harvard were alone again, the former remarked in his quietly even tone:

"Bingham, it has been a business rule with me never to put all of my eggs into one basket; which is to say that my account in this bank is not the only one I have on this side of the Rio Grande. I have one in St. Louis, one in Chicago, and another in Boston. So the temporary deprivation of my balance here will not embarrass me at all. Therefore I have a suggestion to make to you."

"Yes, sir?"

"Your paying tellers, your cashier, possibly one or more others of your employees, those detectives, and ourselves are the only persons who have knowledge of what has happened. My advice is that you enjoin absolute secrecy upon all of them, and that the circumstances be kept entirely to ourselves for the present."

"But you—"

"I am your foster father's friend and yours. I do not need that money at present. I do believe that we will recover it—or very nearly all of it—sooner or later. So let's go easy for the present, anyhow."

"If Chilton should have taken it into his head to return to Mexico—what then?"

"He won't do that. I feel assured of that much. If he should— well, I'd get him quicker than you could get him here. No. He won't go back to Mexico. *My* belief is that he will stay right here in New York City. I know the man. I know his nerve. I know his resourcefulness. I will admit to you now that I had an inkling of what might have happened before I arrived in New York."

"You did? How was that, sir?"

"I was detained two days after the time I had set for leaving Mexico. The stated reason for my detention was a mere subterfuge, and I knew it, but I could not avoid it. I half suspected that Chilton was the cause of it, and it made me think. I was not entirely unprepared for what has happened."

Harvard picked up the two checks that Chilton had signed, which he had ordered sent in to him, examined them attentively, and then asked Van Cleve to write his name.

Then he put the forgeries down on the desk in front of him, one on either side of the genuine signature.

"It is the most remarkable forgery I have ever seen," he said after a moment.

"Yes," Van Cleve replied, also studying the three signatures. "Chilton is what you may call a 'free-hand' artist. He is really wonderful with his pencil, in sketching faces, reproducing expressions and all that. That same talent has enabled him, with practice, to reproduce my signature with exactitude. A signature should be more easily copied in that way than the expression depicted in eyes, mouth, nostrils, and contour of a man's face. But it does not concern us as to *how* he did it; the fact that stares at us is that he *did* do it, and that he got away with it."

When Van Cleve had gone away, and Bingham Harvard was alone, he sat very still at his desk for a long time, thinking deeply and intensely upon the problem that confronted him. Then he pulled out a drawer of the desk and took therefrom a photograph of a police officer in the uniform of a lieutenant. The face was a handsome one in its way, although possibly it suggested rather too much of what might be called "bulldog" characteristics. It was the picture of Detective Lieutenant Rodney Rushton, who was, at the time, serving out a long prison sentence for complicity in the theft of $136,000 from that very bank. The picture was one which the lieutenant had given to President Chester, long ago, at a time when he possessed Chester's entire confidence.

Harvard studied the pictured face long and carefully. Then, silently, he told himself:

"Rushton is the man! He has got the ability, and, if given the opportunity, he can, and he will, make good. I wonder if it can be done? I wonder if I can get him out of prison, on parole, for this specific purpose?"

"It is worth trying, anyway, and it will give him an opportunity to redeem himself. Set a thief to catch a thief! By Jove, I'll try it."

Harvard reached for the telephone and called up the office of the district attorney.

CHAPTER VIII

THE MAKING OF A MAN

The private office of the district attorney of New York County, four days later; Wednesday of the succeeding week. The district attorney and Bingham Harvard were alone together. They had the air of having exhausted the topic that was the object of their meeting at that time and place. They seemed to be awaiting the arrival of a person expected. After a somewhat extended silence between them, the county official remarked, casually:

"I regret, Harvard, that I have not the confidence in this experiment that you possess. The fact is due, I suppose, to my official training. Honestly, as I told you when you suggested this thing, last Saturday, Rushton is the very last man I would have selected for this form of leniency."

"Nevertheless, I believe that he will make good," Harvard replied, smiling confidently.

The district attorney shrugged.

"He was a grafter from Graftersville," he said, shortly. "He is a convicted felon. He has served less than two years of his ten years' sentence. He is—"

They were interrupted by a summons at the door.

"He has arrived, evidently," Harvard said quietly. "Will you leave me quite alone with him, please? And I would rather that you did not address a word to him now. Wait until I have had my talk with him."

"Oh, all right, Harvard. Just as you say."

The district attorney left his chair and threw open the door. Three men stood outside, waiting: two detectives of the district attorney's staff, and between them, Rodney Rushton, handcuffed to one of them.

"Take off those irons, Snell, and leave Rushton alone with this gentleman," the district attorney ordered, and passed outside.

A moment later the door closed, and Rodney Rushton, unfettered and unhampered, stood alone in the presence of the man he had once so foully wronged, and who had been the direct cause of the prison sentence he was enduring. Rushton's eyes were furtive, suspicious, sullen. With his close-cropped hair and shaven face and lip, he looked more the bulldog than ever. The angry scowl on his face and in his eyes deepened the instant he saw and recognized Bingham Harvard.

"You, eh?" he said, with a half snarl, bending slightly forward toward the man he thought to be his sworn enemy. His eyes were blazing with ill-suppressed fury. His fingers twitched. Every muscle in his body was tense and strained in the visible effort at self-control.

"Say, Harvard, if I didn't know that you possess the strength of ten ordinary men, I'd take a chance right now, and try to choke the life outa you."

"Sit down, Rushton," Harvard replied calmly. "Take that chair. I have considerable to say to you."

"Oh, you have, have you? Say, what did you have me brought down here for, anyhow? Wanta get some more testimony out o' me—eh?" Rushton snarled; but he dropped into the chair that Harvard indicated.

"You were a good detective, Rushton," Harvard replied, speaking slowly but with quiet emphasis. "By nature, and by training, and because of experience and a natural aptitude for the work, there was none better qualified than yourself when you were at headquarters. If you had kept straight—if you had not gone money-mad—you would have been the peer of all of them down there. You know that, don't you?"

"Say, Mr. Man, is this here guff you're givin' me intended for a sermon?"

"Possibly; but I want you to listen to me to the end. You admit, do you not, that what I have said is true?"

"Maybe it is, and maybe it ain't. What of it?"

"This: I am going to ask you a question straight from the shoulder, Rushton—and I want you to reply to it, straight from your inmost heart. This is it: If you were given a chance to redeem yourself—if you were freed from prison on parole, and given the opportunity to make good, would you do it? Would you be on the level?"

Harvard paused to study the effect of his words. And then:

"Would you play square and open? Would you be honest and straightforward, and do your utmost to win back the place in the world that you have lost, and to deserve once more the respect and confidence of your fellow men? Would you, Rushton?"

Harvard bent forward in his chair as he put the compound question. His level gaze bored into Rushton's soul, and the convict's eyes widened, his face became a shade whiter than its prison pallor, and his lips parted in an effort to speak, although for a space no sound issued from them. But at last, in a voice that was gruff and husky with emotion, he faltered:

"As sure as there is a God in heaven, Harvard, I would! *I would*!" Then: "Say! What are you givin' me, anyhow? What kind of a stall is this that you're workin' on me? I ain't no candy kid, Mr. Bingham Harvard. What are you tryin' to dig out from under my breast-plate, Mr. Alias the Night Wind?"

Harvard leaned back in his chair again, smiling.

"I'll accept your reply to my questions and strike out those *you* have asked," he said. "I am here to offer you just that chance, Rushton. You are here to accept it, or decline it, as you may prefer."

The convict seized upon the arms of his chair and gripped them until his knuckles became as white as chalk. He breathed hard. He attempted no reply. He had begun to realize that the man by whom he was confronted was not merely talking—was in earnest in what he had said.

Harvard spoke again, in a low tone, and quietly.

"You have been, in the past, about seven-tenths to the good, and three-tenths to the bad, Rushton—and that is pretty nearly the make-up of almost every man you will meet and pass in the city streets. The difference is that the badness takes different forms in different men. Yours took the form of money-madness. You have been trained in an atmosphere of graft. You came to look upon it as a sort of inherited right. With time and opportunity it spread, like a rash on your skin, all over you, all through you. And then it got you 'in bad,' and it dumped you, and put you where you have been for almost two years. You want to get out of it, don't you?"

"You bet your sweet life I want to get out of it, Mr. Harvard. Honest, don't play with me or fool me, for God's sake! *Is* there a chance? Say, *is there one*?"

56

"Yes, Rushton, there *is* one. Will you take it?"

"Will *I take it?* Good God, *won't I take it!*"

His lips trembled. He wheeled in his tracks until his back was toward Harvard, and stood so for a moment with his face buried in his hands. Then he turned slowly around again, and with solemn face but shining eyes he said quietly: "I will take it, Mr. Harvard, and I will make good."

"Fine," said Harvard. "Sit down again now, and look this over." He took a folded document from one of his pockets and gave it to Rushton. The latter read what it contained, with distended eyes and set jaws. Twice he looked up incredulously, unbelievingly. Then he read on to the end of it. Then he folded it and sat very still, holding the document tightly in one clenched hand. He did not speak; possibly he could not have done so at that moment.

Harvard spoke again quietly:

"It is, as you see, a parole, granted at the instance of the district attorney and myself and signed by the Governor of the State. It gives you your freedom under the stated conditions. A dishonest act on your part would end it. Either the district attorney or myself can have you returned to prison at any time—but neither of us will ever think of doing so unless you give us cause. You cannot leave the State save with the written permission of one of us, but I shall give you that written permission to go wheresoever you will at once."

"But why, *why*? Why have you done this, Mr. Harvard? For me! You, of all men! Why? I do not understand it. I—Say! I'll go through hell for you for this, and I won't get so much as a hair of my head singed, either. I'm done with crooked ways. I'll make good! *I'll make good!* You have given me the chance; you watch. I—I wish I was a woman for half a minute; I'd like to cry. Honest."

"Go ahead and cry. It won't hurt you."

"I can't, and that's the hell of it. Honest, Mr. Harvard, why did you do this? Because—I know that you're the one who has done it."

Harvard smiled as he replied:

"Partly from a motive of selfishness, Rushton, and partly because I have the utmost faith in that seven-tenths of good in you. I have got a case for you to work out—quite an important one. I believe that you can do it. I have convinced myself that you are the *only* man who *can* do it quickly, in the right way and as I want it done. It would not do the State of New York any good, or me any good, or you any good, to keep you locked up in prison eight years more. To have you outside and busy and redeeming yourself as well as serving the State and county, will do us all good. You were never a criminal from choice and selection; you became one because of environment and an insidious 'system.' I am going to put you on the track of a man who is a criminal from deliberate study, selection, and self-education to that end—the kind of a man whom it is best to put into a prison and keep there. Do you want the job?"

"You bet I do. Just lead me to the place where the trail begins, that's all."

"The trail begins in my private office at the bank, Rushton. I am its president now. Mr. Chester has retired. We will go there together. But first"—he pressed a button beneath the edge of the desk—"we must say good-by to the district attorney."

That official entered a moment later. Rushton sprang to his feet in greeting. His face was transfigured. He looked another man than the one who had stood at the door a little while before, handcuffed to an officer. His eyes shone with enthusiasm and confidence. He stood straight and solidly upon his feet where he had half slouched before.

"Mr. District Attorney, I want to thank you for this," he said. "I want to promise you that you won't be sorry—that you will never regret what has happened to-day. I am going to make good. I'm going to win back all that I lost. Why, I can't believe it all, even now. It's—it's wonderful; just wonderful. You believe me, don't you, Mr. District Attorney?"

"Yes, Rushton, I think I do—now. I did not, though, until now. Go ahead, Rushton. Try it out; and win out. And don't thank me; thank Mr. Harvard. I never would have taken the chance if he hadn't badgered me—and the Governor, too, for that matter—into it."

"Well, sir, you take it from me, he won't lose; nor you; nor the Governor. And I'll win. I swear it!"

"You are beginning to make me think that you will, Rushton," the official replied, with a kindly smile.

Not until Rushton and Bingham Harvard were seated together in the private office of the Centropolis Bank did the latter refer to the matter which had been the direct cause of liberating the ex-lieutenant from prison. Then he related it exactly as we know it here, adding to it that information concerning the mysterious disappearance of Chilton from the Pullman stateroom on the Chicago train. Rushton listened with close attention to all of it, occasionally interjecting a pertinent question, making few notes, concentrating his mind upon everything that was told to him in a way that pleased

Harvard very much indeed. It was not at all the old-time, blustering, bullying, bluffing Rushton who listened; it was the Rushton who, years before, had started out upon a promising career, filled with hope and alive with ambition to succeed in his chosen calling.

"I'll get him, Mr. Harvard," he said at the finish of it; "and I will get the most of that money, too. It's a cinch that he's got it planted somewhere by this time, and it's a pretty safe proposition that he planted it somewhere in the city of New York, too."

"I am sorry that he got away with those pictures of himself," Harvard suggested.

"They wouldn't be any good to me at all," Rushton replied quickly. "He ain't wearin' that hair and beard any more; and I guess a lot of that tan on his face was artificial—the same as the gray hair. This ain't a case where pictures would do any good; it's a case for honest-injun, straight-from-the-shoulder detective work—and I'm the guy that can do it."

CHAPTER IX

ROLLING A CIGARETTE

Rodney Rushton was a man transformed. And Bingham Harvard had given him permission to see Lady Kate that evening, to secure her approval of what he was to do to redeem himself. The whirlwind events that had entered his life within a few hours impressed him with the force, and faith also, of a miracle; for Rushton in his youth had had a mother who had talked much of such things into his young ears. And it was as Bingham Harvard had said to him: his instincts were naturally good ones. Only the environment of that octopus-like police system of old New York which was the growth of many decades, which had been planted and had flourished amazingly in the days of Tweed, and which had grown and spread unbelievably, had led him astray from the paths of rectitude and virtue that his mother had once lighted for him. Many like him have been thrust into the mire, to sink deeper and deeper into it with each struggle to escape; and many had gone down, never to escape; some had succeeded in withdrawing (like his friend Lieutenant Banta, for example); and others, by good fortune rather than by intent, had escaped altogether.

Also, it was as Bingham Harvard had said in reference to Rushton's abilities as a detective officer. His superiors at the central office had formerly acknowledged that there was none better; and if, in the past, he had relied upon his intelligence rather than upon his shrewdness, and had stuck to honest methods rather than use the questionable ones that had offered themselves unsought, his name already would have been a household word for ability. And he was wise enough to recognize the facts, without egotism, when he came away from the bank after his interview with Harvard in which he had been told the story of the coming and going of Holbrook Chilton.

He saw himself as others saw him—and he saw it all, without self-apology. The days and nights that he had passed in prison had tilled and enriched this soil in which this act of Harvard's, aided by the district attorney, had planted the seed of rehabilitation.

Rushton walked out of the bank, not a new man, but the former man restored. His face was illuminated. His eyes shone with resolution and purpose. He had cast aside the garment of shame, remorse, and reprisal, as he might have thrown an old coat into the dust-heap. He looked at men as he passed them in the street and smiled into their faces, conscious that he no longer would have reason to avert his gaze; and there was a bounding sensation in his heart and uplift in his soul, a clearness of his moral vision, which made him very, very glad.

He sought his old home in a house he owned and which had remained, undisturbed during his absence. It was in a street east of Union Square. Relatives still occupied the lower floors, but the top one that he had occupied remained as he had left it. When he came forth later, dressed and equipped for the campaign he was to undertake (for he had made several purchases on his way there), the erectness of his bearing, the spring in his tread, the lofty impulse in his soul, lent to him a dignity that he had almost forgotten and which he had thought never to possess again: the dignity that belongs with right-doing.

There was still much time to kill before he could present himself at the home of Bingham Harvard, for he had asked very earnestly for the privilege to see and talk with Lady Kate and to secure her approval before he should actually begin the work he was to do. He occupied part of it by a visit to the restaurant and by ordering for the first time in many months exactly the sort of a meal he wanted; and there was still time to spare when he came out of it. He sauntered through a side-street to Fifth Avenue, turned north along that thoroughfare, and walked on and on, sometimes nodding familiarly toward certain towering buildings that looked good to him, and glancing askance at others that had sprung into being during his absence; and so he came, after a time, to the Hotel Mammoth.

At the entrance he halted, ostensibly to light a fresh cigar, for he was ever an inveterate smoker; really to stand there for a while and to look upon the familiar and the unfamiliar faces that passed him going in and out of the great hostelry. Beside him, their elbows almost touching, was a man whose presence and nearness Rushton did not at once notice; until, chancing to glance downward, he discovered the stranger in the act of tearing a yellow cigarette-paper from a little book of them, crease it through the middle delicately, produce a small pouch of embroidered buckskin from which he sprinkled tobacco (crushed and dried leaves of the natural plant, Rushton noticed, too) upon the creased paper, and then deftly roll the combination into a perfectly-formed cigarette.

Rushton watched the man with an abstract sort of fascination; for while his mind was wholly upon other matters, he still took subconscious note of the odd manner in which the stranger rolled the paper around the tobacco. Also he made the barely conscious mental comment, characteristic of his habit of close observation, that "the stranger was too swell a guy to be rolling his own makings." For the first time he took note of the stranger's features. For a man who was so immaculately and perfectly attired and yet who rolled cigarettes with all the deftness of a cowpuncher, and who performed the act with lightning-like swiftness and between the second and third fingers of his hands instead of between the thumbs and fingers, interested that sixth sense of Rushton's which had long ago beckoned him into the police force and had developed him into a detective. It was entirely a casual glance that Rushton cast upon the stranger who stood beside him. He saw a man somewhat taller than himself, perfectly put together, splendidly formed for athletics, graceful of pose, distinguished of appearance, handsome of feature, with dark hair and red-brown eyes that were large and full and immoderately glowing behind the shell-rimmed glasses that were worn over them.

The stranger inhaled only a few deep breaths of smoke from the cigarette he had made. Then he cast it aside and did something which the observing Rushton regarded as being distinctly more appropriate. He produced a beautifully monogrammed case from one of his pockets, extracted a gold-tipped Egyptian cigarette from among the many that it contained, and lighted that. And he made a wry face over the first whiff of it as he did so.

"He don't like that kind, but he's tryin' to learn to," was Rushton's mental comment.

Other things attracted the former detective's attention. When he turned again to glance toward his neighbor the man had disappeared. Rushton shrugged his shoulders and forgot him, never imagining that within another hour or so he was to meet him face to face and be introduced to the man according to the recognized customs. But the stranger had not once turned his eyes upon the former policeman who had been standing so near while the cigarette was manufactured, so it was not likely that the recognition would be mutual when the two should meet.

Rushton, however, never forgot a face. He possessed much the same qualities which had given renown to one of his former compatriots at headquarters, who had been known variously as "The Moniker Man" and "The Man with the Camera Eye" and "Second-Sight Bill." He never forgot a face that he had once seen; and invariably he could remember when and where he had seen the face also.

He looked at his watch and discovered that he would just about use up the necessary time if he walked slowly from the Hotel Mammoth to Bingham Harvard's home, which was located on the same avenue at some distance above the Plaza. So he strolled forward. And ultimately he came to Bingham Harvard's house, as we shall see.

So did that other man arrive there later; and heralded, too, by a card and a brief note that he had previously despatched to Bingham Harvard's wife; to Lady Kate, as Rushton always thought of her. For she had been "Lady Kate of the Police" before she met and wedded the man who had won the alias of "The Night Wind."

For Rodney Rushton there remained only one thing to be attained now, that Harvard had bestowed his confidence, and that was the approval of the act by Harvard's wife; by Lady Kate. And it was with a fervent prayer in his heart and soul that Rushton walked forward on his quest to secure that approval, never doubting that it would be accorded him. And so he came presently to the door of the mansion that had once been the home of President Chester of the Centropolis Bank, and which that same splendid old man had bestowed upon the bride of the man whom he loved as a son.

CHAPTER X

SOME OF RUSHTON'S "DOPE"

Experts have repeatedly insisted that every man possesses two characteristics which are impossible of perfect and continuous disguise: his voice and his walk. It is certain, nevertheless, that the man called Holbrook Chilton succeeded in accomplishing both supposedly impossible feats. We shall see presently how he did it.

The evening of the day of Rodney Rushton's deliverance from prison and his assignment to the case of running down the forger, Chilton, Bingham Harvard spent at home with his wife. Until then he had told her nothing concerning his plan to give the ex-lieutenant of police a chance to redeem himself.

In fact, he had not felt entirely assured that Katherine would unqualifiedly approve of his philanthropic efforts concerning Rushton. The experiences that she had encountered and overcome in association with him while she was connected with the detective bureau down at headquarters were not calculated to predispose her in his favor.

There had been a time, approximately three years antedating the beginning of this history, when, because her father, who was a prominent Kentuckian, had insisted upon her marrying a man she did not love, she had left her home in the Blue Grass country and gone to the great city of New York. Her father having been a United States Senator, and she having spent much time in Washington as a girl and a young woman, she found it possible to find the kind of influential backing she wanted. With it she had sought and obtained an appointment—on probation—to the detective bureau of the New York police. As "Lady Kate of the Police" she had made good; as Lady Kate she had first been brought in contact with Bingham Harvard, alias The Night Wind, and with Bingham Harvard's true and tried friend, Tom Clancy; and with Lieutenant Rodney Rushton, then an active and more or less important quantity at the Central Office.

Now she had become the wife of Harvard and her police experiences were relegated to the past. She had settled down to the young-matronly pursuits of a thoroughly happy and contented domestic atmosphere. But who shall say that yearnings for the concentration and excitement of her career as an accredited detective did not at times possess her? They did. The fact that she made no mention of them to her husband was merely a matter of judgment and expediency with her; but she found a great deal to interest her in keeping pretty close tabs upon the "doings" at police headquarters, and in working out mentally (and often to her own satisfaction) some of the cases that puzzled the authorities. And she had written many a letter of modest suggestion to the deputy commissioner and the inspector in charge of the bureau.

Chilton's masterly theft of three hundred and ninety-seven thousand dollars did not, however, get into the newspapers. It was a closely-guarded bank secret, following out the suggestions voiced by Mr. Anderson Van Cleve. The regular police were not called into the case at all. The national agency, whose chief with two operatives had been summoned to the bank to meet Van Cleve and ex-Lieutenant Rodney Rushton, were the only parties at work upon it; nor did they work together. Rushton greatly preferred to work alone.

Naturally, however, an announcement of his parole from prison by the Governor at the joint request of Bingham Harvard and the district attorney, was printed and appeared in the evening papers of that day. There are always newspaper reporters around the office of the district attorney, and they were not slow to see and recognize the ex-lieutenant and to ask pertinent questions concerning him. Lady Kate saw that announcement and questioned her husband about it over the dinner-table. He related the whole story from beginning to end, and having a well-trained mind, she listened without comment until he had finished.

"Where," she asked when he had done, "did you acquire your superlative confidence in the ability of Rodney Rushton?"

"I have always had it, Katherine, ever since I first knew the man," Harvard replied. "Mr. Chester felt the same way about him up to the time when he knew that Rushton had gone wrong. You may be sure of that, else Rushton could never have made him believe—"

"Yes, yes; I know," she interrupted. Then after a pause, she added tentatively: "Sometimes, Bing, I wish that I were back in the harness again. I wish it now, to-night. I do, really. I would like—nothing could give me more genuine pleasure than to work on this case myself"—and she looked across the table beneath drooping lashes with a glance that was at once whimsical and appealing.

"Nonsense, Kate!" he replied.

"I mean it," she said. "I do, really."

"Possibly you would like to assist Rushton?" her husband suggested ironically.

"I would," she retorted. "For one thing, I would like to determine for myself if Rushton is to be trusted—completely. I shall not feel assured as to that until I have seen him and talked with him."

Harvard glanced at his watch.

"All right," he said. "You will have an opportunity inside of an hour. He asked if he might drop in here for a few moments to pay his respects to you, and I told him he might. He said he wanted to start even and that he did not feel as if he could quite do it without *your* approval."

Lady Kate nodded.

"That has a good sound," she remarked. "The impulse to come here to see me is reassuring. All the same, I am rather sorry that he selected *this* evening."

"Why?"

Instead of replying in words she passed an opened envelope across the table to him, and he took from it a card and a short written note which he read aloud. It was merely a request that the writer might be permitted to call and pay his respects that evening, and to renew a valued and cherished acquaintance of long standing.

"Who is Benton Keese?" Harvard asked, restoring the note and card to the envelope and returning it.

"Did I never tell you the name of the man whom my father wanted me to marry? The man who was the unconscious cause of my leaving home and coming to New York and becoming a police-woman?" she asked smilingly.

"No; I don't think I ever heard it."

"The man was Benton Keese; and really, Bing, I think we are under obligations to him—don't you? If he had not done as he did, if he had not sought to influence my father to coerce me, I would not have left home, I would not have come to New York, I would never have been connected with the police, *and I never would have met you.*"

"Oh, well, I don't blame him for loving you, little lady. I don't quite see how anybody can help doing that. Poor devil, I suppose I ought to feel sorry for him because he lost you—only somehow, I don't."

Soon after they returned to the library from dinner Rushton was announced. He had made good use of his time. He was well and fashionably attired, and but for the closely cropped hair he would have borne little resemblance to the man who had been taken that day to the district attorney's office handcuffed to an officer. There was definite purpose in his face, a new expression in his eyes. Not a *new* man, but the *real* man, stood before them in Rodney Rushton's shoes.

Lady Kate stepped quickly forward the instant he appeared and offered him her hand. He took it and held it for a moment while he searched his mind for words in which to express the emotions he felt because of her reception of him.

"I guess, Lady Ka—Mrs. Harvard—that I wronged *you* even worse than I did *him*, when I framed up that crooked deal against the best guy that ever stood in shoe-leather," he faltered lamely. "But I did want to see you, Lady. I did wanta hear you say that you'd forgiven me. That's why I asked the Night Wi—Say; I'm makin' bad breaks, all right, ain't I? Anyhow, that's why I wanted to come here to-night. Thank you both for lettin' me."

"Why, lieutenant," Katherine replied instantly, "if you had not worked that frame-up, Mr. Harvard and I might never have known each other at all."

"Say, I hadn't thought of that. I guess, maybe, that's right, too. And there's another thing that wouldn't have happened, either; I wouldn't have stood just where I do now. I'd have been the same crooked cop, graftin' to beat the band, framin' up lies and other things on innocent parties, and—"

"Well, Mrs. Harvard, this guy that's talkin' to you now ain't the same Rushton that you knew downtown; not so's you could notice it."

"I believe that thoroughly," Katherine replied with feeling.

"I have been telling Mrs. Harvard about the affair at the bank, Rushton," Bing remarked, to change the subject.

"Gee, Lady Kate—There I go again, callin' you by that name. But it comes sort o' natural, you know. You'll have to excuse me when I make breaks like that."

"Call me Lady Kate, if it comes easier. I rather like it," she replied. "What were you about to say?"

"I was goin' to say that I couldn't help wishin' that you were goin' to help on this case, same's you did on that other one. Of course it's a foolish wish, but—"

"Perhaps not entirely foolish. I may be able to assist. I will, if I can—only the affair could not end as the other one did; I couldn't marry the criminal, you know." At which remark they all laughed aloud happily. Rushton turned to Bingham Harvard.

"Say," he said, "I've been dopin' this thing out in my mind ever since we had our confidential chin down at the bank."

"Well, what do you make out of your dope?" Harvard inquired smilingly.

"That fellow Chilton is some slick article, Mr. Harvard. He's smoother and slipprier'n watch-maker's oil, take it from me; and he's got nerve. I'd lay my pile against a brick medallion that he ain't got no criminal record, and that he has just been layin' by an' studyin' out this big play for months, maybe for years. To get Van Cleve's bank-roll, I mean; not necessarily to pinch it in just the manner he did do it finally. He belongs to that breed of gamblers that stake their whole stack of chips on a single turn of the cards."

"Very likely, Rushton."

"This thing didn't come onto him sudden. He'd been thinkin' of something of the sort for months and months—sure as you're born. He'd been practicin' that signature all the time, too. I've doped it out that he meant to bury Van Cleve somewhere down in Mexico and to come here afterward and pass himself off as the dead man. And then this here opportunity fell onto him all of a sudden."

"That sounds reasonable," Harvard commented; and Lady Kate nodded her approval of it.

"Then, another thing. His disappearin' from that Pullman the way he did couldn't have meant but one thing."

"What thing?"

"That he was comin' back here to New York. That heavy tan on his face was *painted* on, I'll bet a cookie; and for two reasons; to make him look as dark as a Mexican and to keep off the real tan, so that when he got rid of the paint and his beard and his long hair and

68

other identifyin' marks, his complexion would be white enough, and evenly white at that."

"It is your idea, then, that Chilton is, even now, right here in New York City?"

"I'd bet on it goin' an' comin', and straight across the board, Mr. Harvard," Rushton replied with emphasis. "It wouldn't surprise me none if he should have nerve enough to get himself introduced at the bank under another name, so's he could open an account with you. If he ain't plumb full of what you call egotism I miss my target, that's all. Why, I—"

The door opened. A servant entered and brought a card to Harvard, who announced:

"It is Mr. Keese, Katherine. Bring the gentleman here, Bolton"—to the servant. Then: "We will change the subject now, Rushton."

A moment later Benton Keese was shown into the library, and Rodney Rushton caught his breath and with difficulty withheld a violent start of surprise when he saw the man. Benton Keese was the man he had seen in the act of rolling a cigarette before the entrance to the Hotel Mammoth!

CHAPTER XI

TOM CLANCY'S FOOL REMARK

Tall, clean-cut, well built, smoothly shaven, undeniably hand-some and distinguished in appearance, richly and fashionably attired in a garb that suggested the clerical without actually accomplishing it, with tortoise-shell-rimmed eyeglasses, large and round, that emphasized the luster of his brilliant brown eyes, Benton Keese was an attractive figure of a man as he came into the room and bowed low over the white hand that Katherine extended to him in greeting. He was entirely self-possessed; thoroughly at ease, and he turned with a graceful gesture to acknowledge the introductions to "Mr. Harvard, my husband, and Mr. Rushton, a friend."

And Katherine announced him to them as "Mr. Benton Keese, of Lexington, Kentucky—a friend whom I have always known."

"You have changed very little, Benton," Katherine remarked when they had resumed their chairs, and he replied smilingly:

"Outwardly, to the eye, perhaps you are right, Katherine; but inside of me—in my heart and soul and aspirations and ambitions I feel that there has been a very decided change."

He hesitated an instant, and then with glowing eyes added in a tone that was almost inaudible: "A very decided change indeed—with one exception, which can never change."

Harvard and Rushton did not—could not—hear that last sentence that Benton Keese uttered. Apparently he did not intend that they should hear it. It was intended for Katherine's ears alone, and it could have but one meaning: that the man who made it was as madly and hopelessly in love with her then as ever he had been. Keese lowered his glistening eyes when he said it, and he contrived to express the few words in such a manner that they could convey no of-

fense; nevertheless, Lady Kate flushed vividly—but it was with resentment that he had dared to say such a thing to her; not at all because she cared about what he did say.

Benton Keese had never attracted her. He was much older than
she—ten years or thereabouts. And when one is young, as she had
been at the time he had forced his attentions upon her, ten years' se-
niority is an aeon of time. She had liked him—at a distance; had respected him because he was a member of one of the old families of
the neighborhood of her birth; that was all. But now, as he raised his
brown eyes again to hers after making that remark, a vague uneasiness beset her. She recalled that she had fled from her home to avoid
him, because something within her, like a sixth sense, had feared
him; and now, of a sudden, that indefinable fear assailed her anew.
She could not have told why; she could not have explained it. Indeed, she flouted the idea mentally, yet all the while she was quite
conscious that it was there.

The pause between his remark and Katherine's succeeding
question was so short as to be barely noticeable. The flush on her
face disappeared almost as soon as it came. Instinctively she forced
her chair a few inches farther away from Keese.

"You have been abroad somewhere, have you not?" she asked.

"Yes. In China, mostly. In the interior. I have just returned; indeed, I have not been to Kentucky as yet, although I have written
that I am back. As my manner of dress may have partly suggested to
you, I have been engaged in work that was connected with certain
foreign missions."

"You do not mean—" she began; and he interrupted her laugh-
ingly:

"Oh, no, Katherine! I have not taken orders. I went out merely
as an agent; a business agent for the consolidated boards. But I was
informed of your marriage, even though I was at the other side of
the world. I hope you are glad to see me?"

"I am—of course. Very glad, Benton."

He bent nearer to her.

"Do you know, Katherine," he said, "that after you disappeared
from your home, and before I went away, I searched everywhere to
find you, and that I—"

"We will not refer to that time, if you please," she interrupted
him coldly. Then she turned to the others.

"Bingham," she said, "Mr. Keese has been to China. He has just returned." She felt that it was time to include her husband and Rushton in the conversation.

Whatever reply Harvard might have made was interrupted by the opening of the door, and Tom Clancy appeared at the threshold.

"Hello, everybody," he exclaimed, advancing. Then, perceiving Rushton, he halted.

"Well, by Jove!" he ejaculated. "I saw it in the paper, Rushton, but I did not believe it. That is what brought me here to-night, as a matter of fact. So it's true, eh?"

He did not offer his hand to the ex-lieutenant. Rushton, who had risen, stood very still, facing him.

"Shake hands with Mr. Rushton, Tom," Harvard said quietly. "What you saw in the paper is quite true, and more goes with it. Now, let me present you to Mr. Keese, of Kentucky, but more recently from China; an old friend of Katherine's."

Tom, in his usual hearty manner, seized upon Keese's hand and shook it vigorously; and, after he had done that, instead of talking on in his customarily enthusiastic manner, he did what for him was an unusual thing. He kept silence. More, he lifted the hand that had greeted Benton Keese and fixed his eyes upon the fingers of it, as if they were new to him. Then he laughed aloud; and the space of his silence and abstraction really occupied less than a second of time.

"That's some grip that you brought home from China with you, Mr. Keese," he said.

"I am sorry, Mr. Clancy, if I hurt you," Keese replied. "It was involuntary."

"Hurt me?" Tom laughed. "Not at all. It wasn't that. But if I didn't know better I would swear that I had shaken hands with you before—somewhere. Odd, isn't it? That is a pronounced peculiarity of mine—remembering hand-shakes."

After that the conversation became general, and within the hour Benton Keese arose to take his leave. Harvard invited him cordially to call again. Katherine's invitation was perfunctory but lacked nothing of words. Clancy and Rushton bowed their adieus from across the room.

"Who and what is he, anyhow?" Tom asked when the man had gone. "Is he a minister, a mission-worker, or a wire-tapper, Bing?"

"He is the man who sent this little lady here to me," Harvard replied, laughing. "He is the chap she ran away from when she came to New York; the one her father wanted her to marry."

"It's a wonder that you didn't fall for him, lady," Tom said, turning toward Katherine with his humorous grin. "There's no denying that he's a handsome chap. Say, Rushton, what is all this song and dance about you? Is it a sure-enough reformation?"

"Mr. Harvard has given me my chance. I have accepted it; that's all, Mr. Clancy," the ex-lieutenant replied.

"Bully for you! Say, I wonder if you know that I saved your life once? That was when Bing was going out to kill you offhand and I wouldn't let him do it. You owe me one for that."

"Tom," Harvard said quietly, "Van Cleve and I agreed together that the Chilton episode should remain a bank secret. Chief Redhead and a few of his operatives are the only persons outside of our own circle who know about it. But *I* wanted to put Rushton on the job, because I believe that he is the man for it. The district attorney has aided me, has given him a special appointment, with authority to arrest; and—there you are."

Rushton started to his feet.

"And here *I* am, too, when I oughta be goin'," he exclaimed.

"I'll chase along with you, Rushton," Clancy said, rising also.

"No, Bing, thank you. I've got another date. I dropped in for a moment, anyhow."

"Good night, Katherine. I hope you haven't a tender spot left in your memory for that chap Keese, eh?"

"Not one, Tom; nor the suggestion of one," she smiled back at him.

"Well, take it from me, he has got a lot of 'em for you. Judging from his eyes and manner, by what little I saw of him, it's a wonder to me that he did not seize you bodily and carry you off when you knew him down there in Kentucky."

"Frankly, Tom, I was afraid that he would do that very thing. That is why I ran away," Lady Kate replied; and she spoke quite seriously apparently.

Outside of the house Clancy and Rushton walked in silence for a time. Then Tom stopped in his tracks at the corner, and addressed his companion abruptly.

"Rushton," he said, "I am going to make a fool remark that hasn't got the slightest foundation to stand upon other than a mere hand-shake; but everything 'goes as it lays' just the same. The fool remark is this: That guy Keese is the man from Mexico, or I'm a damn fool. If he isn't that fellow Chilton who shook hands with me at Harvard's bank and at my own office, and who got away with

Van Cleve's dough, I'll crawl back into my hole and pull it in after me. And there wasn't a single thing about him to suggest it but just that hand-shake of his."

CHAPTER XII

THE SERPENT—AND LADY KATE

Tom Clancy said nothing to Harvard of his suspicions concerning Benton Keese. The fact was that they were so vague, so devoid of logical foundation, so literally absurd, that he gave very little credence to them himself.

But Rushton took them more seriously. His official experience had taught him that the "little things that are counted trivial" are often the fingerposts which point the way to achievement. He had noticed and had mentally commented upon Tom's attitude at the moment of that hand-shake. He had wondered about it a little, and here was the explanation; and so Rushton decided that he would keep an eye upon Mr. Benton Keese for a time—or at least until he could satisfy himself that the man from Kentucky was everything that he appeared to be.

It was a coincidence that not long before Rushton's summary dismissal from the "force" the performance of duty had taken him to Lexington, Kentucky, to bring back to New York a prisoner who had been arrested there and detained; and so he had made the acquaintance of the then chief of police of that city. Consequently as soon as he parted with Clancy he filed a telegram to that Southern official, as follows:

> Approximately three or four years ago Benton Keese disappeared from your community. Where did he go? What became of him? Please wire full information you possess concerning him and his family.

Before noon of the following day he received this reply:

Left here three and a half years ago, ostensibly for China. Nothing known of him since then. Doubtful if he communicated even with members of his family.

Both parents have since died. Sister Elizabeth, called Miss Betty, twenty-five, occupies old homestead with maiden aunt and servants. Property, valued hundred thousand or so, left by will equally to her and B. K. Community believes him dead. Sister confident he will return. He disappeared shortly after being jilted by young woman when reported about to marry.

No record against him save usual escapades of young gentlemen of his type, such as poker, and gambling generally. Left no unpaid debts.

COCKRELL,
Chief of Police

The message was a substantiation of the account that Keese had given of himself, and Rushton took it to Clancy, explaining what he had done. Tom's comment was entirely characteristic.

"I told you that it was a fool remark when I made it, Rushton," he said. "Just because a chap happened to grasp my hand in a certain manner I immediately associated him with a forger and thief with whom I had shaken hands twice only; and there was not another single thing about Keese—not one—to suggest in the remotest manner the identity of the other fellow."

Lady Kate harbored no misgivings of the kind that impressed Tom Clancy and Rodney Rushton; but she did feel others, although they were of an entirely different character. She said not a word to her husband concerning them; but she thought of them that night while she was composing herself to sleep, and again in the morning after Bing had left her to go to the bank.

Keese had exerted an undeniable and altogether uncanny influence upon her ever since her earliest recollection of him. But he had been able to impress it upon her only when she was actually in his presence. Away from her, outside the house or the room where she happened to be, he was altogether repugnant and repulsive. And yet she recalled that morning how strangely his eyes, his low-pitched voice, his deferential manner, and his spoken words, which always seemed to convey a double meaning, had always affected her. There was an indefinable lure about him that she could not avoid, and which she had infinitely dreaded during the days of her young maidenhood in Kentucky—a lure from which she had incontinently fled, fearing with all her heart and soul that if she remained within his environment she would one day succumb to it, that the day might come when she would not have the strength of purpose to deny him. That was before she knew Bingham Harvard.

Since then, since the great love for the man whose wife she had become had filled her with happiness and content, all of the misgivings and all of the indefinable fears engendered by the subtle, insidious influence that Benton Keese had impressed upon her against her will had been forgotten—until the moment when he was actually before her again, looking into her secret soul (as it seemed to her) with his strangely luminous eyes, speaking to her in that oddly hypnotic voice, battering down her reserve with some occult force which she could neither understand nor resist, and force his personality upon her emotions in a way that frightened her almost into a panic when she thought about it afterward. It was almost as if with his eyes he stripped her bare of her moral clothing, as if he compelled her soul to nakedness, as if he read and understood her fear of him and actually gloried in it, as if he were thoroughly aware of the Satanic lure he possessed for her. It was as if he knew that she hated it and him; and also that she feared both it and him. It was, in effect, the tale of the serpent and the fluttering bird retold and humanized.

In her presence Benton Keese at once became the primitive man, and the very force and masterfulness of him brought to the surface of Katherine's consciousness, resentfully and utterly against her will, the primitive, unstudied, totally unknown and uncomprehended emotions which nobody but this man had the power to uncover. His big, softly luminous eyes seemed to possess arms and fingers and muscles that could reach out invisibly and embrace her, that could hold her, that could momentarily quell her resentment and compel her to return his unspoken messages in kind, even though she hated herself for doing so. She could feel his personality mentally embracing and holding her to him across the width of a room, even when he did not look at her; and yet she could not remember that he had ever uttered a word to her or committed an act against her that she could have resented with spoken words.

But Benton Keese did not have to use words or to commit acts to convey the messages that radiated from his eyes, and, indeed, from his whole lithe, athletic, and handsome physical presence. He drew her forcefully and forcibly as the magnet draws a steel needle, and she hated and feared him most of all whenever that almost irresistible attraction influenced her.

Katherine was restless all that morning after his call. She wandered from room to room in her home—the home that had once been Sterling Chester's, and which he had given to her as a wedding present. She feared Keese might take it upon himself to call again upon her without announcement, and she gave orders that she was "not at home" to anybody that day.

Toward noon she considered seriously the idea of going down to the bank and confiding all of her doubts and misgivings to Bingham; but dismissed the thought almost as soon as it was born. Later she decided to write a message to Benton Keese in which she could tell him plainly that a renewal of their old-time friendly associations would be impossible. Then she dismissed that decision, for she knew perfectly well that *he* would thoroughly understand the meaning and the motives that were behind such an act, and that he would gloat over it in secret. She realized that it would be, in a sense, a confession of her fear of him and that it would give him an added confidence in his uncanny power over her.

Shortly after two in the afternoon she went out. She had herself driven to Altman's store, where she dismissed the chauffeur, saying that she would return in the Fifth Avenue 'bus. From Altman's she went to Tiffany's for a jewel that was being reset for her. When she came outside again Benton Keese was standing near the entrance exactly as if he had been awaiting her.

Katherine flushed, grew pale, and flushed again when he flashed his brilliant eyes upon her, raised his hat, and stepped nearer to her with extended hand which she could not ignore.

"This is indeed a pleasant surprise, Kitten—encountering you here," he said in his softest tones.

"Kitten" was a name of childhood that had clung to her throughout the neighborhood of her Kentucky home. It was quite natural that Keese should make use if it, although she resented it bitterly even while she smiled a reluctant welcome into his glowing, speaking eyes.

"I was waiting for you, I think, although I did not know that you were in there. Shall we walk up the avenue?"

Apparently he did not expect a reply, or he took an affirmative for granted; and although she hated herself for doing it, she nevertheless walked beside him without question.

"I was passing—just strolling down the avenue," he added a moment later. "I sensed your nearness, Kitten, and I stopped and waited. And lo! in a moment more you appeared. It is quite wonderful, isn't it, this telepathic communication between two persons who happen to be thinking of each other at the same moment?"

CHAPTER XIII

TWO CAN PLAY AT THE SAME GAME

Three blocks farther north, at the corner of Fortieth Street, Katherine stopped.

"I shall take the 'bus here," she said with decision. She was angry with herself because she had permitted Benton Keese to accompany her even that short distance; disturbed, too, by the fact that she was aware of a subconscious pleasure she experienced because he was beside her; and she was still considering abstractly that remark of his about telepathy. Was there—could there be such a thing as a form of telepathic communication between herself and this man?

The thought of it was disquieting. It contained an active menace against her continued peace of mind. For Lady Kate knew that she had been thinking about Benton Keese nearly all that day; she knew that her mind had been more particularly upon him since she came downtown—while she was in Altman's, and again on the avenue and at Tiffany's. She had feared and dreaded just that sort of an encounter with him; and behold, it had come to pass. Was it possible, she asked herself, that her thoughts of him had drawn him inevitably to her in spite of her abhorrence of the mysterious attraction?

Her emotions concerning him were not unlike that impulse which many persons experience when peering from a great height into an abyss beneath.

The unnatural cravings to leap off into space, to test the height, to dive into the depths, to experience the unknown emotion of falling through limitless distance to the uttermost bottom and to feel the shock of oblivion at the end of it, were clamoring within her consciousness—and so also was the shuddering horror of the consequences. In metaphor Katherine was actually poised upon a pinnacle above a bottomless abyss whenever she was in propinquity with Benton Keese. His fathomless, caressing eyes spoke without words the invitation to her to make the leap. And alas! she knew that whenever her own gaze was inevitably drawn to meet his it responded. She hated herself for it, but she could not deny it nor quell it, nor could she keep her gaze diverted. There was something about his nearness which forcibly drew to the surface of her own nature every elemental impulse of her flesh and bone and blood; and it was all the more terrible in its vague suggestiveness, because it was so utterly mysterious, so entirely unknown, and so foreign to every desire she had otherwise or elsewhere craved.

"I will ride with you," he replied; and Katherine could not have told why she found it quite impossible to deny him, save that downright rudeness on her part could alone have repulsed him.

They went inside the 'bus and rode in silence for a time; then he announced, as if there had been no hiatus in their conversation:

"You will be glad to see my sister Betty again, of course. You used to be such great friends. I telegraphed to her last night to come here. At noon to-day I received a reply. She will arrive to-morrow morning."

"Oh!" Katherine exclaimed with genuine pleasure. "I am glad."

Then impulsively, and before she could think twice of the possible consequences: "You must bring her directly to me, Benton. A hotel would be no place for her; but with me—"

She stopped, confused. A partial realization of the privileges which the invitation would also extend to the brother startled her. She had intended to find a way to avoid him in the future, to deny him at her home, but it was too late to do that. The invitation was already given, was already accepted. With Betty as her guest, Benton Keese would quite naturally hold the open sesame to her home.

They got down from the 'bus at the corner nearest the house. Keese walked with her to the door. Then he followed her inside without awaiting an invitation to do so. He took it for granted, accepted as a privilege that belonged to him. He made use of the hospitable customs of the South, and ignored the empty formalities of Northern etiquette.

"It is kind of you, Kitten," he began; but she interrupted him with impatience.

"I don't want you to use that name," she said shortly; and he smiled and bowed his assurance that he would not offend again, adding, as if there had been no interruption:

"Most considerate of you to ask Betty to come here. I will confess that I had thought you might do so." He did not think it necessary to add that he had sent for his sister for that express reason.

"She had never visited New York when I went away; I doubt if she has done so since. Perhaps I can induce you to go with me to the station to meet her at ten to-morrow morning?"

"No," Katherine replied quickly. "But I will go alone to meet her, if you will defer your own reunion till later."

And so it was arranged. Strangely enough, too, that careless acquiescence in an impulsive suggestion was chiefly instrumental in directing the destinies of at least two lives in being—and others yet unborn. Also—although nobody even dreamed of such a thing—it provided the first step in the ultimate success of Rodney Rushton's effort to "make good."

Benton Keese was far too wise to linger in Lady Kate's presence that afternoon. He rose to take his leave as soon as Betty's reception and entertainment at Katherine's home was arranged. Kate gave him her hand in parting when he put out his own, and he held it rather longer than was necessary—not forcibly, but with a warm pressure which for some unknown reason she found irresistible. It was neither offensive nor suggestive, and yet it set her hand and arm to tingling, and her pulse a-throbbing, so that she started away from him and turned her head to hide the flush that she knew had swept into her face.

"Dear little playmate," he said softly, as if to himself; and turned and went swiftly from the room.

Lady Kate stood quite still after he had gone, a frown between her eyes, her lips in a tightly drawn line of self-derision. Then she crossed the room and stood before a mirror that gave back a full-length reflection of herself.

"What is it? What can it be within me that responds so riotously to Benton Keese's lightest word or touch when I know deep down in my heart of hearts that I loathe and despise and hate him, as I have always done since my earliest recollection?" she asked of her own image mentally.

"Why am I, who have never known fear of any other, horribly afraid of this one man? And what is it about him that I fear?"

She turned from the mirror without attempting an answer to any of her unspoken questions, and with her hand at the knob of the door she stopped again. This time she murmured spoken words, scarcely aloud, but audible to herself.

"After all," she said, "it is not the *man* I fear; it is myself. And—I will be afraid no more."

Benton Keese, strolling leisurely down the avenue, gazed complacently toward the green foliage of the park, and told himself unctuously, if mentally:

"If I had persevered in my effort to find her she would never have married Bingham Harvard. She would have fluttered into my arms like a bird."

"But—it would not have sufficed then. I was poor—rotten poor—then. Now I am rich. And," he chuckled audibly, "it is never too late to mend. Never! Perhaps—who knows?—perhaps—"

His mental commentary stopped at that point, but the perspective, thinly veiled from his egoistic vision, was, at the least, not at all disturbing.

Somewhat farther down the avenue Keese, although he was walking slowly, overtook and was in the act of passing another pedestrian who seemed to be in even less haste than himself; but having a quick eye and being by nature discerning, he recognized the broad shoulders and the back of the other man even before he had advanced far enough to observe the profile.

"How do you do, Mr. Rushton?" Keese inquired blandly and in his softest tones. He really possessed a wonderfully attractive voice. Rushton gave a start of well-assumed surprise.

"Why—hello!" he returned. "You are—er—mister— Names always get my goat, somehow; but I met you last evening at Mr. Harvard's. Glad to see you again."

"Ah! Now I have it. You are Mr. Keese, from Kentucky."

"Quite right, Mr. Rushton. Fine day, isn't it? You reside in this neighborhood, I assume."

"Me! Not so's you could notice it, Mr. Keese. My income wouldn't stand the strain of livin' around here. But I've got friends who do. Say! After bein' in China two 'r three 'r more years, it must seem kinda good to you to hit the pavements of little old New York again. Huh?"

"It certainly does, although I must confess that I never knew very much about this city of yours."

Thus they chatted idly together until Fifty-Ninth Street was reached, where Rushton uttered a hasty word of parting and boarded a west-bound car.

Benton Keese stood for some time at the curb on the corner gazing after the blue car that was bearing Rushton away. His eyes were narrowed; they would have impressed an observer as being introspective, rather than interested in the moving car and its latest passenger. But presently they resumed their normal fullness and softness behind the round, shell-rimmed glasses, and a slow smile showed at the corners of his mobile lips.

"That chap was watching me. I wonder why?" was his mental comment as he crossed the street and entered the Savoy, where he sought the café. He ordered a toddy, which he sipped slowly while he thought on:

"He wears the earmarks, or the hallmarks, of a typical New York cop; and that hair-cut looks to me like it was done without his asking for it and without cost to him either."

Keese paid for his drink, called a taxi, and had himself driven to the Hotel Mammoth, where he occupied a suite of rooms. From the suite he made use of the telephone and called a number that was printed on a card that he took from one of his pockets—the card of a somewhat obscure detective agency which (whether Keese was aware of it or not) was none too particular about the character of its investigations.

Within half an hour another card was taken to him. It bore merely the written inscription: "Mr. Roland." But inasmuch as that other card from which he had taken the telephone number was inscribed with the name of "The Roland Detective Agency," it may be surmised who the dapper little man was that was presently admitted to Suite 777.

"Be seated, Mr. Roland," Keese said, indicating a chair. "I assume that you are at the head of the detective agency that has been so highly recommended to me?"

"Yes, sir. I am Mr. Dudley Roland. I am the proprietor and the general manager of the agency; and I may say that—"

"Never mind your assurances of excellence. You shall have an opportunity to establish that. I shall probably require more or less service from you for a few weeks. Just now I want some quick information which I have no doubt you already possess."

"Has there been within your recollection, a man connected with the New York police whose name was Rodney Rushton? I want all the information concerning him that you may happen now to possess."

"Yes, sir. He was a detective-lieutenant at the headquarters bureau until about two years ago. Then they got something 'on' him and he was dumped. He was mixed up in the robbery of a bank—"

"What bank?"

"The Centropolis."

"Oh. Well, what more?"

"He was indicted, tried, convicted, sent to prison, and served nearly two years of a long sentence. Only the other day he was released on parole. If you had been reading the papers you wouldn't have had to ask me about it, Mr. Keese."

"Never mind that. What more is there to tell me?"

"If you should ask me *why* he was released on parole, or what is expected of him in return for it, I'd have to tell you frankly that I can't even guess at the reason. Only it strikes me as a bit funny all around, because the man who was behind it was the very man that Rushton had wronged the most. It was he—Harvard is his name; he used to be called the Night Wind, but I'll tell you about that later—who interested the district attorney in the matter, and so got Rushton out."

"So. I see," Keese meditated aloud.

"Well, Mr. Dudley Roland, I will give you three days in which to find out for me the true reason why Rodney Rushton was paroled from prison, and why the district attorney deemed it wise to recommend such an act. Do you think you can do it?"

"Yes, sir. I think I can," was the confident reply.

CHAPTER XIV

SHE CAME FROM OLD KENTUCKY

Katherine in passing through the Pennsylvania Station just before ten o'clock next morning met Tom Clancy, who was hurrying in the opposite direction. He stopped, however, and shook hands with her, hat in hand, while he explained that he had gone to the station to see a friend off who was to be a long time absent, that he was already far overdue at his office; and all in the same breath demanded in his usual impetuous way what it could be that had taken her there at that hour of the morning.

"I won't tell you, but I will *show* you, Tom," she replied mischievously. "That is, if the multitude of affairs at your office can stand the strain of waiting another half hour upon your arrival there."

"Huh!" said Tom; and turned about to return with her. "I don't think any cataclysms would happen if I should not show up down there at all. I assume, from your manner, that you are here to meet somebody. Eh?"

She nodded. "Quite the prettiest girl I ever knew," she assured him.

"I don't like 'pretty' girls," he told her.

"The most beautiful, then."

"That sounds better; but—"

"And altogether the most charming, fascinating, alluring, puzzling, inviting—and elusive creature I can imagine."

"Then my business can go hang," Tom announced with decision. "With all of those pronouncements tagged upon her your expected friend must be a wonder. Who is she?"

"Wait until you have seen her," was the enigmatical reply.

The expected train was on time, and presently Tom Clancy saw a vision of loveliness that would have made him gasp with pleased astonishment anywhere rush into the embrace of Lady Kate and cling to her with affectionate enthusiasm. A steady flow of the softest and most entrancing Southern exclamations of pleasure and endearment that he had ever heard rippled from the lips of the girl.

"I certainly am right glad to see you, Kittie, dear," was one of the many things that Tom overheard while he awaited an opportunity to be introduced.

"Ben telegraphed to me that you would meet me at the station and that you meant to take me home with you so that I wouldn't have to go to a horrid hotel."

Miss Betty's words flowed on in her eagerness and delight, each sentence ending in that exquisite and inimitable drawl which must be born with the tongue and can never be acquired by an outsider. But there did come a pause even in the mutual enthusiasm of the two girls—for Katherine was as much the girl as Betty and the affection between them had always been very genuine and deep—and the opportunity for which Clancy was waiting came.

"Tom," Katherine said, disengaging herself, "I want to present you to Miss Betty Keese. She is my dearest friend. We were playmates in childhood, schoolmates in girlhood, and chums ever since either of us can remember."

"Betty, this is Mr. Clancy. He stands in just about the same relation to my husband that you do to me. And I *do* so want you two to be good friends."

"It's up to Miss Keese, then," Tom replied, with his inimitable and engaging smile. "I am captive already."

Betty smiled delightfully—entrancingly, Tom thought—as she put her small, gloved hand into Clancy's. Her seal-brown eyes sparkled, and the dimples that showed in her cheeks seemed almost to possess eyes of their own, they were so fascinatingly alluring.

"Oh, I reckon that we will be good friends," she assured them both, dimpling and smiling even more brightly. "I can see that you like Mr. Clancy immensely, Kittie, and that is all the recommendation *I* need."

"Where is Benton? Isn't he here to meet me, too?"

The question came like something of a shock to Tom. He had heard the name of Keese when Betty was introduced, and he had repeated it; but he had not, for some unknown reason, associated it with the Benton Keese whom he had met at Bingham Harvard's house—and whom, he suddenly remembered, he had instinctively distrusted and disliked. Looking upon her again as she turned once more toward Katherine and admiring her personal charm, her lithe, small figure, and her perfect features more gravely and critically than he had done at first, he discovered instantly the unmistakable likeness she bore to her handsome brother.

"Whatever the brother may prove to be, there is no doubt about the physical and spiritual loveliness of the sister," was his mental comment.

And when, later he undertook to analyze the actual estimate in which he held Benton Keese, he did that person as well as himself the justice to admit (to himself) that there was no plausible reason why he should not regard Miss Betty's brother with the utmost friendliness.

"Tom," Katherine asked, when the three were walking through the station toward the street, "do you remember that you once asked me if I had a sister to whom you might be properly presented?"

"Perfectly," he replied, nodding and smiling. And he added coolly: "I also remember *why* I asked you. It was because Bing found you first—and I thought, possibly, if you *did* have a sister— Words fail me, Katherine."

Lady Kate laughed outright and frankly. Betty shot a glance of mischief from the corners of her eyes at Tom, and Lady Kate continued:

"Behold her, Thomas Clancy. For in everything save the tie of blood, Betty and I are sisters indeed; and—there is Julius with the car. Hurry to your business, Tom, and come to dinner with us this evening."

"By Jove!" Clancy commented to himself after they were driven away. "By Jove!" he muttered again as he hurried toward the "L" station at Thirty-Third Street. "By Jove!" he repeated aloud inside the car.

And presently an acquaintance who happened to be seated opposite stepped across the car and dropped down upon a seat beside him that had just been vacated.

"Hello, Tom!" he said laughing. "This is the first time I knew that you had ever been 'make-up' editor on a newspaper. When was it? How long ago was it?"

"What's the answer?" Clancy inquired, shaking hands.

"You are reading your morning paper upside down. Only make-up men do that."

"Oh! I see. That's so. Well, you see, I have just been sort of turned upside down myself—and I suppose that accounts for it."

Inside of the automobile that had taken the two young women from the station and at approximately the same time Katherine was asking:

"Well, Betty, don't you think he's nice?"

"I certainly do, Kittie—that is, if you happen to mean Mr. Clancy," the Kentucky girl replied frankly. "If your Northern men are all like him—well, I shall just naturally fall in love with all of them. But you might have waited until I had really arrived and had had an opportunity to make myself a little more presentable before you tried to throw me right at him."

"Oh, I did not *invite* Tom Clancy to be present, Betty. I shouldn't have permitted you to see each other for at least a week if I had had my own way about it. He was just *there*, that's all."

"He isn't exactly what you might call handsome," Betty commented mischievously, after a pause. "His hair is almost red; he has got a turn-up nose, and he wears freckles, and—"

"But, dear, did you ever see more beautiful teeth in a man's head? and such straightforward, earnest eyes—when they're not twinkling? And such shoulders? and—and—and—"

"It's a wonder that *he* didn't get you, Kittie, instead of the man who did," Betty broke in when words failed Katherine; and she added, without waiting for comment upon what she had said:

"You never did get over your aversion for Benton, did you? Poor Benton! Why every girl in four counties—Bourbon, Fayette, Scott and Harrison—would have given up their eye-teeth to get him, the only one that he really wanted just plain, sure-enough, ran away from him without so much as saying good-by. Do you know, Kittie, that there were heaps of times when I came mighty near to breaking my word with you and telling Benton where you were. Yes, indeed."

"But you did not do it, Betty."

"No, dear. And I am glad—now; for one has only to look at you to see that you are *perfectly* happy."

"I am. Yes, indeed, I am. I have got the best husband, and the handsomest, and the—"

"I know all the rest of it, dear, and I don't doubt *any* of it; not in the least. But all the same, Kittie, I have got one bit of right good advice to give you."

"What is it?" Katherine asked, without turning her head, keeping her eyes directed toward the street.

"It's this: I don't believe that Benton has changed a bit, so far as you are concerned. He went away not very long after you disappeared, and I have not set my eyes upon him in all the time since then. But I know that he was just *mad* about you, dear; and—I know Benton Keese, my brother though he is."

"That is not advice."

"No; it's a statement—with this much added: He wants you right now just as much as he *ever* wanted you. Benton did not ask me to come here because he cared a picayune about *my* pleasure. He sent for me because he knew that when he told you he had done so you would immediately invite me to go to your home; and if *I* am there, of course *he* can drop in at any old time he wants to, without regard to conventions. I am the catspaw; you are the chestnut, and your home is the fire that you're to be pulled out of—or I don't know my own fascinating, handsome, accomplished, and subtle brother."

"Nonsense, Betty," Katherine exclaimed, but there was little mirth in the laughter. She felt an odd shiver of apprehension as the result of the outspoken comment of her friend. "I haven't heard the advice even yet, dear."

"I'll give it to you in five words: *send me to a hotel.*"

"Why, Betty Keese—"

"Oh, I know you won't do it, but you should, all the same. You just *cannot* shut your door against Ben when I am there, but you should do so, all the same. You *cannot* avoid giving him opportunities to make love to you as long as he can come and go as he pleases; and you can take my word for it that he *will* make love to you every time that he has the merest ghost of a chance."

"Betty, if he should dare to attempt such a thing—"

"Kittie, dear," the Kentucky girl interrupted hastily, "don't you know that he won't make love to you as *other* men would do it? Don't you know how subtle he is? Don't you know that he will never say or do a thing to offend you or to which you can take offense?"

"Have you ever noticed a dog when it plays with a stick in its master's hand, and how the dog will keep right on seizing the stick a little bit higher up and nearer to the hand that plays with it, every chance it gets?"

"Elizabeth Keese, you ought to be ashamed of yourself to talk about your brother in such a manner, and about me, too!" Katherine exclaimed, disturbed and half in anger.

"Dear," Betty replied soberly, "I love my brother with all my heart, but I love you with all my heart and *soul*, too."

"Why, Kittie, he fascinates even me, his sister, when I am beside him. He is dangerous; he is subtle; he is deep and patient. And he knows how to wait—and how to win by waiting. I have learned several things about him since he went away from home that I did not know before. And I know that he is a dangerous friend for a woman to have. I know, too, that I am very glad indeed that you did not marry *him*!"

CHAPTER XV

AN IMPORTANT SNAPSHOT

There was a consultation at the Centropolis Bank, held immediately after banking hours on the ninth day after the arrival in New York of the real Anderson Van Cleve; that is to say, on a Monday. It was also the eleventh day after the first appearance of Holbrook Chilton, who had represented himself to be Van Cleve; it was the fifth day after Rushton's rehabilitation as a man. Therefore, in order to keep our chronology of events correctly in mind, it was the third day after the advent of Betty Keese and her installation as a welcome and beloved guest in the home of Bingham Harvard and Lady Kate.

There were present at the conference Anderson Van Cleve, Tom Clancy, Rushton, the red-haired chief of the National Detective Agency which handled the bank's affairs, his two operatives who had gone there with him that day of Van Cleve's arrival in the city, and of course Bingham Harvard himself. Also, in response to her own earnest request (one might almost call it insistence) made to her husband as soon as she knew that the consultation was to take place, Lady Kate was there.

The meeting was held in the directors' room. It was entirely an informal affair; almost an impromptu one, in fact, and it had come about chiefly because of a suggestion of Katherine's that she had made to Bingham the preceding evening. He had summoned the others by telephone. Clancy was the last of the lot to arrive, and he crossed immediately to Lady Kate and dropped upon a chair beside her, his face and eyes beaming as he demanded, *sotto voce*:

"How is Miss Betty? And where is she? And why is she not here with you, Katherine?"

Lady Kate replied demurely and with exactness, but neverthe-less with twinkling eyes:

"Betty is quite well. She is motoring with her brother, I believe. She is not here for the very good reason that she was not wanted—inasmuch as the reason for this conference is supposed to be a se-cret."

"Huh!" said Tom. Then: "Do you mean to tell *me*, my lady, that you and Miss Betty Keese of Kentucky have spent more than three whole days together and that you have not told her *all about* 'that dreadful thing that happened down at Bing's Bank'?'"

"I do not tell everybody quite *all* I know, Tom," Katherine re-torted with dignity, recognizing the innuendo that women tell all their secrets to their best friends, "in confidence."

"Honestly, now, Katherine," he teased, "didn't you tell Miss Betty—strictly in confidence, of course—that you could not go mo-toring with her and her charming brother this afternoon because you had promised to meet Bingham at the bank precisely at four o'clock? Answer me that?"

"Tom Clancy, I believe you have been talking to Betty over the telephone!"

"I have. I wanted her to go motoring with *muh*; and you were not included in the invitation, either. I was intending to shy this meeting, shamelessly; to pretend that I had made the engagement before I received the message to come here, and all that. See?"

"It serves you right, then, that she could not go with you."

"Maybe so. Anyhow—"

"Hush. Let us hear what Mr. Van Cleve has to tell us," Kathe-rine interrupted.

"I have told several of those present individually practically all that I have now to say in regard to the man Holbrook Chilton, who came to this bank one week ago last Thursday and succeeded in passing himself into the confidence of Mr. Harvard in my name," Van Cleve began.

"For the general benefit of all who are here, I will now refer to him as follows:

"During the few years that he was in my employ in Mexico I never once had occasion to doubt his honesty; and yet always, in-stinctively or intuitively, I did doubt the *man*. That statement is, of course, paradoxical. I doubt if I can explain it adequately. But al-ways during our business relations, after he had left me at such times as we had been discussing my affairs, certain little things concerning his attitude and manner toward me left an unfavorable impression. It was never tangible. It was never anything that I could define, even to myself, in words. It never amounted to more than an uneasy impression."

"Time and again I have resolved that the next time I summoned him to the city of Mexico or that I had occasion to seek him at the mines or at whatsoever place he happened to be employed, I would make a closer and more intimate study of the man. But (and I realize now that this is the remarkable thing about him) inevitably and without exception, each and every time when I was actually with him and talking to him and listening to him while he talked, *I was just as strongly impressed in his favor; I was made to feel just as certain that my misgivings about him were purest folly.*"

"The first time I ever saw Holbrook Chilton he came to me seeking employment. I was at a hotel in Morelia, the capital of the State of Michoacán, at the time. He appeared then"—Van Cleve glanced from Bing Harvard to Tom Clancy—"almost exactly like the photographs that you two gentlemen have seen of him, which were contained with the letter that I wrote and forwarded to Mr. Harvard, announcing my intention of coming North. Also, like this three-and-a-quarter by four-and-a-quarter snapshot that I once made of him myself."

Van Cleve paused while a small Kodak picture was passed around from hand to hand. It completed the round at Katherine, and she held it in her hand when Van Cleve continued:

"The man appeared to possess the very qualifications that I required in such an employee. Down in the country we do not inquire too closely concerning a man's antecedents. I employed him. He remained steadily in my service and performed good and faithful work so far as I know, until the happening of this circumstance. He never volunteered any information about himself—but once. At that time he mentioned, apparently with inadvertence, that he was a native of our State of Virginia. I did not doubt the truth of it; I do not doubt it now. I have frequently detected in his conversation evidences of the truth of it—or I have thought I did so."

"He was—he is—an educated man, and a talented one. He was a freehand artist of unusual ability, but, I should say, an untrained one. In other words, a natural one. Without doubt it was that talent which enabled him, with practice, to write my signature with such a degree of perfection that I would not myself have been able to differentiate between one that he wrote and one that I had written. But I did not know that until a week ago last Saturday."

"Since these revelations concerning him have come to light, I have been thinking deeply about them—and I have done some telegraphing to Mexico. The pictures of Chilton came to Mr. Harvard in an envelope that I addressed to him myself, and which contained a letter with my own signature which I had just prepared. The two pictures of himself that he managed to substitute for mine were mounted on cabinet-size cards, which bore the imprint of a photographer in Mexico named Llorente.

"Señor Llorente has replied to my telegrams with the statement that he did not make the pictures of Chilton, but that he found, after the receipt of my message, that four of his cards for mounting photographs were missing. That circumstance recalls another trivial one."

"The evening of the day when I posed for my own pictures I drove to Chilton's place of residence in San Felipi Neri Street. As I stepped down from the carriage I distinctly saw a brilliant flash of light at the window of one of the two rooms which I supposed to be occupied by my manager. The window was closely curtained, but that flash of light did show through certain crevices and openings so that I saw it. Chilton was, however, in the other of his two rooms, engaged in rolling and lighting a cigarette, when I was admitted. Doubtless he had heard the carriage-wheels when I drove to the door. There can be no doubt now that he was occupied in making those pictures of himself that he later sent here. Another message to the chief of police of Mexico City, who happens to be a friend, has brought a reply which states that he visited the house in San Felipe Neri in response to my request, and that he found there a complete and valuable photographing outfit."

"I mention these things, not because they are of particular consequence to our investigation just now, but as evidence of the undoubted fact that Chilton had for a long time been preparing for some such move as the one he eventually carried out. My own belief is that he intended to murder me, or to have me killed down there, so that I never would return to this city of New York. But that the suddenness of my announcement of intention to leave the country precipitated matters for him so that he was forced to act quickly. It is a fact—and it may interest you to know it—that a very pronounced effort was made to kill me just before I succeeded in getting away from the city of Mexico."

"Now, my friends, Holbrook Chilton was without doubt an assumed name. It is quite possible that his remark that he was a native of Virginia—which I thought to be a 'break,' at the time—was a carefully studied statement. *But there can be no doubt whatever that the man was Southern born.* There are certain twists of the tongue in that section of our splendid country which cannot be mistaken, and which can never be acquired nor correctly imitated."

"Lastly (and this will close my somewhat lengthy statement), looking back upon my association with Holbrook Chilton, I am convinced of the following points:

"His hair was naturally dark, but I believe he dyed it the jet-black it was down there. Sun and wind and exposure did not tan his complexion to the leathery hue it assumed before and retained while he was in my employ. It was created, I believe, by a stain or a pigment, which, in fact, protected his skin. When he did away with it, shaved off his beard, cut his hair, and restored it to its natural color, he would become a changed man entirely."

"Finally, he was the coolest man—and, I might truthfully add, one of the bravest men—I ever saw in the face of danger. He courted it. Nothing rattled him. And there was a certain indefinable charm about his personality which was experienced by every man or woman who came in contact with him. In short, my friends, Chilton was and is now, wherever he may be, a thoroughgoing egotist, and I am convinced that that trait will keep him—has kept him—close to the scene of his latest (perhaps his only) exploit."

"Now, if there are questions concerning him or his relations with me that occur to any of you, please ask them."

There was a short interval of silence after Van Cleve had finished, and it was Lady Kate who put the first question. She did not raise her eyes to Van Cleve when she spoke, but kept them fixed upon the small photograph that she held in her hand. Every eye in the room turned toward her quickly, but she appeared to be unconscious of the fact.

"I have noticed, and I have been taught," she said, prefacing her question, "that every adult person, man or woman, is addicted to some characteristic gesture or mannerism or figure of speech or exclamation to express surprise, pleasure, astonishment, anger, or satisfaction. Your association with Holbrook Chilton, Mr. Van Cleve, spanned a considerable period. During it, being an observant man, you should have noticed such a characteristic gesture, mannerism, or verbal expression, if there was one. Can you give us any information as to that point?"

"Very little, if any. The man was always strangely self-possessed; oddly motionless when not actually engaged in doing something; enigmatically expressionless when not actually giving expression to something he was saying or doing. He had no nervous habits; rather, he gave me the impression of being without nerves. Really, I can recall only one act of his which might be called a mannerism or a characteristic act—and even that one would be of little service to us here in the North."

"He always rolled his cigarettes between the second and third fingers, instead of between the first fingers and thumbs; and always he rolled them backward. I have never seen anybody else do it in exactly that way."

Lady Kate, still with her eyes directed upon the picture she held in her hand, replied evenly:

"The first part of your answer is the reply to my question, Mr. Van Cleve. Thank you."

Rushton, in his corner, nodded a vehement affirmative and shot a glance of admiration toward Katherine.

CHAPTER XVI

THE PICTURE OF HOLBROOK CHILTON

Katherine addressed her next question to the red-haired chief of the National Detective Agency.

"Please give us," she said, "a brief account of what you have learned concerning the movements of Chilton after the moment when he went out of my husband's office at 11.30 A.M., one week ago last Friday."

"He spent two or three hours in going from bank to bank and changing one-thousand-dollar bills into smaller currency. He ultimately returned to his hotel, paid his bill, drove to the Grand Central Station, purchased a ticket and a Pullman compartment for Chicago, and departed. He went into the dining-car as soon as it was available. He returned to his compartment immediately afterward, told the porter that he was not to be disturbed until morning, and locked himself inside. There is no authentic account of his having been seen again after that time; no report of any person not otherwise accounted for leaving that car or that train while it was on its way to Chicago."

"When he did not appear the following morning, and made no response to repeated summonses at his door, it was opened with a duplicate key. The man had disappeared, and with him the smaller of the two satchels he had taken aboard of the train. That smaller satchel without doubt contained the money he had drawn from this bank."

"And from me, also," Tom Clancy interposed. "Don't forget that little item of thirty-six thousand."

"All of the clothing he had worn when he went aboard of the train, even to underclothing, handkerchiefs, collar, tie, *et cetera*, was found in the larger of the two satchels that he left in the compartment," continued the chief.

"There had been six towels in the rack when he took possession of the room. All of them were missing save one; and that one had been used to wipe the woodwork, the nickeled basin and plumbing, the window, and every sort of smooth surface which might have retained the imprint of one of his thumbs or fingers. The compartment was in perfect order. The berth had not been occupied. He had closed it up, apparently, immediately after he locked himself in."

"Of course, the assumption is that the larger satchel contained all the clothing he required for the change he made; that he shaved himself, cut his own hair, washed the stain from his face—and left behind him every article that had been associated with him in the character of Holbrook Chilton."

"One moment, please," Katherine interposed at that point. "Was that train made up entirely of Pullman cars?"

"Yes."

"It made stops—where?"

"Poughkeepsie, Albany, Utica, Syracuse, Rochester, Buffalo."

"Is it not practically impossible for a passenger to leave or to enter one of the cars of a 'solid Pullman' train, particularly during the night, without particular notice being taken of either fact by one of the porters or by the Pullman conductor?"

"It is supposed to be entirely impossible."

"Then, in your opinion, chief—and your experience has been wide—how did Holbrook Chilton get down from that train without the fact being noticed—and remembered?"

"He did not leave from the off-side of the train between two cars where the doors had not been opened, because he could not have closed a door and lowered the platform into place from the outside afterward. He *must* have got off the train in the regular way, and have walked calmly past one or two porters, and probably the Pullman conductor, also, when he did so; and he must have had his small satchel in his hand at the time. How did he accomplish it?"

"I'd like to answer that question, Lady Kate," said Rushton.

Every eye in the room was directed toward him. They waited in silence for him to continue.

"I've doped it out like this—see?" Rushton went on. "He had figger'd ahead on that getaway the same's he'd figger'd ahead on the pictures, and the identification here in this bank."

"Well, Rushton?" It was Bing Harvard who bent forward and put the eager question.

"Chilton worked on a time schedule, same's they run trains on a railroad, from the minute he hit this town till he blew out of it. As Lady Kate says, 'twa'n't possible for him to drop off that train without being noticed. Well, then, there was only one way—*just one*—that he could 'a' done it."

"How was that?" Harvard asked.

"I don't know," Rushton replied; and added: "But if *I* had been in his place, and had figger'd ahead on it as he did, I know how *I* would 'a' done it."

"Tell us, then."

"He didn't lock himself in that stateroom till after the train pulled out of Albany. He had to work like sixty to accomplish all he did and to get ready to leave it at Syracuse. Maybe he went on to Rochester. Anyhow, that's what *I'd* have done. I would have bought a ticket and reserved a lower berth or a seat in a smoking compartment on that train from Syracuse to Rochester several days ahead of time—and I'd have gone to Syracuse to do it. I'd have had that ticket and reservation inside of my jeans before I ever showed up at this bank—and I'd have made the reservation of a stateroom out of New York in the name of Chilton a day 'r two ahead of time, too. I'd have made the changes, shaved an' done the rest of it that had to be done between Albany and Syracuse."

"At Syracuse, bein' ready, I'd have peeked out o' the stateroom, then slid outside and locked the door after me. Then I'd have drifted through the car toward the one in which I knew my reservation to be, from Syracuse to Rochester, *and* which I had previously located. When I passed a platform where the doors were opened to the station, I'd have called down to the porter 'r the Pullman conductor standin' at the step before the open door and I'd have asked: 'Say! Where's car two?' (or three, or whatever it was); and I'd have given the impression, although I wouldn't have *said* so, that I had come aboard of the train at one of the other open doors. See? That wouldn't have excited no comment, nor notice, nor remark."

"Bimeby, after the train started on, the conductor would have hunted me for my ticket. I'd have cussed some because I had to make that night trip when there wasn't time to make it worth while to go to bed—and I'd have walked off of the train like any other regular passenger when she blew into the station at Rochester."

Rushton turned to the chief of the agency.

"If I had been on your job as soon as you was, chief, I'd have quizzed them Pullman guys about a passenger from Utica 'r Syracuse to Rochester 'r Buffalo that night; and then I'd have talked to the ticket-agent at the place where such a passenger got on at; but it wouldn't do you no good now, because I have done it."

"What did you discover, Mr. Rushton?" Van Cleve inquired.

"Well, what I've just told you as bein' the way *I* would have done it turned out to be pretty close to the way Chilton worked it himself. The original of that there picture that Mrs. Harvard's hanging on to did buy a ticket to Rochester and make a reservation at the Syracuse station a week ago last Wednesday afternoon, and he did have it stamped so's the date was the second day afterward. That is, a week ago last Friday."

"And—" Katherine said, bending forward in her chair.

"There was a gray-haired guy with mutton-chop whiskers, an' a plug hat, an' a raincoat buttoned up to his chin, an' spats over his shoes, and a limp in his left leg who did get aboard of that train at Syracuse that night, and who did get off at Rochester, and who did sit in the smoking compartment and snooze all the hundred miles between them two stations; anyhow, that is what the conductor and two porters agreed on in telling me."

"And, of course, that was Chilton?"

"Sure. And he shed the gray hair and the whiskers and the plug hat and the raincoat and the spats and the limp pretty soon after he got off at Rochester, more than likely."

"And then returned to New York?"

"I'd bet the gold out o' my eye-tooth, Lady Kate, that he ate lunch in New York the very next day," Rushton replied with settled conviction.

Then he turned to Van Cleve.

"And," he added, "if you will give me the number of that house in San-Philip-Something Street, in the city of Mexico, and a letter to that chief of police friend of yourn—can he talk United States so I can understand him?"

"Yes. He speaks English very well indeed."

"Well, if you will give me a letter to him I'll leave to-night for Mexico; and I won't stay there more'n a day after I get there, either. Where'd you say that office of yourn was down there?"

"In *calle* Gante; that is, in Gante Street."

"I suppose that everything that was in it has been rotted out by this time, eh?"

"No. I merely looked at it and left it just as it was. My lease of it runs for another year. It may have been entered since I came away, but I hardly think so. Those who know me down there, with the exception of the chief of police to whom I telegraphed, do not know that I have left the country."

"Well, that's all right. I'll take a chance on finding what I'm going after. It is worth the effort, anyhow."

"One might ask what the devil you *are* going after, Rushton?" Tom Clancy interjected.

Rushton half closed one eye while he fixed the other upon Tom and replied, grinning:

"I'm going down there, Mr. Clancy, to start a brand new revolution; and if I can do it all, one full day will be about all I'll need."

Then, to Harvard: "I ought to make it in about two weeks; and, as I said before, the thing I'm after is worth the effort."

"Don't you want to tell us what it is, Mr. Rushton?" Katherine asked.

"No, please; I don't."

"Probably the lieutenant is of the opinion that Chilton has returned to Mexico by this time," one of the operatives of the national agency remarked with a touch of sarcasm.

Rushton turned upon him and replied, evidently with hidden significance:

"I'll bet a hundred dollars that you have looked straight into Chilton's eyes more than once in the last ten days and didn't suspect it. I'll bet that you will look into them again while I'm away and won't even guess at it. And I'll bet that when I get back here, or soon afterward, I'll be able to prove to the satisfaction of everybody present that what I've just said is true. Are you on?"

"We certainly hope that you will be, Rushton," the chief interposed before his operative could reply, "and when you do get back, if we have not nailed the fellow in the meantime, you can rely upon each one of us standing in line to help you. I think I know what you are going there to get; and if I am right, it is a good move."

"Well"—Rushton left his chair—"I guess this meeting is about ready to adjourn. I'll take a walk along with you, Mr. Van Cleve, if you'll let me. I want to dig up a little more information out o' you, if I can."

"And I," Katherine said, also addressing him, "would like to keep this picture for a time, if I may. I think there is—I have an idea that I would like to study it in connection with certain things you said about the man himself."

"Certainly. Keep it by all means," Van Cleve replied at once.

Tom Clancy, bending closer to Katherine, said in an undertone:

"I was just about to ask Mr. Van Cleve to lend *me* the picture, Katherine. I wonder if my reason is the same as yours. Eh?"

She shot a startled but half-puzzled glance at him and replied quickly:

"It could *not* be, Tom. It is impossible."

"Maybe so," said Tom; but he left the impression with her that he did not think so, nevertheless.

CHAPTER XVII

THE MESSAGE FROM MEXICO

Rushton and Van Cleve, when they left the conference at the bank together, called a taxicab and were driven directly to the Hotel Mammoth, where Mr. Van Cleve was staying.

"I think that I *must* go to Mexico," Rushton announced with an air of finality as soon as they were started.

"Is it necessary, Rushton?" Van Cleve asked quietly. "A trip like that takes time. The whole country is unsettled just now. Journeying through it at present is not what it might be, and you are likely to be detained much longer than you plan for." [The time was after the overthrow of Díaz by Madero.]

"I know it."

"But you think that you *must* go there?"

"Somebody must."

"Could not some person down there perform the service you require? Could the matter be done for you in any way?"

"I hadn't thought of that, Mr. Van Cleve. But if somebody was there who knew *how* to do it and who *would* do it for you, and if we could get a telegram or a cable to that man that would explain exactly what it is that I want done—well, it *might* do the trick. And I wish to Heaven that it could be done, so that I would not have to go away just now."

"That is precisely the feeling that I have about it, Rushton."

"Do you think it can be worked, sir?"

"I am sure of it—provided it is anything confidential. But you have not told me what it is yet."

"I want finger-prints and thumb-prints, if there are any to be found down there, of Mr. Holbrook Chilton. That's what I want, sir."

"Good. That will be easy—if there are any there to be found. And—I think it is quite possible that there are some."

"You do?"

"Yes. I am sure, for example, that my office is still closed in the *calle* Gante; that it has not been opened or entered since I left it, and will not be for some time to come. The same rule would apply to Chilton's rooms in San Felipe Neri, and there should be many finger-prints of his there on the camera he used in making the pictures, on the plates he touched and did not use, on the furniture generally. Oh, I have no doubt of it."

"Good."

"And, at my office, while he talked to me the very last time he was there, I remember now that he stood for a time leaning over a table that was between us, and that the fingers of both of his hands rested upon the smooth and polished surface of the top of that table at the time."

"Fine! Then he has left the print of them there, all right."

"There is not a doubt of it, I think."

"Now, who is the man you have in mind to do this work for us, Mr. Van Cleve?"

"His name is Tranquilino Corona—but that will mean nothing to you. Also, he is my very good friend, and has been so for a long time. He is a man I can trust thoroughly."

"That is all right, too. But is he a chap that can do the trick—who will know *how* to do it?"

"Without a doubt. Before Madero came into power, before President Díaz was ousted, Corona was the president's right-hand man in the secret service down there. He is a thoroughly trained detective, Rushton. Díaz once sent him to Paris to study the methods over there. I know that he is familiar with the finger-print business."

"Then he is just the man for us."

"I *know* that he is."

"When we get to your rooms at the hotel, we will get up a telegram to send to him, no matter what the length of it or what it costs—eh?"

"Certainly."

"And you will sign it with your name and—I've got another thought right here."

"What is it?"

"Can you fix it so that his replies will come direct to me under another name than my own, do you think?"

"Easily. I will tell him in the body of the message how to address his replies. But why that, Rushton?"

"Because I am thinking that I will disappear from this locality for a time. I am thinking that it will be just as well—and better—if we let the others, all of them, believe that I *have* gone to Mexico. I think that I can do better work in that case."

"It is a good idea, Rushton. I approve of it. Only you will tell Mr. Harvard and—"

"I'll tell nobody but you, sir. Not a soul—only Banta."

"Who is Banta?"

"He is the gray-haired chap that sat next to you part of the time this afternoon. We are old friends—old pals—used to be side partners on the force. He is with Chief Redhead now since he retired. I'm goin' to take him in with me on this deal—and what Banta an' me can't pull off together won't be worth pullin' off, believe *me!*"

"Very well. You know best, Rushton."

"Say, it's a thousand to one that Redhead, now that he knows that I am bound for Mex, will have me trailed; or will wanta send somebody with me. If he does it will be Banta that he will pick. So Banta an' me'll make the start, all right, all right; but we won't go very far on the way at that."

"But why is that necessary?"

For a moment Rushton turned and looked straight at Van Cleve, as if there was something that he was about to say. But evidently he changed his mind, so he replied presently:

"I've got still another idea that I ain't sure about, Mr. Van Cleve; and until I *am* mighty sure I don't want to give it out. But I will say this much right now: If that guy Chilton is playing the game as I think he is playing it, and if he is the man I think he may be, right here in this blessed city now, *there ain't any human way short of them finger-prints to prove it.* There ain't any other way to nail him to the cross. And—here is the point—if he *is* that man it's pretty dead certain that he will be keepin' tabs on Harvard an' Clancy an' you an' me—mostly me, too—from this out—see?"

"Who—whom do you suspect, Rushton?"

"I ain't sayin' just yet. I don't want to say it now. But I will say this much: I know a guy that rolls cigarettes just the way you talked about at the bank to-day."

106

"Very well. I am content. I believe in you, Rushton. I think that you are the right man in the right place."

"Thank you, sir."

"Is he—is the man to whom you refer one whom we see and know, do you think?"

"Tryin' to put me through the third degree, Mr. Van Cleve?" Rushton asked with a smile. "Honestly, I don't wanta talk about that just yet."

"Very good. We will drop the subject. Only I wish to assure you that I have every confidence in your ability."

"Say, don't rub it in too thick, sir. You might get me stuck on myself."

At the hotel, in the privacy of Van Cleve's suite of rooms, the message to Mexico was concocted after a great deal of labor. But it was very much to the point. Words were not spared to render perfectly plain what was wanted to the man who was destined to receive it. Every instruction was given to him regarding how to proceed; how to secure the finger-prints, how to preserve them once they were secured, how to pack and forward them, and the name and address in New York to which they were to be sent—a name and address that Rodney Rushton supplied. In all, the message contained one hundred and thirty words; but nothing that could add to its efficiency or to the necessary instruction of Tranquilino Corona was omitted—and the message itself was finally filed for transmission at the main office of the telegraph company.

Afterward Rushton sought Banta at Banta's home, and the two conversed in private for a long time after that. They were old side partners who had come together again, and who were both equally delighted at the prospect of working once more in unity and harmony. And when Rushton finally sought his own quarters there was a smile of intense satisfaction and content—and confidence in the outcome, too—in his eyes and upon his face. He thought that he could see far enough ahead of him, then, to know just what the possession of those finger-prints would do.

CHAPTER XVIII

LADY KATE'S PERIL

In the meantime Betty Keese and her alluring and hypnotic brother were motoring together in Westchester County in the high-powered roadster that was his newest possession. But notwithstanding the fact that he had owned it only a few days he was thoroughly master of the craft of operating it—just as he very quickly became the master of whatsoever he undertook to perform. The two were oddly silent at the beginning of their ride. Very little more than the commonest civilities were exchanged between them during the first half-hour or so of it. The rumble seat behind them was unoccupied. They were as utterly alone, in so far as confidential conversation between them was concerned, as if they had been upon a mountain-peak.

"Well, Ben?" Betty remarked when they were going along within sight of the Sound, going only at a moderate pace.

Then, when he made no reply, she added: "You did not bring me out here this afternoon just because you were crazy for your sister's company, you know. Don't forget that I *am* your sister."

He turned his head and shot a swift glance at Betty. His eyes glowed appreciatively, and the corners of his mouth twitched with a glimmer of amusement.

"Quite right, Betty," he said—and drove on again in silence.

"I reckon I already know the drift of what you want to say," she went on; "but I will wait for you to say it, just the same."

"You see," he remarked, after another short period of silence, "there is never an opportunity for a word alone with you at Harvard's house. Kitten or Harvard himself, or that everlasting and ever-present Bolton, the butler—one of them is always butting in. Or, if it is not one of them, it is that new maid whom, you tell me, Kitten has engaged only since your arrival."

"A brother and sister aren't supposed to have state secrets to discuss, Ben," his sister said, with a toss of her head. Then she half-turned in her seat and demanded:

"Say it, Ben, whatever it is? You did not send for me to come north, for any other purpose than to make use of me. I know that perfectly well. Now—what is the use to which you intend (if you can) to put me?"

He shrugged. Then, although he still looked straight ahead of him over the steering-wheel, he smiled. A moment later he chuckled audibly.

"You are so sudden," he derided her, and laughed aloud.

Then, sharply, and with unexpected directness, he announced: "I am here to win Kitten away from Bingham Harvard, whom she calls her husband. And I am going to do it. And *you*, Betty, are going to help me."

"I knew that that was about what you were going to say, Ben," his sister replied, with slow deliberateness. "This is my answer: I would sooner see you tied down on a white ant-hill and slowly devoured."

"I haven't a doubt of it, Betty," he replied, with another shrug. "But, you see, I know you better than you know yourself. If I were tied down as you say you would cut the cords, all right. And you will help me to sever the bonds that hold Kitten and Bingham Harvard together, too. You have *got* to do it!"

Betty was silent.

"Haven't you?" he insisted.

"I prefer to hear all that you have to say on the subject before I reply to that question," she said then.

"I accumulated a good deal of money while I was in China, Betty," he stated, with an abrupt change of subject.

"*Were* you in China?" she demanded, without raising her voice, and with her head turned so that she was gazing out across the Sound.

"Naturally—since I tell you so. I brought back a small fortune with me, too. It is in cash, and is therefore available. I can afford to give you as much as fifty thousand dollars of it, Betty—if you want it badly enough to do as I say."

"So my affectionate, sisterly services are to be purchased, are they?"

"If you prefer to put it in that way—yes."

"Suppose I decline the proposition?"

"I think I know you well enough to feel assured that you will not—*quite dare*—to do that."

He half-turned his head and looked straight at Betty when he used the two threatening words.

"And I know myself well enough to be able to assure you that I can, and will, make you accept it, dear sister."

"Kittie hates you, Ben."

"She *thinks* she does—when I am not present. It is quite the contrary whenever I am in touch of her. She is a little bit afraid of me, that's all—and she doesn't quite know what it is that she is afraid of. She has not studied it, because she has feared to do so. She flutters about like a bird in a cage when I am near to her. She flushes and pales: she tries to escape, but inevitably returns; she avoids my eyes all she can, but always I can draw them back to mine; she catches her breath, she breathes quickly or slowly, as I will her to do. She feels, all in the same instant, the impulse to strike me dead at her feet and to fly into my arms and to lie there. She cannot commit the former act; she will—she *must*—do the latter."

"Ben"—Betty turned to her brother with sudden earnestness— "Kittie is happy now. She loves her husband. She adores him. He is her idol, her world. Go away and leave her alone, won't you? Please!"

He laughed harshly.

"Go away and leave her to another man—to *that* other man, who, in spite of every concentrated energy and effort of my soul, won her away from me! Go away and leave her to the man who took possession of her, owned her, and held her in his arms, and won her caresses and her embraces, while I was absent?" Benton Keese cried, his handsome face dark with anger, his eyes flaming with sullen, smoldering fires.

He guided the car to the side of the road and stopped it. He half turned in his seat to face his sister. The sinister beauty of his shapely features was never more remarkable than when he was in one of his fits of passionate temper.

"Do you know me so little as to expect that, Elizabeth?" he asked, smiling cruelly. "Did you ever know me to relent after I had once determined upon a projected course? Don't you know that I would sacrifice everything—you, and even Kitten herself in the end—to win her *now*?"

Betty shrank away from him in spite of the fact that she believed that she knew him better, and therefore feared him less, than others did. She trembled inwardly, wide-eyed and frightened. She could see, through the smoldering glare of his eyes, the devil that dwelt inside of him. It had always been there. Their own father, now dead, had been afraid to arouse it. Their mother had dreaded it and had always been frightened by it. The negroes had called him "that little devil" when he was a boy. Betty could remember, when she was five and he was fifteen, how he had shocked her and filled her with horror by acts of cruelty that he had committed, and how frequently, and almost in the next moment, he had won her again with kindnesses and by the power of his strange personality. She was not afraid for herself, but she was frightened—terribly frightened—for Katherine, and it was because she did know her brother so well, because she understood his subtle power to charm, and realized his daring.

But all of the subtlety that had descended from the Keese ancestors had not been bestowed upon Benton. Betty had inherited some of it herself. She had no thought other than to be unswervingly loyal to her friend; but she knew, also, that she could not successfully battle against her brother in the open, even in the service of Katherine. She was aware that to combat him she must meet him on his own ground, in his own way, and that she would have to be as subtle, as far-seeing, and as resourceful as he was.

So, when that momentary burst of passion had swept over him and spent itself, she asked him quietly:

"What do you want me to do, Ben?"

He started the car ahead before he replied.

"I don't know—yet," he said after an interval. "But I must know that I can depend upon you. When the time comes to act you must be ready to act with me and for me. No matter what the emergency may be, I must know that you will stand with me through it and to the end of it."

"Ben," Betty entreated, "you will not use—you will not attempt to compel Kittie to go away with—Oh, dear—*you must not*—"

He interrupted her calmly.

"I will use persuasion to the limit," he said deliberately. "If that fails I will employ other and more certain methods. And you must help, if it comes to that."

"Ben"—she reached out and rested one hand lightly upon his arm—"don't you know that Bingham Harvard will kill you in the end, no matter *how* you may accomplish what you have started out to do? No matter even if you fail at the last? Don't you know that he will kill you, even if you have *tried* and have failed?"

He shrugged and did not answer.

"Do you know anything about the history of Bingham Harvard?" his sister asked him.

"I know *all* about it. I know *everything* about it."

"Are you sure? Do you know all about him when he was called '*Alias the Night Wind*'?"

"Yes; and if he were ten thousand Night Winds rolled into one, the fact would make no difference. I want *her*—his wife. And I'm going to *get* her. And, if I have to kill *him* in order to do it, why—I will kill him; that's all."

"My God, Benton—"

"No heroics, if you please, Elizabeth."

"Have you been told about the terrible strength of the man, and of his awful temper, when it is aroused? Do you know about—"

"I tell you I know *all* about him; everything. And you know mighty little about your beloved brother, if you think that you can frighten me. Now, listen to *me* for a moment."

"Well?" Betty turned her head away while she listened.

"I have not given myself any too much time to do all that I intend to do. Two weeks—or three, at the most, is all that I care to allow myself. I intend, then, to disappear. And Kitten shall disappear with me. Do you understand that?"

Betty nodded her head affirmatively. She could not have spoken just then.

"Willingly, if she will; by force, if necessary, she shall go away with me. But I think—I intend in the meantime—to compel her to a willingness, if not to an eagerness, to escape from Harvard, and to go anywhere, even to the uttermost ends of the earth, with me. Do you understand *that*? If you do not, I won't explain. If you do, you need not think too much about it. But my plans are made. I shall carry them out to the end. I waited too long a time for Katherine Maxwilton to let any consideration for Katherine Harvard stand in my way. And as for the man who stepped into the ring and caught her when I was not present to prevent it—?"

"I will find a way to be damned well rid of him, after I have—" He stopped.

"Have done what?" Betty asked, breathlessly.

112

Keese replied slowly, his eyes boring into his sister's as he did so:

"After I have taken possession of what belongs to me. After I have made her mine; and when she would not go back to Harvard even if he would take her back—why, then I'll either kill him or have him killed; one or the other. There won't be room enough in the world for both of us, afterward."

CHAPTER XIX

AN ELEMENTAL PUZZLE

Lady Kate and Tom Clancy left the bank together. Tom's car, that had taken him there, waited at the door directly behind Katherine's. But he dismissed his own and followed Katherine into the limousine after a nod of friendly greeting to Black Julius, who had been her faithful servitor since her childhood, and who sat like an ebony statue under the steering-wheel.

"Katherine," Tom said when they were seated side by side and the car was headed uptown, "I am in love. I—er—don't suppose it surprises you so very much to hear me say that, does it?"

Lady Kate threw a bright smile at him and replied gently:

"It does not surprise me at all, Tom; and it pleases me greatly. Why, it has been printed all over you as big as a signboard ever since the moment you looked into Betty's eyes. I knew even then that the little god had made a bull's-eye. To tell you the truth, I rather thought it would be so, from the moment I knew that Betty was coming."

Tom nodded his head with silent emphasis. Presently he said:

"Cupid does not always shoot both ways at once, does he?"

"Meaning—?" she inquired, raising her brows.

"Meaning this, Katherine: I am wondering if the little chap scored a bull's-eye *for* me, as well as *on* me?"

"'Faint heart,' Tom; you know the rest of it."

"Sure. And I'm not faint-hearted; you know that. And I am not worrying particularly about that other bull's-eye, either, for I mean that it shall be one before very long, if it isn't so already. So there!" he concluded with a light laugh.

"Modesty is not your hazard, at all events," she returned, smiling again.

"Katherine"—he turned his head and looked straight into her eyes—"I am in love with Betty Keese. I knew I was in love with her before I had walked a block that morning after I left you two at the entrance to the Pennsylvania Station. I know, too, that a man doesn't get it in the neck—I mean in the heart, of course—like that, without the shock being mutual; or reasonably close to mutuality, anyhow."

"Modesty, Tom, as I have already observed—"

"Never mind the 'modesty' part of it, Katherine. There isn't any of *that* kind of modesty in the game, when a chap is in love—the way I am. But the circumstance, take it all in all, places me in rather a peculiar position toward you. That is what I am leading up to, Mrs. Bingham Harvard, if anybody should ride in on a biplane and ask you."

"Toward me?" Katherine stared at him in entire uncomprehension.

"Uh-huh." He nodded. Then he grinned. "When you introduced me to Betty you said that she was a sister in everything but the blood-tie. You stated, also, if I remember correctly, that she stood in the same relation to you that I do to Bing. Well, then, if Betty and you are sisters, and, by the same axiom if Bing and I are brothers, that makes *you* my *double-sister*, doesn't it?"

"You are not very clear, Tom, but I will admit that it does, in order to hear what more you may have to offer on the point."

Tom absently took a cigar from his pocket, bit off the end of it, returned it to his waistcoat, and replied:

"I am going to talk to you, Katherine, exactly as if you actually were my sister; precisely from the standpoint of a real brother. If you do not happen to like what I say—you won't like it; that's all."

"It begins with this statement: That brother of Betty's is *not* a healthful and wholesome chap to have around your fireside."

Katherine's lips parted. Her eyes dilated with surprise. She was on the point of replying when he interrupted her.

"Wait a moment, little lady," he said. "Let me get this out of my system before you butt in. If I were not exactly what I am, to you, and to Bing—and, I guess, to Betty, too—I don't suppose that I would have seen or noticed a thing. But, being just what I am, to all of you, I get a viewpoint from four sides at once. See?"

She made no reply, and he went on:

"I take a squint at Benton Keese—and I see a whole lot. I throw a side-glance at Betty, when she is not aware of it, and when she is stealing a look at her precious brother—and I see a whole lot more. I turn my eyes in your direction, and—well—I read another hidden chapter. Then, Katherine, when I make a composite, mental picture of the whole shooting match I'm scared stiff. And it is not that handsome he-cat that scares me, nor what I read in Betty's mind. It's *you*."

"I?"

"Yes. You are afraid of him. I wouldn't dare to say this if I weren't your 'double-brother.' But you *are* afraid of Benton Keese. And you are not one to be afraid of anything without good and sufficient reason. Now, little lady, I want you to forget everything except that I am just what I am to you and Bing, and tell me exactly what it is that you are afraid of. Wheeew! Maybe you think it did not take some courage to get that off my chest!"

His attempt at levity passed unnoticed. Katherine stared straight ahead of her at nothing during a considerable interval before she replied. Then she said, almost inaudibly, and with hesitation:

"I—do not—know."

"You admit that you are afraid of him?"

"N-no. Not exactly that. No; I am not afraid of him." She still spoke in a low tone, and with evident hesitancy; but it was the hesitation of uncertainty, not of reluctance.

"Then—what is it?"

"I don't know, Tom." Katherine's eyes still stared straight ahead of her.

"You do know, don't you, that the man is madly in love with you? His kind of love?"

"His kind of love—yes." She nodded with conviction. "Only—I do not know the kind. It is utterly strange to me. It always frightened me. My fear of him—if it *is* fear that I feel—must be due to the force of habit. I can account for it in no other way, Tom."

"Habit?"

"I *was* afraid of him, always, when I was a child. I dreaded his presence—and flew into it the instant he appeared. He is five years older than Betty is—than I am. When I was five and he was ten, I was horribly afraid of him. When I was ten and he was fifteen, it was the same, only more so. But he fascinated me, always, if he chose to do so."

"And—does so, now?"

"No. Not that—unless it may be that form of abnormal fascination which is attracted by things that are most repulsive."

"How was it when you were still older? When you were fifteen and he was twenty? And afterward, until your parents wanted you to marry him, and you ran away?"

Katherine turned her eyes to Tom's for the first time since the beginning of the subject.

"I hated him," she said with half-breathless vehemence. "He made my flesh creep, and my hands cold, and my cheeks flush—and my heart throb with anger, every time he looked at me. He had a way with him that—"

"Please go on," said Tom.

"I can't. I don't know how to continue. It is all so inexplicable."

"He has a way with him still, has he not, when he is near you? When he looks at you?"

"I am—afraid—that he has—Tom."

"How does it affect you? Can you tell me that much?"

"No. I do not know. It's a mixture of attraction and repulsion: of liking and of loathing. It attracts me by its very balefulness. It is utterly fearsome while it fascinates. It is like looking into the vortex of a terrific conflagration and longing to approach it for a nearer view, yet knowing that the touch of it will consume and destroy. Do you understand it, Tom? Can you explain it for me?"

"Is it, do you think, a form of hypnotic influence?" he asked, without replying to her question.

But she shook her head instantly and with decision.

"It is not that," she said. "It is not even mental suggestion. It is not mental at all. It is not physical. Mentally, physically, spiritually, I utterly loathe the man. It is primordial; elemental. It is—" She stopped again.

"Well?" Tom encouraged her.

"Tom Clancy, if there were such a thing as reincarnation—if I could accept the theory of pre-existence—I would readily believe that Benton Keese and I had known each other and loved or hated each other, then; and that one of us had murdered the other; and that (I almost hate myself for saying it, even to you, Tom) history is trying now to repeat itself. He attracts me, he pulls me, he draws me to him, in spite of myself, but the impulse that is upon me at such moments is to strike, to destroy, to *kill*."

"Good God, Katherine!" Clancy exclaimed, astounded.

"I tell you it is elemental. And it is nothing that is even remotely akin to love, or that ever could have been, even in that chimerical past existence. It is hate—diabolical, relentless, chaotic, destroying hate. Love is one great extremity of life. Hate is the other—it's opposite. The second is as positive in its attraction as the first."

"By Jove!" Tom said under his breath and leaned back against the cushions.

Then: "The danger is not exactly what I feared it might be, little lady, but it is just as great—or greater, even. For, take it from me, Katherine, it is not the second one of those two extremes that *he* feels. It is the first one. He is the one who is in danger; not you. And upon my word, just now when you said what you did, you looked—and spoke, too—as if you might strike and destroy and kill if he should ever thrust himself across the dividing line."

Katherine bent nearer to him. She rested one hand gently upon his arm. She spoke with intense earnestness.

"You have opened my eyes, Tom," she said quietly. "You have made me understand at last what it is that I fear. I am afraid that he will attempt to cross that dividing line and that the elemental feminine within me will destroy him if he does so."

The car drew up at the curb in front of Katherine's home and stopped. Another that had approached from the opposite direction did the same at the identical moment. As they stepped down to the pavement Benton Keese and Betty did likewise from the other car. The four entered the house together.

CHAPTER XX

THE SWEETEST STORY EVER TOLD

"Miss Betty, were you ever in love?"

Tom asked the question softly. Betty was seated at the piano with her fingers running lightly over the keys and improvising the harmony they produced. Her shapely chin was tilted slightly upward so that her exquisite face was in full view of his devouring eyes and her lips were parted mischievously.

"Oh, heaps of times!" she assured him roguishly. "I cannot even remember all of the times."

"In that case," Tom said with calm conviction, "you will know exactly how to sympathize with a poor chap who suddenly finds himself in that predicament."

"Is it a predicament?" Betty inquired archly, while her fingers strayed into the refrain of a love-song.

"Quite so." Tom nodded his head with undoubted emphasis. But he held to his position at the end of the piano and nothing in his attitude or manner betrayed the earnestness of his words. He wondered if Betty intended that the air she was playing to be significant of her attitude—or if she was merely making fun of him.

Benton Keese, at the far end of the room, was idly turning the loose leaves of a portfolio. Both he and Tom had been asked to remain for dinner, and the arrival of Bingham Harvard was momentarily expected. Katherine was temporarily absent from the room.

Betty played on for a time without response. Then—

"Who is the poor chap to whom you refer?" she asked, bending slightly forward over the keyboard—but not so far as to prevent Tom from seeing the deeper color that had flooded the shapely cheek and chin.

"I am," he replied boldly, still holding to his distance—but doing it with evident difficulty, as the enforced rigidity of his upright pose sufficiently demonstrated.

Betty's fingers strayed again. This time they touched upon another old-time melody which everybody whistled and sang only a few years ago.

"Love me, and the world is mine," Betty's fingers said to him; and he had the almost ungovernable impulse to seize her, to lift her from the piano stool, and to crush her warm and supple body against his own. But he succeeded in resisting it.

She was silent again until she had played nearly through the once popular song. Then, with face and eyes averted, she asked, in so low a tone that he barely heard the words:

"Who—is—the—the other one?"

"You are," he replied instantly.

Crash! Betty's slender fingers fell upon chord after chord of harmony, each one softer and yet fuller than that which had preceded it, and her tapering, dainty fingers, directed by her whimsical but receptive mood, modulated from key to key until with the delicacy of a subconscious thought they drifted into the air of De Koven's "Oh, promise me!" She bent still lower over the piano while her hands found the notes that seemed to be intended for her answer to him.

Tom Clancy's face became, for an instant, as pale as wax. He held himself in hand with difficulty. It was hardly possible to mistake her meaning, then.

"Do you mean it, Betty?" he demanded breathlessly, bending a trifle nearer to her in spite of himself. "Do you mean it, dear?" he went on, recovering in part his mental equilibrium, and stoically condemning himself not to betray by a single act the near-tragedy of the situation. For he knew, without looking in that direction, that the eyes of Benton Keese were watching them, and he realized that what Katherine had been enabled to see so plainly must also have been discernible to Betty's keenly observant brother.

"Do you mean all that the music tells me?" he asked yet again. "I know that it is awfully soon for me to tell you about it; but—but—I *could* have told you the very same thing even before I let go of your hand the first time I ever saw you, down at the Pennsylvania Station."

"I knew it then; right then. Honest, I did. And I told Katherine all about it only a few minutes ago, while Julius was bringing us here in the car. And *she* thought that—maybe—you liked me a *little* bit, you know. Betty, won't you look at me, please? Won't you raise your eyes to mine just once, if it's only for an instant? I'll fly into little pieces in a moment more, if you don't. My heart is swelling so that it will explode like a stick of dynamite in another minute unless you look at me, or say something. I love you, little Betty; with all my heart and soul and strength I love you. And you know it, too. You *have* known it as well as I have, since three days ago, when *I* found it out, all in a blessed minute."

She did not look at him, just then, in response to his plea. She did not dare. Possibly she realized that if she did so, she would, herself, betray to her vigilant brother the very thing that Tom was trying so hard to conceal. But her fingers strayed over the piano keys into the melody of a still older song—"Because it's you"; and he mentally repeated the first verse of it in response to the touch of her singing fingers:

"If I could have my dearest wish fulfilled,
    And take my choice of all earth's treasures, too;
And ask of Heaven what so e'er I willed—
    I'd ask for *you*."

"Betty! Oh, Betty!" he fairly gasped in the excess of his pent-up emotions. "Is that your answer? *Is* it? Tell me. Look up at me and tell me, or I will—"

She obeyed him. Her eyes, moist, limpid, yet wondrously alight and shining through the love-mist in them, sought his own, found them, and rested there for a moment, rapturously. He read her answer there, in the warm glow of them, in the flush upon her cheeks, in the slightly parted lips, in her quickened breathing, in the suffusing warmth of her pulsing nearness—and in his own hammering heart-beats which responded so utterly.

Tom Clancy *knew*, then. There was no need for Betty to speak. A great sigh of supreme content welled within him. The great impulse of conviction, of certainty, overwhelmed him—and steadied him, too. And again, while he struggled to contain himself, Betty's fingers sought out and repeated to him the last bars of "It is the sweetest story ever told." It was almost too much. There is no telling what might have happened then had not an interruption occurred.

The door opened and Bingham Harvard came into the room. Katherine was beside him. Betty swung the stool around so that she faced away from Tom—whose eyes she dared not meet again just then—and left the piano. Benton Keese got lazily upon his feet in greeting. Clancy crossed the room quickly and drew Lady Kate aside, leading her away from the others, so that, for her ears alone, he might safely turn on the "exhaust." He felt that some sort of a safety valve had to "pop," or that he would burst with the wonder of it all.

"I've told her, Katherine," he whispered fiercely. "I've won. I have got her—or she has got me; or—Oh, I don't know what to say. It is all right, anyhow. Glory be, Lady Kate! I am the happiest man outside of heaven."

"Do you mean to tell me, Tom Clancy, that you have been proposing to Betty right here in this room in the presence of her brother?" Katherine asked composedly.

"Uh-huh. Honest. I couldn't help it. It just had to come out over there by the piano. And she, bless her dear heart! answered me with her fingers."

"Really? I did not know that either of you understood the deaf and dumb alpha—"

"Deaf and dumb nothing! She *played* to me. And then, after a little, she *looked* at me. Say, Lady, I've got to hug somebody. Can't I hug you? Eh? Or—I'll tell you what! You go over there where *she* is, and take her aside, and put your arms around her, and kiss her on both cheeks, for me, will you? And you tell her in a whisper to look over your shoulder at me while you are doing it. Go on! Please! I *want* you to. Good heavens, Katherine, what a wonderful thing it is, isn't it?"

But Katherine had already turned away to do his bidding. Tom watched her. He saw her put an arm around Betty and draw her aside just as Harvard left the room to seek his own. For the moment Tom forgot that Benton Keese was somewhere behind him. He had eyes only for Betty, who was at that instant peering at him over Katherine's shoulder. And her own eyes sparkled wondrously, her cheeks were red and rosy, her lips were parted ever so little in a half-roguish smile which Tom thought was the most bewitching and alluring thing he had ever seen. He could scarcely contain himself. He was tense in his attitude, poised, and with his body bent slightly forward as if he were on the very point of leaping forward to seize her. And then he was jerked back to earth again with a jar and a shock that suddenly aroused every impulse of fierce resentment that was in him. The quiet, insinuating, perfectly modulated voice of Benton Keese spoke to him from directly behind.

"You are a regular steeple-chaser in your love-hunting; eh, Clancy? And you take hurdles and blind ditches without a thought of the consequences, I observe," Keese said.

"That was an entertaining tableau at the piano; and very prettily done. But, Betty always does it to perfection. God knows that she has had practice enough."

CHAPTER XXI

AGAIN THAT CHILTON PICTURE

Clancy controlled the angry impulse he felt, even while he turned about to face Benton Keese; and he compelled himself to perform that act very slowly indeed. Tom's impetuosity was a good deal like Theodore Roosevelt's; his brain thought much more quickly, always, than he acted.

"It *was* rather well done, wasn't it?" he replied genially. "I thought so myself."

Keese nodded, a slow smile twitching at the corners of his mouth, his eyes glowing inscrutably.

"If you perhaps had been supplied with a harmonica, Clancy, the scene would have been almost a wordless recitative," he said. "But I suspect that *you* are very much in earnest—most men are when they run up against Betty—and so I suggest that you use your glasses to study the field a bit carefully before you take *all* of the jumps."

Tom's eyes narrowed. Lady Kate and Betty, with their arms around each other, were crossing the room toward them. He replied rapidly, and in a low tone:

"Your metaphor, Mr. Keese, reminds me that in the hunting field one is more prone to warn another rider of danger, when he sees ahead of him a bad jump for his own mount. To stick to the metaphor, 'Look out that you don't fetch a cropper yourself.'"

Keese shrugged his shoulders, and there was a strange and ominous gleam in the depths of his red-brown eyes as he replied, showing his white teeth as he said it:

"Oh, my mount will take me safely over. I fear only for those who may foolishly attempt to follow me. We were speaking of the hunting-field, Betty," he added lazily to his sister. "I was telling Mr. Clancy about that old trick of yours of leading the chase to the most dangerous jumps, and then falling—so that you might safely jeer at your pursuers when they floundered in the ditch."

The double meaning of what he said compelled itself upon each of his listeners, although they were differently impressed. And Keese, who flew from one conversational twig to another with the ease and cocksureness of a sparrow, added:

"All of which reminds me that it has been a long time since I rode to hounds. And I pine for it. Really."

Harvard returned to the room at that instant, and, hearing what was said, replied instantly:

"The Forestbrook Club will hold a meet this coming Thursday, Mr. Keese. Katherine will be glad to attend, I know; and I guess that Tom can do the honors of the day. Unfortunately I won't be able to go myself. But I can join you later; in time for the dinner."

"I should like it very much, indeed," Keese replied readily. "Nothing would please me more than that."

"And you, Miss Betty?" Bingham asked.

"Oh, I should just love it!"

"And you, Tom? Can you manage it to act as host for that day?"

"Sure. I'll declare a bank-holiday, so far as I am concerned."

"And we can fit you out with mounts, and everything that is needed," Harvard added, "so we will declare it settled."

Until dinner was served, during it, and afterward, Tom Clancy found not a single moment or opportunity for a word alone with Betty, although he resorted to every expedient he could think of, or create, in order to accomplish it. He was perfectly aware that Betty sought to avoid it, too; but not, he readily surmised, because she dreaded it or even wished to postpone it, but on account of the proximity of her brother, and his evident understanding of the situation. Their eyes sought each other's frequently, nevertheless, and flashes of entire comprehension of the occasion were exchanged between them.

Katherine watched them demurely, and wondered how either of them could suppose that the situation was not thoroughly understood by Betty's brother and her own husband. The truth she thought was plainly enough depicted upon the faces and in the eyes of the lovers whenever their glances met.

In the library, after the informal meal, Benton Keese sought the company of Bingham Harvard, and they chatted together upon various topics, until the young bank president remarked apropos of nothing in particular:

"It is rather odd, Mr. Keese, that ever since your first appearance among us I have had the strange sensation of having met you before, somewhere—although I know quite well that it cannot be so."

"Indeed?" Keese replied indifferently. "It is, I suppose, some vague resemblance to another, whom you have encountered somewhere; and yet, that other man may not at all resemble me, nor I him."

"Quite so," Harvard assented, nodding.

"It is the old Oliver Wendell Holmes idea that when John and Thomas meet and converse six people are talking: John, as John thinks he is; John as Thomas thinks he is; and John as God *knows* he is—and so on, vice versa, et cetera, and all the rest of it. Eh?"

"Doubtless. My lifelong bank-training has taught me to remember personalities, rather than faces and features. It is something about your personality that seems familiar to me."

"Oh! I see. Well, I think I can account for that, Harvard. It is quite simple."

"Yes?"

"It is the personality of the Southerner. We are all very much alike in many of our characteristics, you know, no matter how greatly we may differ in the concrete. All Southerners possess identical traits which are never entirely eradicated in another environment. For example: your wife and I were raised—as we express it—in the same county and among the same people. Practically, although I am older, as you know, we were children and playmates together; and so the familiar notes that I have struck in your memory are the harmonizing notes of Fayette County, Kentucky, which constant association with Katherine has taught you to recognize."

"Probably that accounts for it," Harvard admitted, impressed by the suggestion—yet unconvinced, although he did not say so; and at that moment there came an interruption.

Betty had been idly turning the leaves of a book that was spread open upon her lap, and listening abstractedly to the conversation between Katherine and Tom, who were seated near her. She had heard Tom ask to be shown again a small photograph, which Katherine presently gave to him. Then, as their heads came nearer together, to look at it, she, too, bent forward to see what it was. And then she saw that they were not really looking upon the picture, but into each other's eyes, studiously, earnestly, thoughtfully, as if each were mutely asking a question of the other—and as if each declined to express any sort of a reply. The first glance that Betty had of the photograph, slanting and distant, so that the pose, rather than the costume and features depicted in the picture, impressed her, made her start and bend still nearer, in order to look more closely upon it.

"Why," she exclaimed, "I thought at first that it was a picture of—but of course it isn't. I can see that now." She reached out a hand, and Tom, who held the picture, gave it to her.

"Oh, no!" she said. "I can see now that it isn't in the least bit like him. But what an odd costume! Mexican, isn't it?"

She studied it in silence for a moment, and both Tom and Katherine watched her narrowly, perhaps unconsciously—perhaps also intentionally. Then Betty called to her brother.

"Benton, come here a moment!" she said, and rose to meet him halfway. And that was the interruption referred to.

Clancy rose also and rested an elbow upon a nearby, high-backed chair. Katherine retained her seat, but bent forward slightly upon it, with her eyes fixed intently upon Benton Keese as he came forward to meet his sister. Harvard raised his own eyes indifferently.

"Were you ever in Mexico, Ben?" Betty asked, with scarcely a pause between her summons to him and the question. "Look!" She thrust the picture forward under his eyes. "I really thought, for just an instant, that it was you."

"I?" Keese replied smilingly, and reached out to take possession of the small photograph, but making no haste to look upon it. "I never knowingly have had my picture taken since I wore knicker-bockers," he commented generally to all of them. And he permitted his gaze to rest for the briefest instant upon each face in turn before he dropped it to the photograph of Holbrook Chilton that Betty had put into his hand.

"Why, upon my word!" he exclaimed at once, and with half-excited earnestness when he did look upon it.

Then he looked again at his sister. "How did you come by this, Betty?" he asked sharply. "Where did you get it?"

"Kittie had it. T—Mr. Clancy just now asked her for it. I leaned over to see what it was, and in the very first glance there was something about it that made me think it was you."

"Oh, yes! Of course. Just because we are so different, I suppose," her brother remarked with irony.

Harvard's indifferent glance had become tense. He left his chair and stepped forward nearer to them. Keese was apparently interested in a closer study of the picture, and there was a vaguely reminiscent smile upon his face as he did so.

"Do you know the gentleman, Mr. Keese?" Harvard inquired calmly.

"Know him? Most certainly I know him—or, rather, I *did* know him some years ago. That is a picture of Holbrook Chilton, or else I am very greatly mistaken," and Benton Keese stared straight into Harvard's eyes, as if daring him to deny the statement.

"You are quite right. It is a picture of Holbrook Chilton," Harvard said—and smiled.

"Sure! I knew that I could not be mistaken, although the costume does change him mightily. But it is the same man without a doubt. Is he a friend of yours by any odd chance, Harvard?" He turned toward Lady Kate. "Or of yours, Katherine?"

"He is an acquaintance of mine—and of Clancy's," Harvard interposed before his wife could reply. "May I ask if you have seen him recently? Since your return to this country?"

"Oh, no! In fact I have not seen or heard from him but once since before I went to China; and even then he was merely a passing acquaintance, so to speak. But I liked the man very much indeed, considering how short a time I really knew him."

"Have you any idea of his present address, Mr. Keese?"

"No. I was on the point of asking you the same question. You see, we traveled together in the same Pullman—in the same section, in fact, for he had the upper and I the lower berth—from New Orleans to Los Angeles. I was on my way to California, with no especial object in view. His destination at the time was Guaymas, in Mexico; and, if I remember correctly, his plans for the future were about as indefinite as my own. We parted after a few days spent together in Los Angeles."

"You have heard from him since then, you say?"

"Once; yes. It was before I sailed from San Francisco. I received a letter from him at the hotel address I had given him there. It was postmarked at Guaymas. I replied to it rather hastily I suppose, and told him that I was leaving for China. Later I wrote to him from Singapore, but I never received a reply to that letter, either. In fact, I had entirely forgotten him until I saw this picture. It is a remarkably clear likeness as I remember him—barring the costume, of course. Still, I would have recognized it anywhere."

"I am quite anxious to know where he can be found," Harvard said, turning and resuming the chair he had vacated.

"I am afraid that I cannot help you in that respect," Keese replied thoughtfully and with evident concern. "We were merely traveling acquaintances, you know, and neither of us was much given to personal confidences. I told him that I was a Kentuckian and he replied that he was a Virginian; but I have no idea what part of Virginia he came from."

Betty supplied a suggestion then.

"It was probably Westmoreland County, Benton," she said, wrinkling her brows thoughtfully. "I remember that papa used to correspond with a man who came from there, whose name was Holbrook; and I have a vague recollection of hearing him mention the name of Chilton, too, although I think he referred to another person when he did that."

Keese nodded.

"Possibly," he assented indifferently. "I have some faint remembrance of the sort myself; only it isn't at all definite. However"—he also resumed his chair—"one might readily find out, I suppose, by writing to several of the local postmasters in that locality. That is"—he turned smilingly toward Harvard again—"if you are so very anxious to know about him. Everybody knows everybody else, and who their grandfathers and grandmothers were, in the rural districts of the South. It is odd, isn't it, that I should find a picture of him here?"

"Quite so," Tom Clancy said dryly. "To make use of an expression that is frightfully trite, the world is a small place—when one makes the effort to disappear."

"Oh!" said Keese. "Did Chilton do that? Did he have reason for doing it? Is that—er—the reason why you-all are so anxious to find him? I should suppose, if he sent that photograph to you, Harvard."

He halted in his speech suggestively, but Harvard did not supply the further information as to the source of the photograph.

"It was taken, I think, by a friend and without his knowledge," Lady Kate announced. She was still bending forward, with her chin resting in the hollow of one hand, and her eyes throughout the conversation concerning Chilton had not once wavered from her close regard of Benton Keese, although he seemed to be entirely unconscious of the fact.

Then, rising and crossing to a chair beside her husband, she added indifferently: "Why did the picture remind you of Benton, Betty?"

"Really, I don't know, dear," Betty replied thoughtfully, "for it isn't at all like him when one comes to look closely at it. I think it was something in the pose or in the poise of the head."

"Probably that is what impressed me also," Katherine said absently; and Clancy, who was in the act of occupying a chair beside one that Betty had taken, nodded and murmured:

"Me, too," which was more expressive than grammatical.

Keese, who still held the photograph, reached out and put it down upon the library-table, and Harvard picked it up and began to study it closely.

Just at that moment the door was opened, and Bolton appeared at the threshold, where he stepped aside to permit some one to pass into the room.

"Mr. Anderson Van Cleve," he announced.

CHAPTER XXII

AN EXCHANGE OF WARNINGS

"Mr. Van Cleve, let me make you acquainted with Mr. Keese, of Kentucky; but more recently from China. And my friend Miss Keese. We were schoolmates and chums all our lives until I left home to come to New York."

So spoke Lady Kate as she stepped forward to welcome the man from Mexico.

Keese and Van Cleve grasped hands perfunctorily and the latter turned instantly to acknowledge the second introduction; but his keen eyes that were always peculiarly penetrating in their regard, looked deeply into the red-brown ones of Benton Keese, even in that brief interval.

"There is no need to ask if you are sister and brother, Miss Keese," he said genially to Betty, retaining for a moment the hand she gave to him. "The family resemblance is a pronounced one."

He selected a chair after he had shaken hands with Clancy, and as it happened to be the one nearest to Keese, addressed his next remark to him.

"Lately returned from China, have you, Mr. Keese?" he asked politely. His manner was that of one who was merely "making" conversation; and he added, without awaiting a reply: "I have recently returned from Mexico, so we are both 'foreigners,' in a measure. The latter country is about as remote as the former, in all save distance."

"I have never visited Mexico, so I could not pass as an authority on that point," Keese replied.

"Mr. Keese knows our friend Holbrook Chilton," Tom Clancy remarked in a casual tone. "We were just looking at that picture you took of him, in Guerrero, and he recognized it at once."

Van Cleve, whose gaze had transferred itself to Clancy when the latter spoke, returned it again to Keese with an expression of polite surprise.

"Indeed?" he said, mildly. "Chilton was my superintendent and general manager, in Mexico. He was originally a Southerner, like yourself, I believe. From Virginia, I think he told me."

Keese nodded. "Yes; that is what he told me. Mr. Clancy conveyed a wrong impression, I imagine, in his statement. I do not know Mr. Chilton in the sense that was implied. We were merely traveling acquaintances between New Orleans and Los Angeles, and for a few days after our arrival at the latter place."

"You found him an interesting companion, I have no doubt?" Van Cleve suggested.

"Quite so. I expressed the wish to renew my acquaintance with him, as soon as the photograph restored him to memory. But I had quite forgotten him. Do you, perhaps, know where he is now, Mr. Van Cleve?"

"No. Chilton has disappeared—unfortunately. But—I think I shall hear from him again, sometime."

"Mr. Van Cleve," Katherine interposed at that moment, "we had arranged, just before you came, to attend the 'meet' of the Forestbrook Hunt Club, next Thursday. Could you make it possible to be one of us?"

"I am afraid not, Mrs. Harvard, much as I would like to do so. But the fact is—"

"Mr. Van Cleve has an engagement with me for that afternoon, Katherine," Harvard said when his guest hesitated. "But I will take him down with me when *I* go."

He turned to Van Cleve. "I had already agreed to join them in time for the dinner. There is nothing to prevent you from going down with me, is there?"

"No. No, indeed. I shall be very glad to do that after we have transacted our business."

The turn that the conversation had taken reminded Katherine suddenly of a fact that had entirely escaped her until that moment, and the thought of it sent a vivid flush to her face which receded as quickly as it had appeared, and left it, for an instant only, white and scared. The arrangement, as it stood, paired her—irrevocably paired

132

her—with Benton Keese for the afternoon's cross-country ride; and now, when it was all too late, she realized that there was no possible way to avoid it; at least not without exciting surprise, if not actual comment, from Bingham. She knew, the moment it occurred to her, that Benton Keese would make every effort to keep close to her during the fox hunt, and notwithstanding the half-confidences that she had exchanged with Clancy and the conversation she had had with Betty on the same topic, she knew that those two would forget everybody else but themselves that day.

Lifting her glance she discovered that Keese was regarding her steadily, and that his eyes were shining stealthily, as if he intended to convey to her a silent message of comprehension which he did not wish the others to observe. And again the flush leaped into her face. She felt, for the moment, as if she had tacitly accepted the arrangement which, as she now saw clearly, was directly the consequence of Benton Keese's subtle arts. To her intense relief he left his chair at that moment with the announcement that he must go, much as he regretted to do so; and Clancy, who was torn by several conflicting desires, surrendered to the one which he considered to be his plain duty, and said, as he got upon his feet:

"I'll chase along with you, Keese."

He caught what he chose to consider a reproachful glance from Betty, although in reality it was merely one of surprise; and in another moment the two men were in the street.

"Odd, isn't it, that you should happen to have known Chilton?" Tom remarked after he had lighted a cigar and they were pacing leisurely down the avenue side by side.

"Is it?" Keese replied lazily. He had declined Clancy's offer of a cigar and had lighted an Egyptian cigarette from his own elaborately monogrammed case; the same one that Rushton had seen him make use of in front of the hotel, after discarding the one that he had previously rolled.

At the opposite side of the avenue, unseen by either Clancy or Keese, Rushton was pacing slowly along after them. He was on the job.

"More odd, still, that your sister, at her first glance at his picture should have fancied that she saw in it some sort of a resemblance to you," Tom continued imperturbably.

"There is no accounting for Betty's fancies, Clancy," Keese replied with a light laugh. "They are as sudden and as changeable as shadows—and just about as substantial; and, in that respect it does not much matter what form they may happen to take."

Keese closed the statement with a little chuckle.

"I suppose," Tom said, "that you mean that remark as a sort of continuance of your metaphor of the hunting field."

Keese shrugged his shoulders.

"I mean it as a kindness, at least, Clancy," he said. "Betty wins hearts in just the same way that she picks wild flowers in the woods and fields. She holds them for a moment in her hand, admires them—and chucks them aside for fresher ones."

"Is it a—er—family trait, Mr. Keese?"

"Possibly. I had not thought of that. It is, however, Betty's way. So—be on your guard, my friend."

"Thank you." Tom replied solemnly. "I suppose I ought to thank you, and I do. However, to tell you the truth, if I am to accept as fact what you have said in regard to your sister, and if I am to consider you as representing the 'family,' fickle fancy is not a trait; or, if it is, the characteristic was overlooked when you were fashioned."

"Meaning—just what, Mr. Clancy?"

"Nothing; that is, nothing more than this: If I read you correctly—and for some unexplained reason I think I do—you are one who is very far indeed from being fickle. In fact, it would not surprise me at all if you were to expand at this moment into a burst of confidence and admit to me that you are still madly in love with your *first* love."

"Does your gift of penetration go so far as to suggest who the 'first' love may have been, Mr. Clancy?"

"Quite so. A blind man could see that, you know."

There was an interval of silence which it was evident that Keese did not intend to break of his own accord, and then Tom added, speaking in an apparently careless tone:

"You see we are even now. You were kind enough to warn me, a moment ago, lest I might cast my bread upon waters that would not give it back. And so, gentle sir—my friend, as you addressed *me*—I feel it my duty to return the compliment."

Keese came to a full stop. Tom had won his point. He had succeeded in wounding the heel of Achilles. He had touched a spot which aroused the fiery Southern temper of Benton Keese.

"What the devil do you mean by that?" Keese demanded hotly. Then, before Tom could reply, or had made an effort to do so, he laughed aloud, resumed his way down the avenue, and added, with a well-assumed appearance of forced cordiality:

"Moths like ourselves, Clancy, delight to singe their wings, provided only that the fire is hot enough to suit us. Dear me! Here we are at Fifty-Ninth Street, and I must leave you. Many thanks for the implied warning, old chap; only, really you know, it wasn't necessary. And I am afraid—very much afraid indeed!—that in your case, it was, and is, quite important that you should heed mine."

CHAPTER XXIII

BINGHAM HARVARD'S QUIET WAY

"Bingham," Van Cleve asked, soon after Lady Kate and Betty had gone from the room for an exchange of confidences, following upon the departure of Tom Clancy and Benton Keese, "are you particularly acquainted with the characteristics, traits and mannerisms of Southerners, generally?"

He had lighted a huge, black cigar and was leaning back comfortably in the chair, and his strong, handsome face, eminently patrician in every line of it, expressed nothing more than mild curiosity. Harvard did not smoke.

"I am afraid that I cannot help you as I have only known one intimately," the young banker replied, smilingly, "and that one is Katherine. Why do you ask?"

"*I* have never known any of them intimately," Van Cleve answered. "Unless it was Chilton; and intimacy would hardly be the word to apply to my association with him. But if you had replied to my question in the affirmative, it would have been followed by another one that had occurred to me."

"What is it?"

"This: Does one Southerner whom you meet casually, inevitably remind you, in some inexplicable manner, of others whom you may have known?"

Harvard studied upon the question a moment before he replied. Then he said:

"In the abstract, yes; I think so. I know perfectly well to what you allude, Mr. Van Cleve, and I want to be entirely fair in my reply. There *is* something about Benton Keese that touches a familiar note of memory, and the familiar note does, very remotely, suggest Holbrook Chilton. That is what you meant, isn't it?"

"Yes."

"I was impressed by something of the sort the first time I saw him, although I did not then connect it with Chilton. In fact, I had not done so until this evening; and I doubt if it would have occurred to me even to-night had it not been for a remark his sister made to all of us about the photograph."

"What was that?"

"She thought, from a distance—at her first glance, and before she had really seen the picture—that it was her brother."

"Then it was something in the pose, probably, that suggested the thought?"

"Undoubtedly."

"Of course," Van Cleve announced quietly, "it is utterly preposterous for us to connect the two men in more than a contemplative way. But—I think that the effect that Mr. Keese had upon me at the moment I was introduced to him was very much the same as the impression made upon Miss Betty when she first caught sight of the picture."

"I don't think that I exactly understand what you mean, Mr. Van Cleve," Harvard said, wrinkling his brows.

"Shall I be entirely plain?"

"Please."

"The first swift glance that I had of Mr. Keese when we were introduced brought Chilton as forcibly to my mind as if he had been dropped down into the room in front of me; and Holbrook Chilton was as far from my thoughts at the moment as China or Mexico, or the private office at your bank. But, as in the case of Miss Betty, the notion was instantly dispelled. It disappeared, utterly; and afterward, although I studied the man covertly and closely, I could discover nothing about him to account for that first impulsive idea."

"You just now suggested that it was something about the pose of the picture which brought the idea into Betty's mind. Was it the pose that suggested it to you, do you think?"

"No."

"What should you say it was?"

"I don't know—unless it was something in his eyes. But, I don't see why we are discussing this question at all. Keese is not Chilton. I am as positive about that as I am that he did, somehow, bring the fellow to mind. Besides—" He hesitated.

"Well, Mr. Van Cleve?"

"The whole suggestion is utterly preposterous, as I said before. Benton Keese is the brother of Mrs. Harvard's best friend and life-long associate. Indeed, as I understand it, he was himself a life-long associate of hers."

"The fact remains," Harvard said quietly, "that Benton Keese left his home in Kentucky within a very short time after Katherine came from there to New York—and that was, approximately, about the time of Chilton's appearance in Mexico."

Van Cleve nodded; and he said with a smile:

"That, of course, is a mere coincidence; and also it is partly accounted for by the incident of the meeting between Keese and Chilton in the Pullman car of the Southern Pacific train. Then, again—and this had escaped both of us—if there had been any real connection between the two men Keese could scarcely have permitted himself to recognize, and claim acquaintance with, the original of the picture. But, my dear Harvard, it is utter folly for us even to discuss such a thing. Besides, it is an affront to your guest; and to his beautiful sister who is your wife's best friend as well as guest—and to you, also."

"I could not help noticing that you were studying the man," Harvard said, ignoring the last remark of Van Cleve's.

"I hope that *he* did not notice it. I was not aware that I made the fact so plain."

"I think," Harvard replied slowly, "that Benton Keese is a man who notices most things that occur in his presence. But if he did notice it the effect upon him could have been only one of two kinds."

"How do you mean, Harvard?"

"He should have been either flattered—or frightened."

"Humph!"

"Flattered by your regard, if he is really nothing more nor less than Benton Keese. And dismayed, if not actually frightened by your close attention to him, in case he *has* been masquerading as one Holbrook Chilton of our mutual acquaintance."

"Good Lord, Bingham! You don't for a moment think that possible, do you?" Van Cleve fairly gasped the question.

"No." Harvard replied with deliberation; and he added, carefully selecting his words: "No. I do *not* think that. And yet, barring your non-recognition of him—and mine also—the situation is just possible."

Van Cleve was about to reply, but Harvard went on quickly:

"Wait a moment, Mr. Van Cleve. I want to make myself entirely plain, if that is possible. You know next to nothing concerning an experience I passed through while I was paying-teller at the bank; and I will not burden you with a recital of it. You do know enough about it to understand what I shall say."

"Possibly."

"It was a bitter experience, and the fact that in its utmost extremity I discovered Katherine and won her love is its only atonement. But it taught me that things are not always what they seem to be; that circumstances of past associations cannot always be relied upon; that truth is frequently much harder to establish than falsity."

"I think I understand you. It is your idea to give this man the benefit of the doubt—both ways. That remark is a free translation of a Spanish proverb which I have sometimes thought is very apt. All the same, it is quite plain to me that you do not like Mr. Benton Keese."

"No. My dislike for him is instinctive rather than actual. In a measure, too, it is the consequence of a very human prejudice. Keese was formerly a suitor for Katherine's hand in marriage. He had the active support of Katherine's parents—more, I think, because of old family relations and associations than anything else. I am telling this to you, Mr. Van Cleve, precisely as I would tell it to Mr. Chester."

"I understand, Bingham."

"There is no doubt of the insistence of his suit. It was because of his perseverance in spite of her negatives, and of the pressure that he induced Katherine's father and mother to put upon her that she fled from them and came to New York."

Van Cleve nodded comprehendingly.

"Neither is there any doubt that Keese was deeply—desperately is possibly a better word to express it—in love with Katherine. Nor can there be any doubt to the mind of one who is ordinarily observant that he is so now."

"Surely you are not—"

Harvard interrupted with quiet laughter.

"Jealous? Hardly that, sir. But the elemental, primitive man inside of me resents the *fact*. You understand that, don't you?"

"Yes."

"I can see, too, that Katherine recognizes it—and resents it much more bitterly than I do. To me it is a condition with which, in an abstract way, I can sympathize; but to her it amounts to very little less than a positive affront. I am sure, because I have observed closely, that were it not for the presence of Betty in our home Katherine would find an excuse for not receiving him. And—I hope you will not misunderstand me now—I am inclined to believe that Keese brought his sister here from the South purposely to avoid that very exigency."

"It seems to me," Van Cleve remarked uneasily, "that we are drifting away from the original topic, Bingham."

"No. On the contrary I am getting back to it. I told you a little bit ago that from the first meeting with Keese he sounded a note of familiarity in my consciousness."

"Yes."

"I have thought upon it, and studied it constantly, since then, but not once with the most remote suggestion of associating him with Holbrook Chilton—until to-night."

"But, now?"

"Now, beginning with that impulsive exclamation from Betty, and followed by a much more careful observation of the man himself, the association—in my mind at least—is unmistakable; and yet, like yourself, I am entirely unable to put my mental finger upon a single characteristic, gesture, or feature, tone of the voice, glance of the eye or mannerism, that will afford even the vaguest support to the idea. And so—pardon me yet another moment—a few questions which possibly you can answer, occur to me."

"We are drifting very far afield, Bingham."

"I know that—and we will either drift farther still, or we will be brought back to the home base for a new start."

"Well, what are the questions you would ask?"

"You were more or less closely associated with the man Chilton for some time. You are observant. Very little escapes you. There are certain features about every human being which cannot be thoroughly disguised—or at least that is the claim of criminologists. They are, roughly, the expression, shape, color and habit of using the eyes; the shape of the ears, particularly at the tops, and the lobes, and as to position in relation to the other features; the shape and position of the nose, not in profile, but in full front view, and in the measurements from the tip of it to the lobes of each ear; the lines of the mouth and the flitting expressions of those lines—not the staid ones. Not the outer lines of the lips, which might be concealed temporarily by mustache and beard, but of the mouth itself, which is never entirely concealed."

140

"A moment ago you referred to the eyes of Benton Keese, and so I ask you—what of them, or of any feature I have named, suggests Chilton?"

"Upon my word, Harvard, save for that vague impression of suggestion which still remains, there is not one expression, one feature, or one mannerism to support the theory," Van Cleve replied with studied conviction.

CHAPTER XXIV

A LEOPARD—AND HIS SPOTS

Anderson Van Cleve entered the hotel where he was staying temporarily shortly after eleven. When he called for his key at the desk an envelope was also handed to him. It contained the card of Thomas Clancy.

On the back of it Tom had penciled the following:

DEAR MR. VAN CLEVE:

No matter at what hour you find this card, will you please come to my house to see me before you retire?

T. C.

"How long a time is it since the gentleman was here?" he asked of the clerk who gave him the message; and then remembering that a time stamp would be on the back of the envelope, he turned it over. The clerk replied:

"The envelope was left at the desk by a messenger about an hour ago, sir."

Van Cleve thrust the card and envelope into a pocket and was thoughtful for a moment. He did not perceive that a young man of Jewish appearance who had entered the hotel immediately in his wake, was regarding him furtively. The young man went out again when he did so and signaled to a second taxi after Van Cleve had summoned one.

142

Afterward the second taxi followed the first one until it had drawn up before Tom Clancy's home, where the chauffeur of it composed himself in the attitude of awaiting the return of his "fare." Clancy admitted his caller himself and led him into the library at the rear, where he put forward a box of cigars and other refreshments while he explained the reason for the summons.

"I never would have made a successful diplomat, Mr. Van Cleve," he said, "so I will go straight to the point. I asked you to come here to-night as soon as you returned to your hotel because I believed it necessary that we should discuss a certain person of our acquaintance."

"Keese? Or, Chilton?" Tom's caller inquired with a half smile.

"Both. Or, to be more explicit and direct in my reply, and in order to explain in a single word what I mean—yes."

"The one word, Mr. Clancy, implies that you believe Keese and Chilton to be identical;" and Van Cleve gave voice to a meaningless remark which is usually spelled "Humph!" only the orthography never properly expresses it.

"I do," Tom replied quietly.

"Why?"

"I'm damned if I can tell you why—and that's flat. But I do, just the same. And the conviction, for it amounts to that, puts me into the very deuce of a pickle all around."

"Cannot you give me some sort of a reason for your conviction?"

"No more than you can give me one for yours; and I am quite certain that your belief is approximately the same as mine, sir."

"No, Clancy, it is not. But I will say this: If I were situated as you are, in relation to this whole affair, I have not a doubt that I would think exactly as you do."

"What do you mean by that?"

"This: You have seen and talked with Chilton only two or three times. I have seen him and talked with him, and hobnobbed with him hundreds of times. I have been in his company for days at a time. We have traveled together across leagues of territory in the saddle, side by side. I have known him when serious danger threatened, and have always found him to be cool, resourceful, self-reliant, and brave, and have been enabled to observe him very closely in such extremities. I have seen him and observed him at Mexican *fiestas*, when there was dancing and music and laughter all around us. I have seen him in my office, engaged in business affairs, and in

143

his own rooms when he was host and I was guest. And always I have studied him more closely than I would have done with another man—because—there was always an indefinable something about the man that impressed me with a vague uneasiness."

"And now—and this is the point—I cannot discover one single characteristic, mannerism, gesture, or feature of Benton Keese's which was also Chilton's. *And I do not believe that it is within the scope and power of any man to disguise himself so thoroughly.*"

"Once upon a time I learned to speak Spanish fluently, Mr. Van Cleve," Tom said.

"Yes? What has that got to do with it?"

"I remember a Spanish proverb that I learned. It has a lot of meaning, too; and it seems to apply just here."

"What was it?"

"Translated to English, and rather liberally, it means: 'When you study the motives of a friend or an enemy, give him the benefit of the doubt, both ways.'"

Van Cleve smiled broadly.

"I quoted the same proverb to Bingham Harvard this evening," he said.

"Were you discussing Keese?"

"Yes."

"Then you were of the opinion that Keese might be Chilton? And Bing had the same idea, did he?"

"I won't go so far as to say that. But the suggestion was made by one of us—that it is within possibility that it might be so."

"Which one made it?"

"Harvard, I think. But you have not told me why you quoted that old proverb."

"I mentioned it because, in studying this question, I have attempted to follow out the rule of that proverb. I have undertaken to give the man the benefit of the doubt—*both ways.*"

"I am still in the dark, Mr. Clancy."

"Do you play chess, Mr. Van Cleve? Yes? Then you know how a good chess player studies his game a great many moves ahead; how he arranges several plans and seeks to anticipate what the moves of his opponent would be, for each plan; and how he finally selects what he believes to be the best plan, and follows it out tenaciously—unless an entirely unexpected move by his opponent *forces* him to change it?"

"It seems to me that we are getting farther and farther away from the significance of the Spanish proverb."

"No. We are getting closer to it."

"How so?"

"If I give Chilton the benefit of the doubt, both ways—studying him from the time that he entered your employ, and assuming that he *is now* Benton Keese; but observing him for the time being only as Chilton—I am brought to the conclusion that the man had observed you and your methods and your business affairs rather closely, before he applied to you for employment."

"Well?"

"The various ramifications of your ventures in Mexico was the chess board. Your mines, your contracts, your investments, your fortune, or a great part of it, and the work you were doing, were the pawns in the game. You were the king he was to checkmate, and you lost your queen irretrievably when you made him your general manager and put him in charge of your affairs. He took away your rooks, your bishops and your knights when your attention was diverted by the unsettled conditions by which you were surrounded. He would have driven you into a corner and checkmated you if you had not made the sudden and totally unexpected move of throwing everything, down there, to the dogs and returning to New York. I verily believe, Mr. Van Cleve, if it had not been for that you would be dead by now, and that Harvard and I would be entertaining Chilton here in your name."

Van Cleve nodded as if he thought so, too.

"But," Tom continued, "you did make that unexpected move, and at exactly the right time. Even so, he has driven you into a corner where you can only move to and fro on a couple of squares while you watch and wait for him, through his overconfidence, to make a false move."

"I entirely understand the simile you draw, Clancy. And, so far as the man Chilton is concerned, I am ready to accept it. In fact, I have done so already."

"But you have said not a thing, as yet, to convince me that Chilton is Keese, or that a man *can* change his spots (I mean his personality, of course) as effectively and completely as Keese has done, *if he was* Chilton."

"You forget entirely the one important thing, Mr. Van Cleve."

"Do I? What is it?"

"Benton Keese is *not* disguised. *Benton Keese* has not changed a spot."

"Eh? I do not—"

"Holbrook Chilton *was* in disguise, from the very first time you ever saw him, until the very last time."

"You mean by that—just what, Mr. Clancy?"

"I mean that every move that Chilton made in the game he was playing with you for an opponent had been previously thought out. That every gesture he employed, every mannerism he used, every figure of speech he adopted, every peculiarity he seemed to posses, was assumed for your benefit. I mean that he was always fully informed of your coming before you arrived, and was prepared for it; that he was surrounded by men who would not notice any change in his attitude or demeanor between the occasions when you were present and when you were not—or, if they did so, would attribute such a change to the presence of the 'boss.' I mean that in all the times when you were together in Mexico Chilton was playing—and doing it thoroughly—a part that he had carefully studied in each and every detail, and that the Holbrook Chilton *you* knew was no more the *real man* than *Shylock* was when Henry Irving played that character. And, lastly, I mean this: That Benton Keese is merely his natural self; that in him you see only the great actor in private life; and, as in the case of all great actors, he does not at all resemble any one of the characters he assumes in his playacting."

"That would presuppose that Holbrook Chilton came into my employ with the deliberate intention of robbing me finally."

"Exactly. And of murdering you, too, doubtless, and so obtained *all* you possessed. But you made an unexpected move toward the end of the game, and so, let us say, saved a fairly good chunk of your bacon."

"But, Clancy, it would also presuppose that the man knew a great deal about my personal affairs. That I am practically alone in the world; that if I should disappear, and he was to assume my name and place—and fortune—there would be practically nobody to question his claim; nobody but Sterling Chester."

"Yes; and in reply to that we have the fact that Chilton somehow knew that Chester was traveling in Egypt, when *you* did not know it."

"The whole thing amazes me, Mr. Clancy. I confess it. And your arguments do impress me. I must admit that, too. But, if your assumption is correct, how are we to establish the truth of it?"

146

"That remains to be seen. Let me ask you this: Have you noticed that you have been followed and spied upon recently?"

"No."

"I have. So had Rushton. So will you, if you watch out. I'll bet you a hat that you were followed to this house to-night, and will be followed back to your hotel when you go out. What for, and by whom, and all the rest of it, you wish to ask? For the ultimate security of Benton Keese, and by operatives from the Roland Detective Agency (so Rushton informed me), which I suspect is employed by Keese. And the 'all the rest of it' is easy enough to guess. Mr. Benton Keese, *alias* Holbrook Chilton, wishes to anticipate any and all moves that may be made against him."

CHAPTER XXV

THE OTHER SIDE OF BENTON KEESE

As for Benton Keese, our good friend Rodney Rushton followed after him. When that person parted with Clancy at Fifth Avenue and Fifty-Ninth Street he went directly to his hotel, which, as it happened, was the same at which Van Cleve was staying, the Mammoth; and he went at once to his rooms, where he waited with a considerable show of impatience the anticipated arrival of a certain Mr. Dudley Roland, who, nevertheless, did not make his appearance until after one o'clock. But when he did appear, Rushton, who was waiting and watching, saw him and knew well his business and where he was going.

Keese motioned the man to a chair and glanced rapidly and impatiently through the written reports contained on several sheets of paper which Roland gave to him. But he crushed them in his hands and tossed them into an open grate, where he touched a match to them before he had half scanned their contents.

"I want no written reports of what you do for me," he said sharply. "You might be hit by an automobile or drop dead when you are bringing them to me. And I don't care a damn what Operatives No. 1, or 2, or anybody else does. I want results."

"So, now, suppose you tell me as concisely as possible just what those reports contained. I did not read them all."

"Van Cleve, Clancy, Redhead and two of his operatives, Mrs. Harvard, and ex-Lieutenant Rushton were all at Harvard's bank late this afternoon, in private conference in the directors' room. I don't know anything about the subject of the conference."

"The subject does not matter. Go on."

"Rushton and Van Cleve left the bank together. They came to this hotel and spent more than an hour together in Van Cleve's rooms. Rushton left here shortly after five o'clock. He went to his own home, remained inside the house only a few minutes, came out with a small grip in his hand, went to the Pennsylvania Station, bought a ticket for St. Louis and went away. My operative left on the same train."

Keese lifted one hand to enjoin silence, and spent a moment in deep thought. Then:

"Go on," he said.

"Clancy came out of the bank with Mrs. Harvard, dismissed his own car and rode home with her—but you know that, because you reached there at the same time they did with a lady."

"I thought I told you that your operatives were not to know *me* at all," Keese said sharply.

"They do not, sir. I happened to be on that part of the job myself."

"Well?"

"Harvard remained at the bank until nearly six. Then he went home. Van Cleve dined here at the hotel, smoked, and read the paper at the table afterward, and then walked all the way to Harvard's house. You came out of the house with Clancy—"

"Never mind what *I* did. I am reasonably well informed as to that."

"When you parted with Clancy at Fifty-Ninth Street he went home. Half an hour later a uniformed messenger boy appeared at the house and came away a minute or so afterward with a letter in his hand. He brought it to this hotel. My operative used a nearby telephone a few minutes later and inquired of the desk-clerk if a messenger had lately left a letter for Mr. Van Cleve and if Mr. Van Cleve had yet received it. The message from Clancy was for him of course."

"Van Cleve arrived at the hotel a little after eleven. He read the letter from Clancy and went outside at once, called a taxi and was driven to Clancy's house. He stayed there an hour. He is now in his rooms on the tenth floor of this hotel."

"What about the man you call Redhead and his two assistants, who attended the meeting at the bank?"

"One of the operatives trailed Rushton and Van Cleve when they left the bank together. To make it short, that fellow stuck to Rushton and finally left New York on the same train with him. He kept in the background, and I do not know whether Rushton is aware of the man's nearness or not. The presumption is that he *does* know it, and that the two are traveling together without having the appearance of doing so."

Keese shook his head with emphasis.

"I don't agree with you," he said. "But that doesn't matter. Where did the remaining two go?"

"To Redhead's office. I had them dropped there."

"Will your man who followed Rushton stick to him?"

"Surest thing you know, Mr. Keese."

"Is he a good man? Can he do the job without being caught at it, even by so clever a fellow as Rushton?"

"He is the very best ever. If he can't do it, nobody can. He will hang to the trail if Rushton leads him around the world."

"Do you know anything about the other follow? The Redhead operative who is on the same train?"

"I know *all* about him."

"Who and what is he?"

"He used to be a headquarters detective. He was retired a few years ago and went with Redhead. His name is Banta. I'll say this for him: they don't make any better detectives for the regular force than he was. He used to be a side partner with Rushton down there, and that is what makes me think that the two are really together. Rushton may not have known that Redhead was sending Banta away with him when he started, but you can bet your last dollar that he knows it by this time. I'll receive a wire from Lazarus as soon as they get to St. Louis."

"I think that will do for to-night," Keese said. "Make an extra effort to know everything about Clancy and Van Cleve from now on. Never mind Harvard for the present. He is not likely to need watching on my account until Rushton gets back. To-morrow, by noon, I want a complete and thorough report from that new maid of Mrs. Harvard's. You said that she was one of your people, or that you could own her. Was that true?"

"Yes. I'll prove it to-morrow noon," Roland replied, and bowed himself out.

CHAPTER XXVI

WHEN IT WAS BETTY'S MOVE

"It is your move to-day, Betty."

The Kentucky girl lifted her glance quickly to her brother's eyes and regarded him with a steady gaze. But she made no reply in words, and Keese went on in his quietest tone, which had something of the suggestiveness in it of the purring of a tiger-cat, and with a faint smile showing about the corners of his attractive mouth:

"Don't forget about that fifty thousand dollars I have promised you—and don't forget that you have no choice about earning it, either. You've *got* to earn it, Betty; or, if you do not, I promise you that you will wish you had."

"Are you threatening me, Ben?" she asked her brother quietly, and with a brief flash in her eyes, to which he gave no heed even if he noticed it.

"Yes," he replied calmly, as if it were the most natural thing in the world to suggest threats of dire consequences to his own sister. "I am warning you, if you prefer that expression."

She shrugged her shapely shoulders and turned her head to look across the field, all dotted as it was with riders in hunting costumes, with men and women afoot and in the saddle, with gaily colored groups gathered here and there, with prancing or plunging mounts that were all eagerness to be off in the chase. A throng of automobiles, carriages, vehicles of all description, saddled cobs and spectators on foot, was drawn up beyond the barrier awaiting the signal of the M. F. H. The day was perfect and the meet was always an event. Betty and her brother had drawn a little apart from their immediate neighbors—or, to be more explicit, he had signaled her to ride aside with him. Katherine Harvard was surrounded by a group of friends, of whom Tom Clancy was one, close at hand. Hounds were baying, horses were neighing, men were calling greetings or comments across slight spaces to other men. The time for the start was near.

Miss Keese made no reply to that last remark. Her brother waited an instant for her to do so. Then he said:

"Walk your hunter a little way beside me. I want to make a few suggestions to you, and I do not care to be interrupted. Come."

She obeyed him. And in another moment he utterly amazed her by the question he asked, which was not at all what she had expected.

"How much in earnest are you in this affair with Tom Clancy?"

Betty's face flushed to a crimson instantly. Her eyes flashed ominously as she turned toward him and replied with almost child-like petulance:

"That is none of your business, Ben Keese."

"Granted, and without a murmur, my dear sister—unless you force me to make it my business," he replied with a smile that was not pleasant, since being his sister and knowing him as she did, she understood the menace of it.

"How much of that music-talk that you played to him last Monday evening did you mean, Betty?"

"That is none of your business, either."

"Which, for you, is another manner of saying that you meant all of it," he said, and the half derisive smile on his face grew wider. "Oh, I was listening, and watching, too, sister. I heard it all and saw it all. A deaf man and a blind man might have done the same, I think. Well, Clancy has got plenty of coin and he comes of a good family, so I haven't the slightest objection to your—"

"As if it would make any difference if you had!" she interrupted him hotly.

"Oh, it would make a difference; a very great one, my dear sister. I could spoil your little romance in a jiffy, if I wanted to; and I *may* want to. That all depends upon you. Do you understand that?"

She shuddered in spite of herself; not because she believed what he said, but because all of her life she had feared this brother of hers and his subtle and unholy ways with people who offended him. He saw and understood that shudder, and laughed quietly.

"Do you understand that?" he repeated.

"I know what you intend to imply by the words you use," she answered.

"Then that is sufficient. You have a good mount under you, Betty, and there is neither man nor woman here to-day who is your superior in the hunting field. I know that, and you know it, too."

"Well?"

"I am not going to impose a difficult task upon you."

"What is the task that you *would* impose—if I should consent to it?" she demanded, still with some heat; and there was nothing in her manner to indicate that she had any idea of consenting to anything that he might ask.

"You have only to hold up a finger, Betty, and Clancy will nod his head. He will sit up and speak, lie down and roll over, play dead, or eat out of your hand at your slightest command."

Keese bent a trifle nearer to her and added: "I want you to lead him on a chase that he won't soon forget to-day; and I don't care *where* it takes you, if only it is far enough away from Katherine. Do you understand that, also?"

Betty made no reply. Her brother pulled in his horse and turned about so that he faced in the direction from which they had come. She was obliged, perforce, to do the same. Keese nodded his head toward the group they had just left and they could see that Katherine and Clancy had drawn a little apart from the others and appeared to be engaged in earnest conversation together. Benton Keese indulged in one of his inscrutable smiles.

"I know exactly what Kitten is saying to Clancy," he told his sister. "I know it as well as if I could hear the words. She is telling him that she wants him to keep as close to her as possible during the hunt; she is asking him to ride beside her, from start to finish, if he can—even if he is compelled to desert you to do so; and she is agreeing to square him with you later. *And* he is promising. How is that for reading lip movement when I am so far away that I cannot even see their lips?" he asked, and chuckled.

Betty was still silent.

"What is the matter? Have you lost your tongue?" he demanded sharply.

"No; nor my ears, either."

"That is fortunate, at least. Are you going to do as I asked?"

"No."

"What's that?"

"You heard me, I think."

"Do I understand, Elizabeth, that you refuse to do what I have asked?"

She nodded without speaking.

"Is this mutiny, my dear? Are you defying me?" he asked with his slow smile.

"Ben Keese, I am not going to do one single thing that will give you an opportunity to make love to Kittie. Not one. I am not going to do a thing that will give you a chance to be alone with her for one minute, if I can help it—and I think I can. You can take your old fifty thousand dollars and go hang with it, for all I care. I would not *touch* it, even if I were starving and did not have a home to go to. So, *there!*"

She brought her hunting crop down sharply upon the flank of her horse simultaneously with that last exclamation and shot away from his side before he could reply to her; and he only shrugged his shoulders and smiled while he jogged slowly after her.

The eyes of many women sought and followed Benton Keese that day. He was undeniably handsome, eminently graceful, and he was at his best in the saddle—a circumstance of which he was quite conscious, although he was wise enough not to show it. There were a few women whom he did not affect in much the same way that Lady Kate felt, and resented, propinquity with him. They were inclined to seek his eyes and to flush and withdraw their own instantly. He seemed to possess the occult power to strip them of their moral armor with a glance; to compel within them, unknowingly but inevitably, a quickening of the heart-beats and to bring to the surface the unwelcome blush of elemental consciousness. Always they lowered their eyes or turned them away from his bold gaze with a sense of startled modesty and an uncomfortably rapid pulse—and just as certainly would they seek his glances again, stealthily, covertly, and often without the power to resist the mysterious attraction he exerted upon them.

With the hunt itself and with the gay throng of people who were assembled there at the great event of the year with the Forestbrook Club, we have nothing to do; only with the events of which shaped themselves because of that occasion.

Betty Keese had spent much time in thought after the occurrences of the preceding Monday, when her brother had taken her to ride in his new car solely for the purpose (as she was well aware) of compelling her to his will in the matter of aiding his mad scheme for the undoing of Katherine Harvard. His proposal to give her a large sum of money had shocked her not because he had offered to pay it to her for a service she was to perform for him and which he demanded in return for it—for Betty knew her brother, and that was like him. But she was shocked because he possessed that much to give, knowing that it could represent but a small part of what he had in store, else he would not have offered it. And she had not doubted his earnestness.

What she did doubt—and she had no reason for doubting other than her intimate understanding of this man who was her own brother—was that he could have become possessed of so much money honestly. Betty understood Benton's principles thoroughly; or, rather, his lack of them. She knew him to be entirely unmoral, and that he was thoroughly an egotist, a self-worshiper, a person without a conscience as she understood the meaning of the word.

Not for one moment during her conversation with him that Monday afternoon had she wavered in her loyalty to Katherine, although she had permitted him to think that she appeared to do so reluctantly. Nor did she believe that his passion for her friend Kittie was what she would have called the real thing. Katherine Harvard was merely something that he wanted and that had been withheld. That was all, according to Betty's understanding. But what she did know, and what she did fear with all her heart and soul, and what she was determined to prevent at all hazards, was that he would get Katherine by fair means or by foul ones, if the slightest opportunity offered or could be forced. She also knew that Benton Keese would not stop at the commission of any brutality that might seem to him necessary or vital to his selfish interests and designs.

Then, during the evening that followed, had happened the episode of the photograph and her impulsive exclamation at the first sight of it. Betty believed in "first impressions"—first impulses. Likewise there had remained with her always certain memories of her childhood, when she was a little girl and her brother was a big boy, which the flashing of that picture upon her consciousness had very prominently brought to mind. In a word, Betty was just as shrewd and subtle in her own sweet and pure way as her Brother Benton, and there had remained not the least doubt in her secret thoughts (although she had spoken differently at the time) that the picture really was a photograph of Benton, even though he preferred to deny it.

And she had sensed, too, the undercurrent of interest that had affected the others who were present at the time, although she had not understood it at all. She had asked herself mentally many times since last Monday evening why her brother had denied the picture and his own connection with it, and who and what Benton could have been and done in the character of Holbrook Chilton; and always with the thought of it the memory of his fifty thousand dollars offer to her returned. Angered and incensed as she was at the moment she turned from Benton and rode galloping away from him, stirred to the depths also by her unswerving loyalty to Katherine, and roused to a pitch of entire defiance of her brother's schemes against her friend by her intuitive horror of them, the scene in the library of Harvard's home last Monday night nevertheless came back to her forcefully before her mount had covered half the distance that separated her from her friends.

As in a flash, Betty saw, or believed that she did so, and clearly, Benton's apparent reason for denying the photograph. Instantly she understood that in some manner it was associated with his possession of so much money—and she read, in the memory of that scene, the fact that there had been during it an undercurrent of excited interest in the absent character of Chilton which every person in the room, save herself, had felt.

Suddenly, then, while she was still at some distance from Tom and Kittie, who were drawn apart and evidently awaiting her, she wheeled her horse sharply around and faced her brother again. And he, mistaking her attitude for one of surrender, pulled in his mount and rode leisurely up to her; nor did he make any effort to conceal the half smile of triumph that glowed in his eyes as he approached. Betty sat very still in the saddle, waiting; and when he was quite close and had come to a stop she said coldly:

"Benton, I don't know why you denied that you were the Holbrook Chilton of that photograph last Monday night. But you did deny it, and you made everybody but me believe in your denial. You even thought that you made me believe it, too—but you didn't. And I could read something between the lines of that scene that was not at all to Mr. Holbrook Chilton's credit; something that is known to Mr. Van Cleve, to Mr. Harvard, to Tom Clancy, and even to Katherine; something that only I, of all who were present, did *not* know. But I propose to find out exactly what it is all about, Ben Keese, and if you persist in persecuting Kittie I won't spare you when I do find out, even though you *are* my brother."

"You have dared to threaten me, so now I give you back threat for threat."

She touched her horse with the crop, but her brother bent forward and grasped her bridle-rein. For a moment after that he glared into her defiant eyes menacingly, while a slow and cruel smile bared his white and even teeth. Then, with careful emphasis, he said, and in a tone that made her shudder in spite of herself:

"You will regret this attitude bitterly, Elizabeth; and, believe me, you have only succeeded in hastening the destruction of your friend—and your own undoing, too."

Then he released her bridle-rein and rode swiftly past her toward the waiting group of hunters.

CHAPTER XXVII

WITH THE PACK IN FULL CRY

Benton Keese was quite correct when he quoted to Betty what he believed to be the subject-matter that was passing between Katherine and Clancy, for she had been saying almost those very words to Tom. But for their talk together on the subject the preceding Monday, Katherine would not have ventured upon it; but, encouraged by that fact and by certain intangible misgivings by which she was beset concerning the possible incidents of the coming chase, and with the positive knowledge that Benton Keese would cling to her side throughout it, she did ask Tom to keep as near to them as possible during the run. And Clancy promised, never doubting that he would be able to keep his word.

Nevertheless, he was unaware of the possibilities of Benton Keese's subtle craft; for Keese had foreseen the likelihood of such a request from Katherine and its undoubted interference with his own plans. And those plans, be it said, he had determined to hasten to a consummation in a marked degree, and he had been urged to that decision by reason of the several incidents that had occurred during that memorable Monday afternoon and evening.

During the episode of the photograph, in Harvard's library Keese had distinctly the advantage over the others because of his thorough knowledge of the character of Anderson Van Cleve—and he read plainly enough that certain undoubted suspicions remained in the mind of the miner-contractor afterward. Nor had Keese any fallacies in his own mind concerning the attitude of Clancy. He knew that Tom suspected him, and had done so from the beginning. Also, he had reasoned it out that Clancy had passed his suspicions on to Rushton. More than all, he could read in the eyes and manner of Katherine that she, too, harbored grave doubts and surmises which were none the less threatening because they happened to be, as yet, indefinite.

And then had come the developments of the night that had followed, brought about by the report of Dudley Roland; the conference at the bank, the interview that followed between Rushton and Van Cleve, Clancy's summons to Van Cleve to go to him, Rushton's departure for Mexico—for he understood perfectly what the ticket to St. Louis meant. He thought, too, that he knew what Rushton had gone after, and he cursed his own lack of sufficient forethought (the only lapse of the kind that he had been guilty of) that had rendered the success of Rushton's journey possible.

So from Monday night until Thursday he had kept himself carefully aloof from all of them and had concerned himself with the completion of arrangements which he believed would make his final move possible and successful in every way. Just what those arrangements were will presently develop; but in perfecting them it is certain that he saw much of Mr. Dudley Roland, that he paid over to that person some considerable amounts of money and made promises of still greater amounts to be paid upon the happening of stipulated incidents, that he made several trips to one section of the suburbs of the greater city and that he passed the most part of, at least, one afternoon and night in the café of a certain hotel where one heard only the Spanish language spoken—and where there had been some sums of money passed from him to these persons whose services he had thought it wise to engage.

The passion of Benton Keese for Katherine was a madness and it had been aggravated a thousand-fold by the fact that another man had won her and possessed her. The money he had stolen was only a means to accomplish the fruition of his mad hopes. All that it could buy, all that it might procure for him, all that it was capable of mastering for his own benefit counted as nothing at all without the accomplishment of the one initial passion of his life—Katherine. And he had in his immediate possession, ready for instant use, a great sum in cash. He had not a doubt that he would be able to meet every emergency and to overcome any and every obstacle that might stand in his way. And there would not be one qualm of conscience to hold him back when the moment came to throw his winning cards face upward on the table in the game he was playing. After that—?

Keese only shrugged his shoulders when he thought of the "afterward." He would meet and reply to that question when it was presented. At least he would have conquered Kittie Maxwilton by then—and he believed that he knew how he could make terms with his enemies when the time should come to do so. Like all schemers, he failed to give due credit to the resources of his enemies, although he did realize that the first great coup of his plans must be accomplished before the return to New York of Rushton.

Betty was not a moment behind him when he pulled rein beside Katherine's thoroughbred mount and her eyes were still flashing with spirit when she drew up at the other side. But if there was something in her thought to which she had intended to give expression, it was interrupted by Clancy's cheery announcement:

"We are going to have a dandy run for our money, Miss Betty. This is the Forestbrook's great day of all the year, you know. And, say, isn't the day itself a perfect corker?"

Then he bent forward in his saddle and said in a lower tone which the others could not hear: "All the same, Betty dear, I'd chuck the whole business in a minute to steal away somewhere with you, alone."

Betty flushed and paled a little. Then, with quiet directness, she replied:

"If you really wish to please me to-day, Mr. Clancy—"

"I won't try to please you at all if you address me in that manner," he interrupted, frowning.

"Tom, then; because I *do* want you to do one thing to please me."

"What is it? Quick. We have only a moment, now."

"Stay as close to Kittie as you possibly can," she announced in a half whisper.

"Play interference against his nibs, your brother, eh? Is that it, Betty?"

She nodded. "Don't leave them alone together if you can help it," she said earnestly. "I will promise not to be very far away any of the time. I can ride."

"You don't need to tell me that," he replied, with enthusiasm.

In the meantime and while they were talking Keese had remarked to Katherine with his face turned from her so that he was apparently studying the general topography that surrounded them:

"You are thoroughly familiar with the ground we will ride over, I suppose?"

"I know it fairly well," she replied.

"So do I." He turned his head and smiled at her. "I have been studying it—that is, maps of it. For instance, yonder is the Rudolph place, isn't it? And beyond that, to the right, the great estate of Algernon Sessions? And over there, beyond that hill, there is a deep ravine, isn't there? with a bad climb after one crosses it—if the chase should lead us there?"

"You are well informed," Katherine said, in surprise.

"Oh, yes; from maps—and some personal information. I spent nearly all of last Tuesday in riding over this country with a guide and asking questions. Over beyond that ravine, several miles from here, I found a very interesting place, too. I wonder if you happen to know about it, Kittie?"

"Do you mean the Ghost house?" she asked with some indication of interest, raising her eyes to his for the first time and encountering them with level gaze.

"Yes. It is a queer story that I was told about it—but quite in keeping, I should suppose, with the careers of people who were burdened by such a name. Fancy being addressed as 'Mr. Ghost!' or as 'Mrs. Ghost.' Or the emergency of having to entertain the 'Ghosts.' No wonder that the people down here froze them out. Eh?"

"And no wonder," she replied, "that being frozen out, that having been literally driven out, they should refuse to sell the little place at any price, preferring to have it go to rack and ruin and to become overgrown with a tangle of young trees and bushes that have become impenetrable, so I am told."

Katherine spoke eagerly, not because she felt any interest in the Ghost house or in the people who owned it and refused to live in it or to sell it and who seemed to delight in permitting it to become an eyesore to the surrounding neighborhood, but because the subject was an eminently safe one between Benton Keese and herself.

It had been given out that the fox was a wise and crafty old Reynard that would give the hunters "what was coming to them," if appearances could be counted upon. He proved it in a very short time after his release; and almost as soon as the start was made shouts and calls of congratulations sounded from one end of the field to the other. The riders soon spread out, some with what they believed to be sagacious forethought, to make shortcuts to intercept the chase at another point, others to loiter far behind because they preferred to do so, and still others to cling tenaciously to the pack with all of the enthusiasm of the seasoned fox-hunter. Riding to hounds amounts almost to a profession with some people, to a mere pastime for others, to a relaxation with another class—and to an enthusiastic sport that gives intensest joy to a very small proportion of those who attend the meets.

Betty Keese belonged to the last of these classifications; so did Tom Clancy. Katherine, too, felt the thrill of it scarcely less than did her two friends, for it had been her favorite sport at home, in Kentucky.

For a time the four rode in comparative silence, although there were occasional calls and replies between Tom and Betty, for one was quite as exuberant of spirit as the other and neither was ever a very long time silent. They kept in the van, too, with very few riders ahead of them and with many others stringing along behind as the dogs led the chase toward a lower section of the deep ravine where there was an old wood road, as Katherine remembered, which led directly to the bottom of it. But Reynard apparently had preferred the more difficult trail along the brow of the hill to the possibility of becoming bottled in the gully, for the dogs had gone that way and the few hunters who still led the chase followed.

Tom and Betty rode side by side, fifty or sixty yards ahead of Katherine and Keese, and had also made the turn and were riding up the hillside along the brow of the cliff when there came back to the practiced ears of Benton Keese a confusion of shouts and directions mingled with a new and more eager tuning of the hounds which he readily understood. He and Katherine were directly at the turn, at the moment, and were side by side. Toward their right the way led up the hill in the direction their leaders had taken; toward the left, a few rods distant, was the opening crest of the wood road which led to the floor of the ravine.

"Wait, Kittie!" Keese called out—and in the excitement of the chase, in the thrill of the tuning of the hounds and the loud and encouraging cries of the hunters, she forgot her determination not to be left for a moment alone with him, and she obeyed; and so they came to a stop with the shoulders of their horses almost touching, and waited, and listened.

Then one of the dogs gave tongue again, seemingly from the bottom of the ravine, but much farther up its tortuous course; and Benton Keese shouted aloud with an enthusiasm that was apparently due only to the excitement of the hunt.

"Come! This way! We will gain the lead of them all!" he added, at the same time forcing his hunter forward in such a way that Katherine's horse was compelled to turn—and in another moment the two riders were galloping down the wood road toward the bottom of the ravine, neck and neck and closely side by side. Chance—or was it partly design?—had supplied Benton Keese with the opportunity he craved.

CHAPTER XXVIII

GHOST HOUSE

They rode into the ravine at the shallowing point where it began to widen into the comparatively level reaches beyond. As they made the turn at the bottom of the wood road the dogs, which had been silent for an interval, gave tongue once more, and their voices appeared to follow straight up the bed of the gully.

Katherine thought as little of altering her course then as did her companion, although their reasons for clinging to it were widely different; only Katherine could not know that fact. All of her enthusiasm was bent upon the chase itself; Keese cared for the hunt, and listened for the tuning of the hounds only because both were playing directly into his hands.

And Keese wisely kept himself in the background just then, preferring to efface himself by giving her the lead, knowing that she would think less of his nearness while he was behind her and so out of sight. He did not doubt that she had temporarily forgotten her fears of him. He knew, too, that somewhat less than a mile farther along there was a rough untraveled path, which led to the top of the hill at the opposite side of the ravine; he knew, because he had ridden over it that preceding Tuesday when he had gone there to make a study of the neighborhood—and to perfect the final arrangements of his plans.

He did not care now whether the fox would finally lead them all the way across the ravine or not, for in either event he had succeeded in drawing Katherine away from the others. But that it would do so he did not doubt. Almost any wise old Reynard would do that very thing, experience told him—and besides his guide of Tuesday had assured him that if the fox ever hit that ravine near the bottom "he

164

would make up it, and head for the opposite side somewhere near the three beeches." So the sequel proved, and very soon.

Keese called out to Katherine to stop a moment when the voices of the dogs told their story. With the horses at a standstill they could hear the hounds as they swarmed down the steep hillside on one hand and up it again on the other; they could hear the shouts of the riders, the crashing sounds of the young trees and bushes that were disturbed by the passing steeds, and the ringing instructions of the M. F. H. to those who followed after him. But they could see nothing of it. A bend in the ravine shut out the view, and they waited in silence until the voices of the dogs should give them more definite information.

And in the meantime Keese worked his horse around to the offside of Katherine's mount so that when the moment did arrive for which he was prepared he would need only to force his own hunter ahead in order to turn hers in the direction he wanted it to go perforce.

"This way!" he shouted when the pack was in full cry again. "Straight ahead, Kittie. There is a path beside that big rock. It leads to the top on the other side—and that is where we have got to go."

Forcing his own horse sharply forward, he shouldered her mount into the rugged path while he talked, and before she could have prevented it had she chosen to do so; but she did not, nor had a thought of it. It was steep, insecure of footing, clogged by roots and stones, and otherwise offered a precarious method of arriving at the top of the ravine on that side; but there was no such thing as turning back once they had begun the ascent. They made it finally, but their horses were winded and spent, and stood silently and with drooping heads once they were at the top.

It was then that Katherine bent her head to listen; and soon again she raised it and looked at Keese with a startled expression in her eyes.

"I can hear nothing," she said. "I do not hear a sound. Do you?"

He pretended to listen—and shook his head negatively.

"Come, please," Katherine exclaimed. "We must be going."

"Wait," Keese replied, resting one hand lightly upon her bridle-rein. "The horses are winded by that climb. We must rest them a bit, Kittie."

He swung from the saddle as he ceased speaking, and added:

"Get down for a moment, won't you? It will rest you to walk a little—and the horse as well."

But she shook her head with decision.

"No," she said, and remembered suddenly and not without a twinge of fear that the very thing that she had sought to avoid that day had happened. She was indeed alone, and very much alone, with Benton Keese.

"I will stay where I am, thank you. And if the horses are not too tired I prefer to go on. We will lose all directions of the chase if we do not."

He nodded and started forward, leading his own horse, and retaining his hold upon the bridle-rein of hers. Once she tried to shake it free from his grasp, but apparently he did not notice the act. At least he paid no heed to it. She did not repeat the attempt, thinking it wisdom not to do so. There was no sign of a path where they were, and Katherine had no idea of the direction he was leading her save that it was straight away from the bank of the ravine; and it was her belief that they ought to cling to it, or at least keep it in view.

Presently, after she had thought the matter out, she ventured the suggestion—for Katherine had no suspicion of the fact that she was even at that moment a victim of the man's subtle craftiness. But he shook his head.

"Just above here the ravine forks or branches. There is another and deeper one which leads into this one at right angles a little way above us. I saw it last Tuesday. We will have to go around it. Fortunately, it is only a short distance," he told her.

Katherine made no reply nor offered further remonstrance. And he was silent, too. If Keese had dared to look around at her then, she would have understood everything. But he did not do so, for he knew that he could not disguise the glow of triumph that was in his eyes, and which would leap in a consuming flame if he should look upon her.

They moved forward slowly, and, imperceptibly to Katherine, Keese constantly bore a trifle to the left of a straight course; for he had a definite route which he meant to follow. It was one which the hunted fox had, fortunately for his plans, materially shortened by taking the dogs into the deep ravine and out of it again, as it had done. For a short while Keese walked forward between the horses' heads, leading them; but the woods became thicker as they had advanced, and they were obliged to zigzag and tangent and half-circle in many places in order to get through at all.

At last Katherine, who was becoming more and more conscious of their utter loneliness—not a sound of the dogs or the hunters had

166

reached her ears since they climbed to the top of the bluff over the ravine—ventured to offer an objection. She pulled her horse in sharply.

"It seems to me we are getting deeper and deeper into the woods, Benton," she demurred. "I do not hear a sound of the chase. The fox must have turned into the ravine again."

"I don't think so," he said, halting, but studiously keeping his eyes averted from hers.

"It must be so," she insisted.

"Well, even then we must keep on as we are going," he answered. "You know yourself that we could not enter the ravine again by that path. Neither your horse nor mine could do it."

She sighed audibly, for she did realize the truth of his statement. He continued before she could speak:

"I was not exactly at this spot last Tuesday when I looked over the country, but I do know the locality. I know that just a little way beyond us there is a narrow road that traverses the woods and comes out upon the highway eventually. The way I am taking you now will lead us to it."

"Oh, I am so sorry that we have lost ourselves!" she exclaimed with a touch of tragedy in her tone.

"Nonsense!" he retorted. "We have not lost ourselves. We will be out of it in a jiffy. If the fox *did* double back into the ravine he'll come out again on this side. We will have the advantage over all the others in that case. If you don't mind following behind me I will try to make that roadway even more directly."

Katherine nodded; but her companion's eyes were still averted, so she replied in a low tone:

"Very well, Benton; only please get out of these woods as quickly as possible."

Then, mentally, she misjudged the man utterly—and smiled to herself with reassurance because she did so. She misjudged him by thinking that he was really doing very nicely by not looking at her as he might have done, to her discomfort—and by his demeanor of aloofness notwithstanding the fact that they were so utterly alone in the depths of the wood. Her heart would have beat much more rapidly than it did had she realized that his aloofness was all a studied pose on his part, done in order that he might not startle his prize— for already he regarded her so—too soon. More distance and more time was consumed. It seemed often as if Katherine would be compelled to dismount or be swept from the saddle by the limbs of trees under which they passed or by the outreaching younger growth of the woods which appeared to draw closer and closer around her.

And then suddenly when she least expected it—when she was on the point of calling out to her companion with more objections—they came out upon the narrow roadway that he had assured her was near at hand. It was narrow. It was closed in by a thick growth of trees and bushes on either side. Above their heads the branches interlaced into a canopy that shut out the sunlight entirely. Beneath them on the ground were twigs and chips and growing weeds and grasses, but no sign of wheel tracks. In advance of them, no matter which way they might turn, the roadway disappeared into swinging curves and gave the suggestion that they were entirely shut in.

An exclamation of dismay that Katherine would have uttered was arrested before it found voice, for Benton Keese, still playing his part—and determined to do so as long as it would avail him—turned and sprang into his saddle.

"I know now exactly where we are, Kittie," he assured her. And he did know, only too well. "Come on. We will be out of this in a very few moments. That way"; he pointed ahead of them toward the direction he wished to follow. "You take the lead, and ride as hard as you like. Look out for the limbs and branches."

She started forward gladly, reassured. The horses were rested, and responded quickly to the wishes of their riders. Overhanging branches made it impossible for them to travel side by side, but Keese followed closely, and even urged Katherine to greater speed as they advanced—for he knew exactly where they were and precisely what the next few moments would develop.

Katherine had often heard about the Ghost house; she had even seen pictures of it; but she had never visited it, and so she could not guess that they were rapidly riding toward it by the only road that could take them there, and that the route to the main highway was directly behind them; that they were riding away from it instead of toward it. Then, without warning, they came out upon a comparatively open space. A high wall of moss-grown and discolored bricks confronted them, pierced by a gateway that stood invitingly open—and the speed at which they had been traveling carried her past it before she could pull in.

Katherine realized the presence of two men, one at either side, as they rode swiftly between the stone gate-posts. She saw directly in front of her a square stone house with wings at either side that was almost completely hidden by a riot of climbing vines and a rank growth of young trees in the foreground. She heard the clang of iron against iron as the gate was banged shut behind her. She recognized from its pictures the Ghost house before her. She saw Benton Keese leap from the saddle to the ground and throw his bridle into the grasp of a man who sprang toward him. She knew then that she had ridden into a trap.

Benton Keese moved quickly to her side and seized the bit of her horse's bridle; and for the first time in more than an hour he looked into her eyes. He was smiling, too—a smile that was triumphant and cruel and evil.

"Welcome to Ghost house, Kitten," he said.

CHAPTER XXIX

THE TRIUMPH OF BENTON KEESE

There is a time when terror amounts to a passion. Intense anger *is* one. Lady Kate experienced both in that instant of revelation. As a curtain is swept aside to expose a wide range of view she saw mentally and understood instinctively every item of the circumstance into which she had permitted herself to blunder. Rage possessed her; terror held her chained. Yet, furious-eyed and in terror, too, she lifted her riding-crop on high and would have struck Benton Keese with it if he had not reached out and torn it from her grasp and flung it aside among the weeds and grass.

Then he came closer to her and held out his hand.

"Dismount!" he commanded her.

Katherine did not offer to move.

Keese waited a moment, smilingly. Then:

"I hope you won't force me to lift you from the saddle, Kitten," he said, with quiet meaning. (Oh, how she hated his use of her childhood's name!)

She glanced around her on this side and on that, dazed. Terror gripped her, but she strove against it with all the fortitude she could summon. Nowhere could she discover a means of escape from the terrible situation. Nowhere was there a sign of life about her, save for one man of foreign aspect who remained near them as if waiting to take away her horse as the other man had done with Benton's; and his back was turned. If he had ears and could hear and eyes and could see, or muscles and could move, he gave no outward evidences of those gifts.

The wall of brick topped with broken bottles and ragged glass that surrounded the house and its outbuildings enclosed two or three

170

acres of ground that was overgrown with tangled weeds which were in turn choked by bushes and sprouting trees.

Katherine already knew enough about the house and its strange story to realize how utterly isolated it was; how rarely it was visited, even by the curious. For the winding roadway that led to it through the woods had long been impassable for automobiles and carriages. Riding parties visited it at long intervals—when the guest of a neighborhood insisted upon seeing the place; but those occasions were rare indeed.

Katherine's talk with Tom Clancy when they rode home together in her car recurred to her oddly then. She knew that if she had possessed a weapon she would have shot Benton Keese dead at that moment. But she was helpless—weaponless. Even her stout crop had been snatched away from her. And all the while—it was less than a minute of time although it seemed an aeon to her—the man who had so foully tricked her stood beside her horse with his firm grasp upon the bit, waiting, smiling, confident, and as relentless in his designs against her as he would be merciless in fulfilling them.

"Get down, my dear," he said softly; and she reached out and struck at him with her open hand; a blow which he easily avoided and concerning which he made no comment.

Katherine called aloud then to the man who waited with his back turned toward them—and who seemed not to hear her when she did call; and Keese announced, imperturbably:

"He is my creature, Kitten, and he does not understand a word of English. I was careful about that. The two men you have seen were Mexican mountaineers—bandits, in other words—before they crossed the Rio Grande into this country to save their worthless and forfeited lives."

"One of them has a wife, and she is here, too. None of them speak English. Don't you think I have planned well?"

He stepped nearer to her as he ceased speaking and held out his hands; but she shrank from him, cowering in the saddle and clinging to it desperately. Then she thought to plead with him.

"Please let me go away, Benton," she asked him piteously. "In memory of your sweet and good mother whom I loved, let me go. For Betty's sake, in the name of your own dear sister, order that gate to be opened and let me ride away, unharmed. I promise—I promise you on my honor as a Kentucky girl that I will never reveal what has happened to-day if you will only do that. For my own sake, Benton. Please let me go away. Won't you, Benton?"

He made no answer by word or sign. His eyes only gloated upon her, lurid with the sure triumph and the sense of possession that glistened within their depths.

She went on again, although she knew that her plea was hopeless; yet she added one other to it.

"We were children together, Benton; playmates. You professed to love me, even then. We grew older, and—Oh, for God's sake, Benton, open the gate and let me go away!"

"No, Kitten." He spoke with exceeding quiet, but with a finality that was adamant. "You are here to stay—for the present. Soon we will go away—together—to the other side of the world, if you will; but together always henceforth. It is written. There can be no other way."

She was white by now—white to the lips; and rigid where she sat in the saddle. A chill gripped at her heart. He spoke again, smoothly, evenly, remorselessly, relentlessly.

"You are mine, Kitten. You always were mine; but you succeeded in evading me. But I have overtaken you at last. You shall not, you cannot evade me now."

She shuddered.

"When you fled from me, I sought you everywhere, high and low; far and near. But my funds gave out. I had no money, and I needed it badly. I knew that I must get some, somewhere; it did not matter how. Mexico has long attracted me. I went there. I believed that I could hold you, as I had always done, in fear and trembling, even at a distance; and I knew that you did not love any other man. I went there, to Mexico. Fate directed my steps to Anderson Van Cleve. In him and his possessions I saw and recognized my opportunity. I meant to have all of his property, instead of only a small part of it. But there is sufficient. I have got enough. Oh, yes; I was the Holbrook Chilton of the photograph."

"Then—I returned. Always I had had the Lexington papers sent to me, but the one that contained the announcement of your marriage, the account of your visit to Europe and of your return was lost. The information did not get to me until very shortly before I came away from Mexico. But I had studied the man I intended to rob. I knew of the moneys he had forwarded to New York and the name of the bank where they were deposited; and I discovered that the president of the bank was the man you had married; that the former president of it, Van Cleve's friend, was traveling in Egypt."

"I swore then that I would take you away from Bingham Harvard. Well, I have done it. I *have* taken you from him. You shall never return to him. These arms"—he spread them widely—"shall be, henceforth, your resting place. You are mine, and nothing in heaven, or on earth, or in hell, can change that fact. Presently, after a time, when there is a divorce if you will have it so and if you can bring Harvard to terms, we will be married. You will be my—"

Slowly she turned her face toward him and at the sight of it he stopped. Marble could not have been whiter or more set and rigid. Horror unspeakable was in her eyes. She swayed in the saddle, and he reached out and seized her and pulled her from it before she could find strength to resist him. She tottered in his grasp, and he passed an arm around her. Then he spoke a sharp command to the waiting Mexican, and led Katherine, unresisting, toward the house.

The sense of triumph within Benton Keese at that moment was great indeed. He believed that Katherine understood the utter futility of resistance, and had surrendered. Indeed it seemed so. She walked beside him, totteringly, dumbly, half leaning upon him and unmindful of his physical support or of his encircling arm. He did not address her again; she did not attempt to speak to him. So they passed partly around the house and entered it across a porch where there was an open door and came upon a room that had been made comfortably habitable, and where a dark-visaged woman with handsome, flashing, questioning eyes, waited.

Keese led Katherine to a low chair, placed her softly in the depths of it, and then did a dastardly act, which, however, Katherine did not seem to notice. He bent over and touched his lips, that were burning hot, to hers, that were like icicles. Then, with an order, spoken in Spanish and an imperative gesture toward the Mexican woman who waited, he passed outside again, and closed the door.

CHAPTER XXX

APPROACHING A CRISIS

The daring and assurance of Benton Keese were superb. Outside of the house, just around one corner of it, he paused to wait; and soon the Mexican woman came out to him, bringing in her hands Katherine's hat and gauntlets. These he seized upon, and with a few hurried but emphatic directions to the woman turned away, whistling a signal of some sort as he went.

At the spot where he had taken Katherine from the saddle he searched for a moment and recovered her riding crop from where he had cast it among the woods. One of the Mexicans reappeared, leading both of the horses and Keese sprang in to the saddle of his own mount. He paused only long enough to utter some further admonitory directions, then the gate was opened for him and he rode away. He crossed the ravine by the same rugged pathway he had followed with Katherine, in spite of the fact that he had assured her that they could not return that way. But he forced the horses to it, caring little whether they might fall and break a leg or a neck, but arriving at the bottom without accident.

At the top of the wood road on the opposite side where with Lady Kate beside him he had paused to listen to the hounds and where he had induced her to follow him into the ravine, he got down from his own horse, made the bridle rein fast to a convenient limb and then went onward up the brow of the hill over the gully, leading the horse that Katherine had ridden. It was not difficult for him to find the place where the fox had turned into the ravine, where the dogs had followed along a ledge of shelving slate and where the hunters had not dared to go because of the treacherous character of the descent. But he went on a little farther and found the place where the

174

riders had taken to the steep hillside, plainly disclosed by the loosened earth and stones and broken twigs.

He nodded with satisfaction and returned to the rocky ledge across which the hunted fox and the pursuing hounds had passed, halting with Katherine's horse just above it. For a moment he stood there looking downward across the ledge, while a slow smile that was not pleasant to see gathered upon his mobile lips. Then he took two steps backward and raised his heavy crop. He struck with it, using all the strength of his arm, and the blow fell smartingly and stinging and without warning upon the horse's flank—and the animal, headed directly for the gulf in front of him and so near to it that his fore feet were close to the edge of the bank, plunged ahead in terror when the cruel blow fell upon him.

The horse slipped upon the ledge and fell. It crashed against a group of saplings, crushing them to earth. Nevertheless, they impeded the force of the fall and doubtless spared the outraged creature the broken bones that he might otherwise have suffered. After that the animal rolled over and over down the steep hill, struggling; and Keese stood looking on with that set smile upon his handsome features, apparently without emotion or pity. Stones were dislodged, bushes and underbrush were crushed and bruised and torn from their roots, young saplings were laid flat—and then the horse brought up against the trunk of a tree that was fifty feet below where Keese was standing, and after a dazed moment of uncertainty it struggled feebly to its feet and stood there trembling.

Keese flung Katherine's hat toward the animal, which frightened it anew, and it started down the hillside, limping. Apparently no bones were broken; seemingly it had suffered nothing more serious than bruises and temporary lameness. Keese waited yet another moment until the horse had disappeared beyond a dense growth of evergreens, then he flung the crop that Katherine had carried after it and followed that with her gauntlets, one by one—but he took the precaution to tear one of them almost in half and to grind them both against the ground beneath his heel before he parted with them.

An hour later he rode in at the club house, and the grooms and members of the club who hastened toward him did so because they had been able to see even from a distance as he drew near that he had met with an accident. He reeled in his saddle but permitted himself to be assisted from it to the ground, where he stood upon both feet and smiled a reassurance toward the anxious faces that surrounded him. One side of his face was smeared with grass-stain and dirt from the ground; his riding coat was torn and badly soiled, his collar was torn from its fastenings and his tie was gone entirely. One of his gloves was ripped up the back its entire length and the other one was missing; his cap, crushed and stained, was on his head. Altogether he presented a sorry spectacle.

And his mount was in a plight almost as bad, so far as dirt and soil and stains were concerned. One stirrup was missing and the strap, or what remained of it, showed plainly where it had been torn apart violently. The bridle was also broken in two places, although not so badly that it had not served for his return to the clubhouse. The saddle-girth had also been broken and tied together again in a knot.

"My girth broke just when I got to the edge of that ravine," he explained. "I have forgotten what you call it. Mrs. Harvard was just ahead of me, but I called out to her what the trouble was and told her to go on; that I would overtake her. Mr. Clancy and my sister were somewhere ahead of Mrs. Harvard, but not in sight."

"Well, I tied the girth as best I could and remounted. Then in my eagerness to catch up with the others and in my ignorance of the country over which I had to ride—and also because the cry of the pack told me that the fox had taken to the ravine—I dived into it, in the belief that I could head off my companions. The fox crossed the ravine and ascended the opposite side—or I believed that it did so. I found a path, or a place that had once been one, and attempted it, and I made the top all right. But up there I discovered that I was all wrong and I made the mistake of attempting to return by the way I had gone."

"My horse fell with me. I reckon that the jolt of it knocked me silly—I fell a little that way, yet—and when I woke up I found the horse waiting for me at the bottom of the gully. Then I managed to get here. And that is all."

It was a perfectly logical tale. Nobody thought to doubt it. Keese was assisted into the clubhouse; he was afforded every facility for making himself presentable again; refreshments were given to him and he was the center of a group of men and women when the riders began to come straggling home. Then, among the very last to make their appearance Tom and Betty arrived. They were not slow to hear of the accident to Benton Keese. It had been one among several that day, all of a minor character, none serious, fortunately; but Betty hurried to her brother just the same, and Tom followed as a matter of course.

A glance told Betty that Benton was not badly hurt, and at once, instead of referring to possible injuries that he might have received, she demanded:

"Where is Kittie?"

"Katherine?" he replied, lifting his brows in well simulated astonishment. "Didn't she return with you and the others?"

"No. She did not," Betty asserted abruptly. "I haven't seen her since the start. She was behind us, with you. Where is she?"

Clancy drew nearer, listening, and watching closely. He saw Keese shrug his shoulders and make a gesture of deprecation. He heard the Kentuckian reply coolly:

"She must be outside somewhere, Betty. I haven't seen her since my girth broke. I called to her then to go on, that I would soon follow; and she did so. You and Clancy were just ahead of us, so she must have followed close behind you. By the time I had tied the girth the fox had taken to the ravine—at least I thought so. Anyhow, I turned down that wood road that you must have noticed when you passed it. I wish now that I had not."

Tom Clancy's eyes had been narrowing dangerously with every syllable that Keese uttered.

"Where were you when you got down to tie your saddle girth?" he asked, quietly.

"Oh! Hello, Clancy. I was right there at the top of that wood road into the ravine. You noticed it, didn't you?"

"Yes. Where was Katherine?"

"Five or six rods ahead of me, following after you and Betty. You were out of my sight at the moment; Mrs. Harvard passed out of it a moment later. I had some difficulty in tying the girth."

"And you did not follow after her when you had tied it?"

"No. I have just explained that I followed the wood road into the ravine."

"Do we understand that you have not seen Mrs. Harvard from that moment to this one, Mr. Keese?"

"Most certainly you do, Mr. Clancy. I crossed the ravine and ascended a steep path at the opposite side. When I tried to return by the same way my horse fell with me. It knocked the wind out of me, and my relish for the hunt as well. I returned here as soon as I was able to do so."

Betty had stepped backward a little, and her bright eyes were boring into her brother's consciousness—or she meant them to. For Betty did not believe his story. Neither did Tom Clancy; but he did not consider that moment the proper time to say so. He turned about abruptly.

"I will make some inquiries," he announced shortly and departed.

Betty stepped forward, nearer to her brother, and looked him straight in the eyes. The two were, for the moment, comparatively alone, others who had been near having withdrawn or been called away.

"I don't believe you, Ben," she said fiercely, under her breath; but her eyes were blazing, her cheeks were flushed, and all her Southern spirit was aroused.

Keese merely shrugged his shoulders and smiled up at her from the depths of his chair.

"You are lying!" she reasserted hotly, but still in a low tone; but he did not even flush beneath the taunt. Instead, he shrugged again, and widened his smile until it became one of defiant derision.

"I warned you," he said, almost in a whisper, and still smiling.

"So! You dare to admit—"

"Only the truth of what I have already told you," he interrupted. "Don't get tragic, Betty. You will attract the attention of others if you do that. And there is no need for it. Go outside and look for Kitten, as Clancy has already done. You will find her there, I haven't a doubt."

"You lie, Ben Keese! You know you do. You have done something to Kittie that is keeping her away from us. I know you have. I can read it in your eyes."

He shrugged again and did not answer; and she bent down until her beautiful, flushed face was close to his.

"You did warn me," she said in a tense undertone. "And I warned you, too. And now I want to tell you this much; Bingham Harvard is due to arrive here at any moment, and if there is no news of Kittie before he gets here I shall go to him at once and tell him everything that you have said to me. *Everything*! Do you understand?"

"Perfectly, my dear sister," he replied; and laughed in a low tone. "Go ahead!"

She turned away and passed through a doorway to the veranda just at the moment when a big touring car drew up and stopped before it, and Bingham Harvard, with Anderson Van Cleve, got down from it. Betty went forward impetuously to meet them.

CHAPTER XXXI

AN INTERCEPTED BLOW

As Betty started forward toward Bingham Harvard with the impulse upon her to tell him instantly all that she knew and all that she suspected, her brother came swiftly through one of the French windows and intercepted her. Benton Keese possessed the faculty of moving swiftly without giving the appearance of doing so, and if there were other eyes turned in that direction just then, they could have noticed nothing to attract their attention.

In reality, however, the act of Benton Keese was anything but leisurely and meaningless. He had gone to that window and stood just within it, watching when Betty had left him with that threat on her lips, and of course he had seen also the arrival of the automobile that brought Harvard and Van Cleve. In intercepting his sister Keese stepped directly in front of her. His hand fell upon her arm above the wrist, and his fingers closed upon it with a pressure that made her wince with pain.

"Let go of me!" She spoke out sharply; but unfortunately the attention of all who were near at hand was riveted upon the new arrivals, and nobody heard. Instead of complying, Keese turned Betty half around, and before she understood what he meant to do he had forced her through the open window into the room beyond it. One quick glance around told him that they were entirely alone.

Betty attempted to pull herself away from his detaining grasp, but his fingers only gripped her arm the tighter as he continued to force her onward, across the room, out of it through a doorway opposite, along the wide corridor which happened (as if the devil himself aided the man) to be deserted, and into one of the several small parlors that fringed one side of the hall. There, he closed the door behind them and swung his sister none too gently into a convenient chair.

Betty raised her stormy eyes to his then, and her lips parted to voice the rage that boiled within. But no sound came from them. She shuddered and shrank backward as if she would withdraw more deeply into the chair. Ever since Betty could remember her brother had been addicted to certain moods and tempers which filled her with terror. Ordinarily, she stood in much less awe of him than others did; but, beyond and behind all of his moods there was one quality that could be roused on occasion, which filled her with the same unspeakable dread she might have experienced if, unwarned, she had been suddenly thrust inside the cage of a couchant tiger. That mood was uppermost just then, and she recognized it; and it frightened her into silence.

He stood directly in front of her, looking down into her eyes with a strange expression on his face, which was not a smile, but which bared his white teeth nevertheless, and transformed the handsome qualities of his features into a menacing horror.

"You poor little fool," he said in a low tone and without emphasis. "Do you think that you could stop me now? Or that Harvard could stop me? Or that all the angels and devils in heaven and hell could change what has already happened?"

Betty shuddered and tried to shrink still farther from him. He went on, in the same quiet tone of awful menace:

"Are you Kitten's friend—or are you Bing Harvard's friend? If you are *his* friend, even to her utter undoing, go to him now and tell him all you think you know and everything that you surmise."

Betty heard only indistinctly the words of his later speech, for that other one that had preceded it was still ringing in her consciousness; and, as if he perceived that it did, he repeated the last part of it that had horrified her so.

"Do you think that all the powers of heaven and hell could change and undo the things that have already happened?"

Repetition of the awful suggestiveness of his question galvanized Betty into action. With a cry as if he had pricked her with the point of a knife, or had jabbed a needle into her flesh, Betty started to her feet and stood quivering but resolute before him. Her terror was turned to fury. She was suddenly become the proverbial female of the species at bay, and cornered. She was transformed into the primitive woman, beside herself with rage and shame and horror, and hate of the man who faced her, even though he was her own blood brother. For just an instant she stood so; then she flew at him, her arms extended, her fingers tense, as if she would clutch him by the throat and tear out the tongue that had dared to utter an inference so vile.

Keese easily repulsed her. He seized Betty's wrists and twisted them until she cried out with the pain; and then he flung her roughly into the upholstered chair again, and took a step or two forward so that he stood over her.

"None of that, you little bobcat," he said coldly. Then he bent nearer to her and said fiercely:

"If you want to go to Kitten, you may. You shall go where she is as soon as we can get away from this place. And she needs you, I think; or *will* need you. But if you utter one word of what you think you know, or with what you are pleased to surmise I—"

He purposely left the sentence incomplete. The implied threat of it was even more terrible so. But Betty grasped at the opportunity to go to Katherine, as he had evidently known she would do. Once more she half started from the chair, but he thrust her back into it again.

"Do you remember the little old red schoolhouse a mile or so back on the road, that we passed on the way out here to-day? The one that you and Kitten exclaimed about, and admired? I know you do remember it. There is a road that is not much used a little way beyond it that leads into the woods. Very well. Get away from these people here as soon as you can. Go there. You can find the way on foot. Follow that unused road until you get into the edge of the woods. Then wait there for me. I will take you to Kitten, if you do that. If you do *not*—it will be the worse for *her*; that's all."

Footsteps resounded in the corridor outside the door. A hand grasped the knob of it, and it was flung open. At the same instant Keese seized one of Betty's hands and began to chafe and slap it; and as he did so he said to her in a savage undertone:

"Remember."

Then he turned his head as the door was opened, released Betty's hand, and stood upright, smiling. He believed he had succeeded in creating the impression that Betty had needed his attention and care.

Tom Clancy came swiftly into the room. He halted midway of the distance between Keese and the open door, and his eyes, burning fiercely, bored into the Kentuckian's for an instant, then traveled to Betty, and then returned their gaze to the face of Benton Keese. It was the policy of Keese not to notice Clancy's only too evident excitement, and he spoke before Tom had an opportunity to do so.

"Betty has been trying to faint." he said with a lift of his brows. "I think—perhaps—that your services, Clancy, will be more efficacious than her brother's."

He moved forward toward the open door, but Clancy stepped directly in front of him and barred the way out.

"Wait!" he said.

Keese stopped, lifted his brows again in questioning surprise, shrugged his shoulders and waited.

"Where is Katherine. Where is she?" Clancy demanded hotly. "You know. You lie like hell itself if you dare to say that you don't know, Keese. Tell me where she is, or by—"

"You are going a step too far, Mr. Thomas Clancy," Keese interrupted. "That sort of talk doesn't go with me."

"Doesn't go with you?" Tom took a stride nearer to the man he had grown to hate so cordially, and his Irish temper had got the best of him. "Doesn't go with you?" he repeated, his hands clenched and his muscles tense. "Anything—*everything* would 'go' with the kind of a cad that you are, you thief! You forger! You—"

Things happened swiftly in the following half second. Keese, enraged, struck out with his fist just as another figure shot through the open doorway and darted forward with the quickness of a shaft of light. Benton Keese's wrist was seized and twisted sharply and he was sent staggering backward half way across the room, and at the same instant Clancy was thrust aside in the opposite direction. Bing Harvard stood between them, and the tall, spare figure of Van Cleve loomed at the threshold of the door behind him.

CHAPTER XXXII

THE TOUCH OF THE NIGHT WIND

Instantly Benton Keese was his suave, complacent self again, although his right wrist, where Bing Harvard had seized and twisted it, tingled with the touch of the powerful hand that had grasped it. It had been a passing touch of the Night Wind, for Harvard had come upon the scene just in time to overhear the last four words that Clancy had used, and to realize the necessity for instant interference.

Now, with both of them silent and motionless, he looked first toward Keese—who shrugged and half smiled, and threw out his hands, palm upward, in a gesture of deprecation—and then at Tom, who was still tense and scowling, and who, in his heart, longed to renew the combat that had been so forcefully halted before it had begun.

Betty had started to her feet, and she stood uncertainly in front of her chair, as if she wanted to run away, yet did not dare to move. Her eyes were wide, her lips were parted ever so little, her bosom rose and fell with the rapidity of her breathing, and her eyes that for an instant lingered upon Harvard, turned inevitably toward Tom. Her glance seemed to draw his to her. Their eyes met. The deep scowl left his face, and he tried to smile; but it was only a grimace that he succeeded in summoning to his aid, for he was still somber and angry and disturbed—and he realized, too, that without doubt he had gone a step too far in his tempestuous assault of words upon Betty's brother. All of this that has been described took place in the briefest instant.

But Clancy's eyes having traveled to Betty's, Harvard's followed them; and he reached out the same hand that had just twisted

Benton's wrist so savagely, touched her fingers, and led her toward the door.

"Won't you find Katherine for me, and say that I will be with her presently?" he said gently; and Betty raised her eyes to his wonderingly.

Had nobody told him? That was her silent thought.

"I—I don't know—where she is," Betty replied falteringly. She had not returned from the hunt when—"

"You will find her without difficulty, I think," Bing interrupted.

Van Cleve stepped aside and Betty passed from the room. Harvard gestured, and Van Cleve closed the door after her in response to it.

"Please stand where you are, Mr. Van Cleve, and permit nobody to enter, for the present," Harvard directed in a quiet tone. Then he turned and faced the two men who remained in practically the same positions that they had assumed when the touch of the Night Wind had fallen upon them and forced them apart.

"Now, gentlemen," he said, "what was the meaning of that scene I interrupted? You, Tom, are a member of the club. Mr. Keese is my guest. Your attitude and conduct toward him, under the circumstances, seem inexcusable."

Clancy was silent for just an instant. During it, however, he realized to some extent the very little that he had had to go upon in charging and attacking Benton Keese as he had done. His belief in the duplicity of the man was intensified rather than lessened, and his conviction that the continued absence of Katherine was in some manner due to Benton Keese was as strong as ever; but he was suddenly aware that he was possessed of nothing tangible in support of either premise. But the dark scowl swept into his face again. His eyes brooded and narrowed. He was determined that he would neither withdraw nor retract what he had said—what he knew that Bing Harvard had heard him say. Fortunately there had been no reference to Katherine in those last fiery words that Harvard had overheard as he approached.

Clancy's silence before replying was so short as to be barely noticeable. Then he said, with his characteristic hot-headed impetuosity:

"I don't know what you heard, Bing, and I don't care a damn, either. Whatever you did hear me say to that man over there, I meant! Every word of it! And more!"

"Hush, Tom!"

"I won't hush—not till I have finished."

"I insist—"

"I don't care a hang for your insistence, Bing. Not a hang. You've got me cornered because you and Van Cleve heard what you did hear, and now you've all got to listen to the rest of it."

Harvard essayed to speak again, but it was Keese who interrupted him then.

"Let him speak, Mr. Harvard," he said, with the utmost mildness, while a sneering smile played across his features and a wicked glint came into his red-brown eyes. "Surely, if there is more to say in connection with the utterances he has already made, we ought all to hear what it is. Possibly there is an explanation which may be distorted into the semblance of an apology."

"Apology!" Tom exploded. Then he turned toward Harvard again. "That man is the brother of the girl I love with all the heart and soul there is in me, Bing. I haven't asked Betty to marry me yet, because I haven't dared—under all the circumstances that I know exist. But I love her, and I'm going to ask her, and she is going to say 'Yes' when I do. So you can—"

"Is this to be the story of a romance?" Keese interrupted with easy insolence.

Tom shot one look of contemptuous hatred toward him, then continued as if he had not heard:

"So you can understand what the accusation I will make may mean to me. I charge that man"—he pointed his finger at Keese—"with being Holbrook Chilton, a forger and a thief. He is the man who stole Van Cleve's money, and mine, and yours. He is—"

"Stop—you!"

It was Keese who spoke the two words. His eyes were aflame. His upper lip was drawn backward tightly across his white and gleaming teeth. His handsome face was distorted into the features of a personified fury. His elbows were partly bent, and his long and tapering fingers, tensed into a semblance of claws, twitched. His face was livid. His body was bent forward as if he had half performed the act of leaping. All semblance of self-control had gone from his attitude. He had been transformed into a demon by the words that Tom Clancy had spoken.

And all of this in an instant of time and while he shouted out the two words like bullets at his accuser. He acted, too, with them; acted instantly. His right hand flew toward his hip pocket, and back from it again, gripping the weapon it had sought, and which Kentuckians

185

are proverbially supposed to carry—which, doubtless, he had carried with him constantly in anticipation of the necessity for its sudden need. Keese was quick in the use of it, too, and the sharp crack of it split the air and crashed upon the momentary silence of the room the instant it appeared.

But for all of that he was not as quick as Bing Harvard. That wonderful swiftness which was the Night Wind's chiefest asset in the days when he was forced to defend himself from his enemies saved Tom Clancy's life and spared the brother of the girl Tom loved from the crime of murder. The bullet, intended for Clancy's heart, imbedded itself in the wall somewhere behind him. The weapon itself crashed against the ceiling of the room and fell to the floor. Benton Keese, with his right arm twisted so that it was almost torn from his shoulder, was hurled backward with a force that might have done him serious injury had not the chair that Betty had occupied stood in the way.

Even as it was he dived headforemost into the upholstery at the very instant that Clancy, beside himself with rage that his life had been attempted, leaped forward toward his assailant. But Harvard hurled him backward also. Then he stooped and recovered the weapon that he had torn from the grasp of Keese, and dropped it into his pocket.

Van Cleve rushed forward and seized upon Keese, and assisted him to right himself, for everybody there could hear the noises of running feet approaching the door of that room. Then it was thrown open. Men and women crowded into the room. Frightened questions were hurled at them. But all that could be seen was the fact that Bingham Harvard stood in the middle of the floor with an automatic pistol in his hand which he was examining with smiling curiosity. But he raised his eyes and smiled the more at the interruption, and said:

"It went off by accident. Nobody is hurt."

Then he looked from face to face among the group around him, still smiling.

CHAPTER XXXIII

WHEN A MAN LIES

What might have happened had there been no interruption just at that moment cannot be known. The situation was tense, and in another instant the eyes of the spectators must have turned from Harvard's face toward Clancy, and toward Keese—and it would have been easy enough to have read what was depicted upon the features of both men.

But a club attendant rushed excitedly into the room and he was calling Harvard's name with all the lung power he possessed; and he discovered the central figure of the group, seized him by the arm, and tried to drag him away while he shouted.

"Mrs. Harvard has been hurt! Mrs. Harvard has been hurt; Mrs. Har—"

Bing grasped him and shook him savagely.

"Where is she? Take me to her!" he demanded, and started for the door, the others following excitedly after.

Even Tom forgot his rage at Keese, and darted forward until he could thrust others aside and get close beside his friend. For the moment Clancy thought that Katherine had been found, dead or terribly injured, and that he had been mistaken in supposing that Keese had anything to do with her continued absence.

Benton Keese himself sauntered after the others, and was the last one to go from the room—for he alone of all who were present knew that Katherine's dead or maimed body had *not* been discovered, that she was in fact, unharmed, and that nothing more serious than a limping horse, a crushed riding-hat, a torn and soiled pair of gauntlets, and a broken hunting-crop had been found. Also he realized that he was "up against it,"—to make use of an expression that is more expressive than elegant. True, the episode of the pistol had passed. No harm would grow out of that.

Bingham Harvard's ready wit had relieved the strain, had reassured the alarmed and excited club-members and their guests by offering a very natural explanation in a few words, and already in the excitement that followed upon the announcement of the club servant, the thing was forgotten. But Clancy would not soon forget it; Van Cleve would remember it; Harvard, he knew, would have something to say about it later.

Oddly enough, it was not Harvard, nor was it Clancy, whom Keese most dreaded just then. It was Anderson Van Cleve. For he knew Anderson Van Cleve as no other man in the United States knew the man; knew him for a quiet, determined, implacable, physically fearless character who had faced all kinds of conditions and dangers in the States of Mexico, with never a flinching, and always to the utter rout of the "other follow." He mentally thanked his stars for that timely interruption, after the pistol had been taken from him and he was rendered defenseless. There was no knowing what might have happened if it had not been for that; he shuddered involuntarily when he thought of the amazing strength of Katherine's husband.

"So, those stories that I was told about him were true," was his mental comment. "He does possess that phenomenal strength of muscle. He is the giant who broke bones like pipe-stems, and threw grown men about like straws in a gale of wind."

Keese was several yards behind the hindmost of those who had rushed from the room with Harvard and the servant, and he lingered still farther behind; for he knew that he had a condition to face in the charge that Clancy had made. He had known last Monday night that both Harvard and Van Cleve would be fruitful soil for the planting of the seed of suspicion. Now it was planted, and with vehemence, and by a hand which would compel those two men to sit up and take notice. And the problem that Benton Keese had to solve during the next half-hour or so—and certainly before the time had arrived for his return to the city—was whether he should disappear at once and entirely or not do so.

Then the memory of his sister Betty returned to him. Through her statement—to which credence would unquestionably be given if she would make one—existed his only immediate danger. And she (he remembered that he had half confessed to her) would take Harvard aside and reveal all she knew, he believed. She would do it for the purpose of convincing Harvard that Katherine was not lying dead or dying somewhere along the route of the chase, if for no other reason. And then, after that—what?

Keese halted in the wide doorway of the main entrance. Everybody else had crowded forward toward a general center of things, and they were "milling" like so many cattle. He looked over the excited heads and waving arms, searching for Betty with a gaze that skipped nobody, but close as his search for her was he did not see her. And then he remembered what he had told her about the road beyond the old red schoolhouse; and he wondered if she had gone there, believing that he would keep his promise and follow her as soon as he could extricate himself from the predicament in which she had left him.

Another swift glance around convinced him that Betty was nowhere in sight. He knew that she would have been among the first to seek the center of the present excitement had she been anywhere near. Therefore he could draw only one conclusion. Betty had gone to the place of meeting and was waiting there for him. He hurried down the steps then and became one of the eager throng that was gathered around the horse that Katherine had rode that day.

But already eager searchers were hurrying towards the stables. Already some of the people had sprung into automobiles and started away. Orders were shouted for hurried saddling; horses were hitched to carriages, dogcarts, drays. Fifty or more persons started away on foot toward the course that the hunt had taken at the start.

Then Keese heard his own name called, and he saw the three men he would have cared most to avoid at that moment approaching him—Clancy, Van Cleve, and Harvard. He went forward to meet them, concern of the deepest sort depicted upon his features.

"Will you take us to the spot where you parted with Mrs. Harvard?" Bingham asked him. He spoke calmly, although his voice was deep with the anxiety he was suffering.

"Certainly," he replied as calmly. "I will gladly guide you there—and Mr. Van Cleve, also. But—not your companion—even under the present circumstances."

Tom's lips parted to utter reply, and it would have been a hot one, judging from the expression of his face; but Harvard put out a hand, grasped him by the arm, and stopped him.

"Mr. Clancy will accompany us, Mr. Keese," he said, coldly, "and I will venture to ask you again to show us the way and the place."

"Very well, sir," Keese replied, and bowed.

"The horses will be brought here to us in a moment. I have already ordered them," Harvard said.

"Where is your sister?" Van Cleve asked. "We would like to have her with us, also."

"I haven't an idea. I have not seen her since she left the room where we were together," Keese answered. Then, as if an afterthought, he added:

"She was very much concerned about the nonappearance of Mrs. Harvard, and was faint when I took her into that room. I was chafing her hands and endeavoring to reassure her about her friend when we were interrupted. It is possible that when she came outside again and did not find Mrs. Harvard she may have started out in search of her."

Van Cleve nodded in acceptance of that theory. So did Harvard. Clancy stood with his back turned to them, tapping his boot with his crop, and made no comment of any sort.

In a moment more they were all mounted and riding swiftly toward the wood-fringed ravine. Clancy clung to the rear. Harvard, who was thoroughly familiar with the locality, led. Van Cleve rode close beside Benton Keese, but never once turned his head, nor spoke a word. But at the same time Holbrook Chilton could feel the iron presence of the man, and was suddenly convinced that the Mexican mine-owner and contractor no longer doubted his double identity. But he smiled inwardly, nevertheless, being convinced also that neither Van Cleve nor any other person would ever be able now to prove the duplicity of his ego. And so they came to the top of the wood road into the ravine and stopped.

"My girth broke when I was there," Keese said, pointing, and addressing the remark to Harvard. "Mrs. Harvard was just at the top of that steep rise, yonder," and he pointed again. "I dismounted and called out to her to go on, and—"

"You lie!" Clancy shouted at him. "I turned and looked back from far above here, at a point where one can get a glimpse of the wood road, near the bottom of it; and Betty did the same. And we both saw you, and Katherine, too, when you rode into the ravine together. So I tell you again, Keese, you lie. *You lie like hell!*"

CHAPTER XXXIV

WHEN KEESE PUT UP A BLUFF

Benton Keese stiffened in the saddle, bending slightly forward as with a quick motion of his left arm he threw one side of the rein against the horse's neck. Then, remembering that saddle-horses are not turned in that manner in the East, he jerked the animal around with the other side of the rein.

At the same instant he reached for the empty pocket where he had carried that automatic pistol. It was not there, of course. He remembered the fact before his hand had traveled half the distance to it; but even so, he had recalled the fact too late, for all three of the men had seen the motion and understood its import—and at least one of them, thinking that Keese might be possessed of a second weapon, had acted.

Van Cleve was that man. He whipped out one of his own pistols on the instant, and before Keese had recovered from the useless gesture—indeed, before he could have drawn—and held it grimly and steadily, with the muzzle of it pointed straight at the heart of Benton Keese. And his eyes were as cold as icicles and as sharp as pinpoints in their intensity. But he said quietly:

"Put up your hands, Chilton. I know you now. That move of yours with the bridle-rein betrayed you. Just imagine that we are back there in Mexico together and that I have got the drop on you. You know *me*."

"Mr. Van Cleve—" Harvard began; but the older man interrupted him.

"Wait, Harvard," he said sharply. "Keep quiet and let me handle things for a moment."

But Keese did not raise his hands, or attempt to do so. Instead, he let them drop to the saddle in front of him and sat very still while a slow smile gathered in his eyes and crept down across his features, relaxing them into the cool self-possessed, fearless individual that he really was. For, to the credit of Benton Keese, be it said that he was always at his best when danger threatened the most.

All this happened while Van Cleve was using his gun, while Harvard started to exclaim a protest and Van Cleve interrupted him. And Keese recovered his reins again as Van Cleve ended that last remark to Harvard. He lifted them, and at the same time touched his horse's sides with his heels. The animal started forward. Keese raised his cap, and even as Van Cleve ceased speaking he said:

"I bid you good day, gentlemen."

"Stop!" Van Cleve called out to him; but Keese rode onward slowly, nor offered to turn his head. "Stop or I'll shoot, so help me—"

"Shoot and be damned!" Keese called back, amusement rather than fear or anger in his tone; and he continued on his way, but without attempting to hasten the speed of his horse.

"By heaven, but I wish we *were* in Mexico," Van Cleve ground out between his teeth savagely, and restored the weapon to his pocket. "Go after him, Harvard. Bring him back here. He's Chilton all right. There isn't any doubt of that."

Harvard started his horse forward.

"Keese!" he called, as he advanced; and Keese reined in and waited. But he did not offer to turn. Harvard rode up beyond him and faced about, blocking his way.

"Will you go back there with me?" he asked quietly.

"No, Mr. Harvard."

"You know that I can *take* you back, don't you, if I attempt it?"

"I don't think you will make that attempt—so I need not reply to the question. I am, unfortunately, your guest here to-day. You have permitted me to be grossly insulted in your presence, twice. It would be a fitting climax to your entertainment of my sister and me, if you should, personally, add to these outrages."

Harvard winced, for there was truth in what was said.

"Keese?" Bingham began again.

"Well, sir?"

"Mr. Van Cleve charges that you are, or have been, the Chilton whom we knew. Are you—*were* you that man?"

"I will overlook the implied insult of that question, under the circumstances, and answer it. Most certainly I was not and am not, and could not be, that person."

"You claimed to have known him."

"I did know him—in precisely the way I have explained."

"Why do you go about armed, as you were to-day?"

"Doubtless for the same reason that Van Cleve does so; because I have always been accustomed to doing so. And that reminds me: I will thank you to return my property."

Harvard reached into a pocket, found the pistol, and returned it. Keese accepted it with a slight nod of thanks.

"It is empty," Harvard told him.

Keese nodded again.

"Is it true that Clancy saw you and my wife ride into the ravine side by side?" Harvard asked then.

"No. It could not have been true, since we did not do so."

"But Clancy says that he and your sister both saw you do it."

"My sister, unfortunately, is not here to support my statement. And, although Clancy appears for some unknown reason to be very deeply prejudiced against me, I will do him the justice to suppose that he is honestly mistaken. There were many riders out to-day. It is possible that others may have descended into the ravine by that road after I had done so."

Harvard was silent a moment. Then without another word he started his horse forward and rejoined his two friends.

Keese rode away slowly in the opposite direction without turning his head; but if any of them could have peered into his face just then, they would have seen a lurking smile hovering around the corners of his mouth.

"Why didn't you bring him back with you, Bing?" Clancy demanded angrily.

But Harvard did not reply. He rode onward up the brow of the hill beside the ravine, toward the place that had been described to him as the one where Katherine's hat and crop and gauntlets had been found, and his friends followed after. Harvard could not believe that Katherine had sustained more than a severe fall which had temporarily disabled her. A sprained ankle, perhaps, so that she could not walk.

And yet—he kept asking himself why the searchers had found no trace of her near the place where her things were discovered. There was no mistaking the spot where Katherine's horse had plunged over the bank into the ravine when Keese struck it with the crop; the disturbed footing, the crushed and broken twigs and shoots of trees and the unmistakable evidences of the animal's having rolled over and over, farther down, were all plainly to be seen.

All three men followed down the course of the hunter's leap and fall—and many other searchers were in the immediate locality, seeking, calling aloud, doing everything that wit could suggest to explain the mystery of Mrs. Harvard's strange disappearance immediately after the accident. And at last, when it became evident that further search in that locality was worse than useless, they gathered into a group, a full score or more of them, and made and listened to suggestion after suggestion and to every possible theory that could be offered as a solution to the problem.

The consensus of opinion was, at last, that she must have been seen to take the plunge over the bank and fall by a stranger who happened to be wandering that way or by one or more outsiders who had joined in the hunt without invitation—a circumstance that is almost sure to happen at a "big day" of the Forestbrook. Such person or persons would have gone to her aid; would have taken her direct to the nearest point of assistance and remedies—and would, by then, have found means to communicate with the club.

So with shouts of reassurance from one to another the search was abandoned and everybody vied with everybody else in a race back to the clubhouse. Night was falling, too, and soon it would be quite dark there in the woods.

Only Tom Clancy among them all was not convinced that news of Katherine would be forthcoming at the clubhouse by then. For he had not changed that opinion that had instantly formed in his mind with the first news of her absence. But he kept his silence while they rode rapidly back, although he clung close to Bing Harvard; and so did Van Cleve, at the opposite side of him. But Tom kept repeating to himself:

"Keese has done this thing, and when Bing finds it out, he'll kill him! Or, *I* will!"

CHAPTER XXXV

THE MASK IS TORN AWAY

There was no news of Katherine at the clubhouse. With the positive information that nothing had been heard from her or concerning her, Harvard, who had not yet dismounted, sat very still indeed in his saddle, his features hardened into a marble-like mask of self-repression and self-restraint. For he knew that he must think; and think quickly and to the point.

And as if by common consent those who were gathered near him were also motionless and silent. The interval thus passed might have been counted in seconds, or minutes; nobody knew as to that; but an interruption came when a club servant edged his way among them and gave a sealed envelope into Harvard's hand. Then came an audible sigh of relief from the waiting friends, for the instant thought was that here, at last, was the blessed news—for information of any character would have been blessed in some degree just then.

Harvard seized upon the envelope and tore it open without so much as a glance at the handwriting upon it. His friends who were gathered around him, eagerly waiting to be told what the message might contain, saw his face harden still more, saw his lips set in a straight line and remain so for a moment before he opened them to speak, saw him cast a swift glance toward Van Cleve, and then toward Clancy. Then, as if decided what to do, he raised the brief note again and read aloud from it so that all could hear.

DEAR MR. HARVARD:

You will, under the circumstances, find excuses
for my sister and me in making our departure from
the Forestbrook clubhouse so abruptly. Circumstances which I will not inflict upon you at this time
have arisen which render it imperative for both of us
to go away at once and without waiting to make our
adieus.

We both feel assured that Mrs. Harvard will have
returned before you receive this note and that whatever accident she may have met with will not have
been a serious one, else some trace of her would undoubtedly have been discovered at the point where it
occurred.

Believing this, as we both do, we feel less reluctance in going; and we desire to extend our mutual
sense of appreciation for the graceful courtesies that
have been extended to us by you and your friends.

Sincerely yours,
BENTON KEESE

A dead silence obtained after the reading of the note. It was
broken, presently, by Harvard, himself, who said:

"I read the message of Mr. Keese aloud to you because I realized that you like myself, supposed it to come from Mrs. Harvard, or
to concern her. Since it explains itself, I need offer no further comment."

"It's a rotten thing for him to do—to leave you like this, at this
time," somebody remarked in a tone that was distinctly audible to
everyone; and there was a general murmur of approval of the senti-
ment from all sides.

But Harvard turned away from it all, and still in the saddle,
pulled his mount away from the others. He knew that they were already organizing searching parties for further effort; and—he
wanted to think it out, alone. But Tom Clancy, who had dismounted,
followed him.

"Bing," he said, in a guarded undertone, when they were at a
safe distance—and resting one of his hands reassuringly upon his
friend's knee—"I've got something hateful to say to you; but it has

got to be said. Will you listen? And will you try to be as patient with me as possible?"

"What is it, Tom?"

"First, upon my soul I do not believe that Katherine has been hurt at all. I do not believe that she has met with an accident—of the kind we have feared. What I *do* believe—and this is the hateful thing I had to say—what I do honestly believe is that Benton Keese, *alias* Holbrook Chilton, is responsible for her mysterious disappearance, and that if we could find him and make him talk, he could tell us where to find her right now."

"Good God, man, do you realize what you are saying?" Harvard seemed to steady himself with an effort, but his fingers twitched as he bent forward, nearer to Tom.

"Yes, Bing, I do realize it. And I mean it, too."

"You are—!" Harvard seemed to choke, and he stopped. "You are suggesting—!" He came to a stop again, unable to proceed. And Clancy understood; and gasped, blunderingly:

"Great heavens, Bing! Do you suppose I meant to imply for a moment that such a thing could have happened with her connivance? Good Lord! I mean that the scoundrel has stolen her away. I mean that he sent her horse over the bluff long after she was out of the saddle. I mean that he tore the gloves, broke the crop, crushed her hat, and—"

"Wait, Tom. Wait. And forgive me. I—I came near to choking you, just now. Wait. No; don't wait. Tell me exactly what you mean. I'll listen. I will listen quietly. I won't interrupt you. I'll hear all of it. I want to hear all of it. I must hear—"

"Here is Van Cleve, Bing, coming this way."

"Never mind. Say it all, in his presence. Go on. Don't wait. He will understand."

"You more than half believe what I have said, now; don't you?"

"Go on, I say. Tell me all of it. Tell me everything that is on your mind. Your conduct has been incomprehensible since I came down this afternoon. Perhaps this will explain it."

"It will explain it, Bing."

"Well? Well? Well?"

"We know—none of we three doubt it now!—that Keese *is* Chilton. Van Cleve knows it. You know it. I know it."

"Van Cleve *does not* know that Keese is the man whom Katherine ran away from when she came to New York, before you ever saw her."

197

"Yes I do. Bingham told me," Van Cleve interpolated.

"Well, then, here is something that neither of you *do* know: Katherine was afraid of him. She feared him, mightily. Not because of what he might do or say, or *attempt* to do or say, to her, but because of what she might, in an extreme moment, do to *him*. She hated him. He aroused in her a primitive emotion that made her want to kill. She told me so herself."

"Katherine told you that, Tom?"

"Yes."

"When?"

"Last Monday, when we came away from the bank together, after the conference."

"Go on."

"She regretted that she had received Betty into her home because it gave Betty's brother the open sesame of the house. She believed that he had sent for Betty to come here for that very purpose. Today, while Betty and I rode together during the chase, she herself admitted as much to me. Even before we started Betty begged me to stick close to Katherine and not to let Ben, as she calls him, get her away alone with him."

"But—great heavens, Tom!—abduction? In this day and age?"

"Bing"—Tom put both hands upon Harvard's knee as he bent nearer the better to emphasize what he had to say—"Benton Keese is more an animal than a man. He would not hesitate to strike, or to use any kind of force, or to choke, and rend, and tear. If his wits did not serve his ends, he used force. If he could not lead her blindly into a trap that he had set for her, he would not hesitate to throw her into it."

"He is an animal! a beast! a monster in the shape and guise of a man!"

Harvard's teeth and lips were tightly compressed. His muscles were flexed and tense. His chest heaved with the intake and expulsion of deep and mighty breaths. But he controlled himself and made no sound.

"Where is Miss Betty? Why is she not here with us, now?" Van Cleve asked.

"God only knows!" Tom exploded. "She was not here when we started out to hunt for Katherine. She was gone, even then— searching for Katherine, as I supposed, then."

"But, now? What do you think about it now?"

"I'll tell you what I think. I burst in upon them suddenly when she was with her brother in that little parlor. I was wild with anger, for even then I believed that he was responsible for Katherine's absence. He pretended to be chafing Betty's hands, but it *was* a pretense. I knew it was, at the time. Betty looked no more like fainting than I did—and she isn't of the sort that faints away. I had just charged Keese with knowing where Katherine was when you two appeared. I had charged him with being Holbrook Chilton and a thief and a forger, when you came. You heard only the last words of it. But I'll tell you something that you did not see, and had no time to notice."

"This: I know—*I know*—from Betty's attitude and manner when I charged that cur with being responsible for Katherine's absence, *that she had been making that same charge against him, herself.*"

"Then, where is she? Why isn't she here?" Bingham Harvard demanded, white now, to the lips.

"I don't know, Bing. I wish I did. You sent her from the room, if you'll remember. You asked her to find Katherine for you. I can only surmise—"

"Surmise what?"

"That just before I interrupted them—just after Betty had made the same charge that I made when I burst into the room—he had worked his devilish craft upon her, somehow. He might even have partially admitted that he did know where Katherine was. He might even have offered to take Betty to her. It would be like his cunning craft, his devilish subtleness."

"And then—?"

"I have made inquiries. I can find no one who saw Betty after she came from that room. *We* remained there for some time afterward. She must have gone away at once. Therefore her brother had said something to her that sent her away."

"Would she have gone like that?" Van Cleve asked.

"She would have gone anywhere in the hope of finding Katherine. She would have gone *nowhere* just then without such a hope. And she *did* go."

"Enough!" Harvard put in sharply.

He was silent a moment, and his two friends waited in suspense for his next remark.

"You have convinced me, Tom," he said in a dead, expressionless voice, presently. "I am convinced. I think now that I have been convinced from the start—only I would not have it so. I have suspected Keese's motives in my house since the first moment I saw him there—only I would not admit to myself that I did suspect. I have coupled him with Chilton from the first—only I would not let myself do it. Now—we must find him. And when he is found I will—"

Van Cleve interrupted in his quiet tone.

"I know the man from the ground up," he said. "I do not think that he will be difficult to find."

"Why?" Harvard asked.

"He will show himself. It is his way. The man is absolutely fearless. If he possesses an abundant passion, it is the love of danger. He will not run away—yet. He will go to his hotel and wait, unless—"

"Unless what?" Clancy demanded when Van Cleve hesitated.

Van Cleve did not reply.

"You mean," Harvard said evenly, "unless his plans were so well prepared that he has been able to get away already, and to take my wife with him. Is that what you mean, Van Cleve?"

"Yes."

"Get the car, Tom. We will go back to the city now. Try to make all these people think that we are starting out to continue the search. Later, perhaps it will be as well—if one of you should telephone here to the club—that Katherine has been found—not badly injured—and taken home—by somebody. It will avoid unpleasant complexities and comment."

Ten minutes later they drove away.

CHAPTER XXXVI

A HOLD-UP AT THE RED SCHOOLHOUSE

Black Julius drove the car that carried Bingham Harvard, Tom Clancy and Anderson Van Cleve away from the clubhouse. It was the same car that had taken Katherine and her company out to that Connecticut "wilderness," which, although it is less than fifty miles from New York, might well be a thousand miles away in its rough and seamed contour and wildness. That was why the Forestbrook Club had chosen the locality. They hunted foxes there, not aniseed bags.

Night had fallen, and since then clouds had gathered thickly. It was unutterably dark. But the glaring headlights of the car like giant fingers picked up and exposed to view every object that appeared upon the highway along their course. And so presently when they shot at racing speed around a slight bend in the road the ribbon-like beams struck upon the red schoolhouse—and upon the figures of two men who stood beside the roadway before it.

The huge car was traveling like a bullet and would have shot past the two men almost as swiftly. But Harvard, who was seated beside Julius, called out suddenly when the lights exposed them to view.

"Stop the car!" he commanded; and the black obeyed.

Trembling, pulsing, heaving, the car came to a standstill. The two men sprang forward and stopped beside the mud-guard, close to the young bank president.

"*Rushton!*" Harvard exclaimed. "And *Banta!*" he added in amazement.

Then: "How does it happen that you are here, Rushton?"

"I haven't been away—not so's you could notice it, Mr. Harvard," Rushton replied quickly, with a broad grin of appreciation of the incident upon his face.

"We sent our *astral* bodies to Mexico, sir," Banta added. "We thought that the physical ones might be more useful right here."

"Mr. Van Cleve knew that I hadn't gone away," Rushton continued, speaking rapidly. "We cooked up another scheme together, which served as well. I figgered it out that there *was* a way for a feller like me to be in two places at once. So, you see, right now I am here! And I'm in Mexico City, *tambien*, as Mr. Van Cleve puts it; which means 'likewise,' 'also,' and 'just the same.' I am here; and I am there, too. And the part of me that is *there* will be *here* by to-morrow, I'm thinking, or by the day after, anyhow. Eh, Mr. Van Cleve?"

"Yes. I think so," Van Cleve answered. "That is how we estimated."

"Get in," Harvard said. "We can talk as we ride on. I am in a hurry. We are after—"

"Mr. Benton Keese. I know," Rushton interrupted.

"You know—Do you know what has happened, Rushton? You and Banta?"

"We know *one* thing that has happened; maybe not all of it," Rushton replied with another grin.

"We must overtake Keese before he can get to his hotel in the city and away from it again. He and his sister are somewhere on the road ahead of us."

"I don't know anything about his sister, Mr. Harvard; but *he*, Mister Benton-Holbrook-Chilton-Keese by name, is attendin' night-school this evenin', and you won't have very far to go to find *him*—buh-lieve me!"

"What?" Clancy cried out, his eyes upon the red schoolhouse.

Rushton jerked his head toward it and grinned.

"Uh-huh," he said. "In there. The door wasn't locked. We thought we'd put him outa sight an' give him a chance to think things over a little while Banta an' me *talked* 'em over and waited f'r you an' Mr. Clancy an' Mr. Van Cleve to show up. And we kinda wanted to see Lady Kate, too. I suppose she's comin' in another car behind you."

"Then you *don't* know!" Clancy spoke up.

"Don't know what?" Rushton's eyes narrowed. His mouth became suddenly grim; and his jaws were set tightly together after the question as he turned to face Tom Clancy.

Van Cleve replied quickly, before either of his companions could do so.

"Something has happened to Mrs. Harvard, Rushton. We do not know what it is. But she has disappeared," and then, swiftly, he explained everything to the two detectives.

Rushton and Banta exchanged rapid glances at each other while Van Cleve talked. As he finished, the distant purring of an approaching automobile fell upon their ears.

"Drive around into that side road, Julius," Rushton directed quickly. "Then shut off your lights so's we needn't be seen hangin' around here an' givin' some guy an excuse to stop an' ask a lotta fool-questions. Banta 'n me'll chase along."

"But," Clancy spoke, "is Keese secure—so that he can't get away?"

"He has got a bracelet of mine on one wrist and a bracelet of Banta's on the other one—and the twin of both of 'em are hitched to the iron legs of two desks inside," Rushton replied. "I guess mebby if it was the Night Wind in there they wouldn't hold him, but bein' that he ain't—"

But Julius shot the car ahead at that instant at his master's command and turned into the same side road to which Keese had directed his sister that afternoon, putting out his lights as soon as he had made the turn and got his bearings properly. Rushton and Banta ran after it and were lost to view of the searchlights when the approaching car shot past the red schoolhouse.

Harvard leaped to the ground as soon as the other car had gone by.

"Take me to him now, he ordered," and started onward toward the schoolhouse door; but Rushton put out a hand and detained him.

"Wait, Mr. Harvard—please," he said with a quiet dignity that was new to his known character, and yet which belonged to him and fitted him; the dignity of an honest man who could face the world unblinkingly.

Harvard stopped.

"Well?" he demanded impatiently.

"I think that we ought to know something about where we're at before we go in there an' throw the gaff into that guy. You see, we ain't got nothin' on him which will let us hold him an' 'take him in,' like you would do with any decent crook you'd pinched. I couldn't take him to a station house, even if I had him over the line an' into New York State right now, and make a charge against him that would go. The lieutenant at the desk would turn him loose in a holy minute."

"Then what *do* you propose to do, Rushton?"

"You see, it's this way: Banta an' me know that he *is* Chilton. *We* know that he is the guy that got away with your coin. But—we can't *prove* that we know it; not right now we can't. And he can't be held as a suspicious character, or for investigation, or anything like that, just because of the way he has been livin' since he came to New York. Why, he's been livin' at your house almost as much as anywhere else; and under his right name, too, which is Benton Keese."

"Then why did you arrest him?"

"We didn't arrest him. We just took him," Rushton replied, grinning.

"Why—if you can prove nothing against him?"

"Well, we figgered that he was bent on makin' his getaway mighty sudden. We thought, when we lamped him comin' along the road just at the edge of dark that he had rung the all-right bell an' was makin' full steam ahead for the sky-line. So we stopped him."

"Where?"

"Right here."

"Was he on foot?"

"Yes."

"And alone?"

"Sure. And bein' as there wasn't anybody around, we just stepped out in front of him and held him up. He don't know that we are cops. Maybe he's got a suspicion that way, but he don't *know* it."

"He knows you, Rushton."

"Well, he didn't know me this trip. Banta an' me tied handkerchiefs over our faces, an' Banta done all the chinnin'. We thought afterward that mebby we'd been a little too precipitate. But when you consider that he's had pretty near the whole Dudley Roland agency workin' for him lately, and that he has been havin' me and you and Banta and Mr. Clancy an' Mr. Van Cleve trailed and reported on everywhere we go, and that now he was doin' the sneaker-act away from that club where you was entertainin' him, it looked to us like he was hikin'. That's why we stopped him, Mr. Harvard; and that's why, instead of goin' on to that club as we was intendin' to do, to talk it over with you three *and* Lady Kate, we decided to wait right here, with him tied up inside of the schoolhouse, an' flag you when you showed up."

"May I ask a few questions, Bingham?" Van Cleve requested, stepping nearer. Then, without waiting for a reply, he added, addressing Rushton: "Have you heard from Mexico? From Mr. Corona?"

"Twice—since you an' me sent that hundred-an' thirty word message to him. Yes sir."

"What did he say?"

"The first one said he had received the dope all right, and the second one said he had found the 'goods' that we asked him to get, an' was forward-in' it by *ex*-press, that bein', in his opinion, safer'n the mail. And it's about due to arrive here to-morrow, or the next day, accordin' to the way I figger it out."

"Corona had discovered what you wanted, Rushton?"

"Yep. Some in your office in that there Gauntlet Street, an' more of 'em in the other place where Chilton lived down there, in Fil-lippy Neery Street."

"What was it that you sent for?" Harvard asked.

"The Bertillion dope, Mr. Harvard—finger-prints, thumb-prints. And there ain't no human way but that by which you can prove that Chilton and Keese are the same man."

"Señor Tranquilino Corona was the most efficient officer in the secret service of former President Díaz," Van Cleve hastened to explain. "He is also a very good friend of mine."

"Lieutenant Rushton realized after the disappearance of Chilton from the Pullman car that it would be extremely difficult to identify Keese with Chilton, and last Monday after we came away from the bank Rushton and I made up the telegram and sent it to Corona."

Harvard turned again to Rushton.

"Did you already suspect, then, that Keese was Chilton?" he asked.

"Mr. Clancy gave me that tip, Mr. Harvard. He got it from a handshake. I had picked one up myself before that; only I didn't know the value of it until later—not until I heard Mr. Van Cleve talk about it that afternoon at the bank. You see, sir, that time when I called at your house—the evening of the day you an' the district attorney turned me loose—and I was introduced to Mr. Benton Keese, it didn't happen to be the first time I'd set eyes onto him. I had lamped him just about an hour before that when he was standin' out in front of the Mammoth an' I was standin' close to him while I waited for the time to slip past before I could go to see you 'n' Lady Kate. And I wouldn't have taken a second look at him then if he hadn't been rollin' a cigarette. But, first off, he seemed like too swell a guy to be usin' his own makin's, an' then it certainly was a queer way he rolled it. But even then I didn't think no more about it till Mr. Van Cleve said what he did last Monday."

"Why did you not tell me about that, Rushton?" Van Cleve asked.

"There wasn't any particular reason, sir; only that I thought that mebby you or Mr. Clancy, if you knew about it, might say 'r do something to flush our bird before I had the gun cocked an' ready."

"Say, Mr. Harvard, do you wanta go inside of the schoolhouse and talk to him? Because I'm thinkin' from what's been told to me that it wouldn't surprise me none if he has had a hand in fixin' that frame-up about Lady Kate's bein' hurt."

Harvard started swiftly ahead. The others followed. The young bank president pushed open the door and entered. Rushton and Banta paused beside him, and with flash-lights taken from their pockets shot penetrating rays toward the spot where they had left their captive—and then into every corner and shadow in the room. But Benton Keese was no longer there. He had disappeared.

CHAPTER XXXVII

THE DISAPPEARANCE OF KEESE

There was no denying the fact that Keese had disappeared. There was evidence enough at hand also to explain the manner of his going, for the two school-desks with iron legs screwed to the floor, to which he had been fastened in the manner described by Rushton, were missing, too. That seems laughable at first; but it was also significant: For the screws had been drawn from the floor by a proper tool, not pried out of it; and the remains of the desk were not scattered about promiscuously. Therefore, they had gone away with Benton Keese, presumably through the small door at the rear of the schoolroom.

Keese, because of the way he had been fastened, could not have reached either of the desks to draw the screws, even had he been provided with a tool for doing it; nor was it likely that he had trotted off with a desk beneath each arm. It was plain, therefore, that assistance had been given him; that another person had been there; that it had been somebody who could obtain immediate access to a tool-box, and that the desks had been taken away with the man simply to avoid the noise that would be necessary in separating him from them.

Rushton absorbed all of those details very quickly and ran for the little door at the rear, and through it into the open at once. Banta followed. The others retraced their steps as they had come and returned to the car. Rushton and Banta rejoined them almost at once.

"Keese had his gray car waiting for him down that side road, Mr. Harvard," Rushton explained. "The tracks of it are there. We found them. It was drawn up at the side of the road among some bushes and headed the other way. So you see it *was* waitin' there for him."

"Yes. But we must not waste time talking here, Rushton. We...."

"Please give me a minute more, sir."

"Go on."

"Banta an' me figger it out that the chauffeur of his car had walked out this way and saw us when we held his nibs up and took him into the schoolhouse. *I* didn't stay in there any longer'n was necessary; hardly a minute; just long enough to help make him fast. I didn't want him to recognize me if it could be helped. I came outside, and Banta came, too, a minute later. Then we stood at the door and chinned for a while and then went out to the roadside. We ain't either of us been inside of that building since we took him in there. See?"

"Yes."

"And it's more'n likely that that chauffeur of his'n got him away before you three gentlemen got here at all. Anyhow, it explains why he was saunterin' along the highway like he was doin' when we lamped him."

"Now—will you all please take a look at this? I picked it up out yonder where his car was waitin'. Mebby one of you can tell who it belongs to."

All three men bent forward to peer closely when Rushton threw the gleam of his flash-light upon an object that he held in the hollow of one hand, and Tom Clancy exclaimed instantly:

"Why, it's Betty's bracelet-watch! It belongs to Miss Keese," he added soberly.

"Then she was out there, too, in that waiting car," Rushton said. "But she wasn't there of her own free will, I don't think. Look closer, Mr. Clancy. You'll see two or three tiny spots of blood on it if you do. It's my opinion, and Banta agrees with me, that she was tied up so's she couldn't get loose, and that she had something over her mouth so's she couldn't holler, either. But that she had her senses with her all the same."

"But—"

"Wait, please. When that chauffeur went away an' left her she musta tried to think of something that she could do to leave a trace behind her that she had been there; and so she must have managed to scrape that bracelet loose from her wrist against the car or something, and drop it alongside of the road. But whether she done it on purpose or it got there where we found it by accident, it *was* there; and it means—"

"What?" Harvard asked.

Instead of replying directly, Rushton turned.

"Julius," he said sharply, "turn on your light and your power. I'll ride beside you. Go as fast as you like till you come to a cross-road or a lane or a turn-off of any kind. Then pull up till further orders. It's a lead-pipe cinch that Keese's car didn't go out of that side road this way."

"Banta is goin' to chase along the main road in the taxi that brought us down here, which is waitin' up the road a half mile or so to head him off if possible. If Mr. Van Cleve will follow my advice he'll go along with Banta. The rest of the bunch will try to follow the trail left by Keese's car. And we can do that, too—till it takes to a traveled road. After that we'll have to do some guessin' an' fig-gerin'."

"Go on, Julius."

Connecticut roads throughout that region which is located back of the Norwalks are rough and hilly and many of them are used but little, and the narrow and bush-fringed one that Harvard's car followed, driven at a rapid speed by Black Julius, belonged in the latter class. It was that sort of a road which is sometimes described as leading uphill both ways.

As soon as they had started Rushton turned in his seat and said to the two men who were seated behind:

"Banta and me had time to do a little examinin' just where Keese's car had been waitin', and the tracks we found told us that the gray car didn't come to that place by the main road."

"It came from the way we're headin' now, and it was turned around so's to head back again toward the way it had come from while it waited—which, as *I* look at it, is pretty good reason to suppose that it wasn't goin' right back to the city this trip. So mebby we can follow it, and mebby we can't. But we're goin' to have a try at it, anyhow."

CHAPTER XXXVIII

WHAT BECAME OF BETTY

Betty Keese, sent from the room where her brother had been called a thief and a forger by the man she loved, and where Keese in sudden rage had attempted to strike Clancy, but was prevented from doing so by the swift action of the Night Wind, was more than ever concerned about the absence of Katherine.

She did not understand the epithets that Tom had hurled at Benton, because she had been told nothing about the "Holbrook Chilton" affair. But she did know her brother better than anybody else knew him, even though much of her knowledge of him was intuitive; and she did not for a moment doubt that Tom Clancy had believed that he had very good and sufficient reason for making such charges, else—for Betty loved him—he would not have made them at all.

And she was certain when that room door closed behind her that Benton did know where Katherine was and that the accident that was supposed to have happened to her was a fake, and had not occurred at all. It never occurred to Betty *not* to go to the red schoolhouse. She had believed that Benton was in earnest in giving her that direction and she followed it the moment she was free to do so with all the speed that she could muster; and her Kentucky training had imparted plenty of strength to her muscles. Accustomed to rural localities and recalling distinctly the appearance of the little schoolhouse, she ran from the club at the end of the veranda unnoticed, struck across the field to cut off the great bend in the main highway and sped onward with rapid footsteps toward her goal.

The schoolhouse door was not fastened and she peered inside breathlessly, really believing that she would find Lady Kate there.

But it was deserted of course. Then she went outside again and around into the side road—to discover that it was as deserted as the schoolhouse. So recalling exactly what Benton had said to her—that she should wait patiently until he came—she selected a seat on a rock beside the road and composed herself to wait. Time passed and the shadows lengthened. The afternoon was changing into evening and night, although the sunlight still gleamed upon the topmost leaves of many of the surrounding trees.

Then she was startled by the purring of an approaching motor, and soon the gray car, which she instantly recognized as the one in which Benton had taken her to ride the preceding Monday, darted into view from around a twist in that wood-bordered roadway and came to a stop in front of her. The man who drove it she did not know; had never seen. But she did not consider that point at all when she stepped quickly forward toward him and said interrogatively:

"I am Miss Keese. This is my brother's car, I suppose?"

"Yes, Miss Keese," the chauffeur replied, respectfully touching his cap.

"He directed you to meet me here, I suppose?" she asked.

"Yes, Miss Keese. I will turn the car around if you will wait a moment."

He did so, and drove it beside the road among the overshadowing bushes where Rushton and Banta were later to discover that it had been standing.

"Why do you do that?" Betty asked as he got down and came toward her.

"I was directed to wait a short time for Mr. Keese, and then to take you to a house in the neighborhood, if he was detained," the chauffeur replied.

"Then take me there *now*," Betty demanded impetuously and with heightened color. "You can return for him—if the house isn't far away. I will go there now, please. There is a friend awaiting me."

The man looked at her oddly, but she did not perceive it. From a distance, at the same moment, came the purring of another motor. The chauffeur stepped nearer to Betty, reached past her, and pulled a light lap-robe from the seat beside the driver's place. He said:

"Will you get in, Miss Keese?"

Unsuspectingly Betty stepped forward and lifted a foot preparatory to getting into the car. For the moment her back was turned to the chauffeur. He stood directly behind it—and it was the situation for which he had been maneuvering. For it would appear that Betty's brother had foreseen every possible incident of that day, and had given his orders accordingly. In fact, the brief directions in Spanish, given to the men at the house where Lady Kate had been taken, had foretold to them the possible arrival there of his sister and had directed what was to be done with her. The instant when Betty's back was turned to the chauffeur he threw lightly over her head and held there the robe that he had taken from the car seat.

Betty struggled and tried to call out; but the chauffeur was a powerful man and held her easily, while the robe over her head deadened the sound of her cries. All the while the man was saying to her:

"You'll not be hurt, Miss Keese. It's your brother's orders. It won't do any good to fight back, because I've got to do it. And you'll be let loose as soon as we get to the house where the other lady is waiting."

While he talked he was fastening a strap around the encircling blanket so that she could not get away.

"I've got to take you there first and then come back here after Mr. Keese," he continued. "I don't like to do this; you needn't think I do. But it's his orders, and I've got to;" and all the time he was working steadily to render her fastenings the more secure.

"Now, Miss Keese," he said finally, "if you will give me your word of honor that you won't call out, and won't make any noise, and won't try to get away, I'll take that robe away. If it was some other man than your brother who had ordered me to do this, you might have good reason to get scared; but being him, and seeing that he *is* your brother, you had best promise, so that I can make you as comfortable as possible."

Betty, furious with anger, reasoned nevertheless. She was going to Katherine; and before her brother came. If she called out, if somebody from that approaching motor which she could no longer hear should interfere, she might be, and doubtless would be, prevented from getting to Katherine in advance of Benton. So reluctantly she gave the promise, and he removed the robe from around her head and face, but did not take it away entirely—so that presently, when she discovered that he had left her, or had withdrawn to some spot where she could no longer see him, she found, also, that her arms were still confined and that the strap that held them was fastened behind her so she could not leave the seat.

212

She called to the chauffeur, but he did not reply. Then she waited impatiently for a time before she struggled to free herself. But she did make the effort at last, and succeeded in freeing one arm, with which she sought to reach around behind her in order to release the strap that held her fast. It was then that the bracelet watch was torn from her wrist—accidentally and not by design, although it served the purpose as well later.

Immediately after that the chauffeur came hurrying back to her, and she could hear him at the tool-box, while he said rapidly:

"Mr. Keese is here. He will be with you in a moment"; and he hastened away again.

A little while later she heard the voice of Benton harshly giving directions to the chauffeur, behind where she was seated. She heard him say:

"Quick, now! Wrench those things loose. Never mind the cuffs. Leave them where they are for the present. Carry those things into the woods and drop them. It's dark now. They won't be seen. Now, hurry; or I'll leave you here."

Then he sprang into the seat beside her and seized the steering-wheel; and Betty saw with the utmost amazement, although dimly, for darkness had fallen in there under the trees, that from each of Benton's wrists something ominous was dangling.

The chauffeur returned and sprang into the rumble-seat of the car. Benton started it forward, and they shot away through the darkness until after they had rounded that twist of the narrow road. Then the lights were turned on. Keese had paid not the slightest attention to the exclamations, protests, and questions that Betty had fired at him ever since his arrival. But after they had rounded the turn in the road he leaned nearer to her and said grimly into her ear so that the chauffeur behind them in the rumble-seat could not hear him:

"I am taking you to Kitten now, and it rests with you only what will happen to you after that. For I have got to go away to-night. And *she* is going with me. You shall go, too, under conditions—or stay. And I'll promise that you won't want to do *that*."

CHAPTER XXXIX

THE COURAGE OF LADY KATE

Lady Kate started to her feet when she heard the voice of Benton Keese outside the door. When he had left her there nearly four hours earlier she had remained in a sort of physical half stupor for a long time, although her brain had been busy enough with the problem she was facing and with her material helplessness to meet and overcome it. Nevertheless her courage, always superb, did not falter even in that extremity. It was a man's kind of courage, which, while it does not belittle the fearsome things that threaten, faces them without flinching and struggles to the last to overcome them, never doubting ultimate victory.

She had remained inert, the better to think and plan and determine what she should do when Benton Keese returned; but during the last hour, after the dark-skinned woman appeared to make a light for her, she had been pacing restlessly up and down the room until the last few moments, when she had again dropped upon the low chair. The woman had entered softly, and had paused just inside the door, tentatively, and with a backward glance over her shoulder. Katherine, following that glance, saw that one of the men who had been outside was there waiting—and watching. Evidently the woman had been warned not to enter Lady Kate's presence unguarded.

Save for the woman's hasty return and exit when she took away Katherine's hat and gauntlets—to which the captive had paid no attention—and when she came later to make a light, Katherine had been left utterly alone. Thus opportunity had been afforded her to recover from the shock of the monstrous trick that had been played upon her and to regain her self-poise and self-reliance. For she had been stunned by the enormity of the act committed against her, rather than frightened by it.

So when after the hours of waiting she did hear the voice of Benton Keese beyond the door that opened upon the porch, and when that was followed by the tread of his feet upon the weather-worn boards, she was entirely her old brave self again, unafraid, defiant and resolute; and she stepped behind the small table that occupied the center of the room under the swinging lamp and waited. She possessed no weapon of any sort; not so much as a stick. And she had searched fruitlessly for something of the sort during the time of her restless pacing to and fro. Still she believed that she was armed, nevertheless, with the moral power of right over a contemplated wrong; with her own individuality and purity and loftiness of soul.

Always, until that moment whenever she had heard the voice and step of Benton Keese, she had been in fear of him. Now, when he was there, and she was his prisoner, and, in a sense, at his mercy, she suddenly feared him not at all. Literally, she was unafraid. She made a picture, too, facing him as she did, when he opened that outer door with a key and entered the room.

He closed it and stood before it, looking at her; and she returned his gaze steadfastly, without a tremor of eye or lip, without the slightest quickening of her heartbeats, and without one nervous dread. For suddenly she had become clothed with entire confidence in her own power to master a situation that was almost unthinkable because of the monstrous effrontery and foolhardiness of it. Her slender figure was erect, her eyes were calm and inscrutable, her pose was one that she might have assumed had an unwelcome guest entered her own home and her presence.

Perhaps that was why Benton Keese came to a full stop inside of the door and stood facing her for a time, speechless. Doubtless he had expected to find her overcome with terror and prepared to plead with him for the consideration and the mercy he had determined not to grant. More than likely he had anticipated tears, protestations, passionate pleadings and prayers to be set free at once and returned to her home. There was no suggestion of any of them in the attitude of Katherine Harvard, the bride, the wife, of the Night Wind. And he was startled, amazed—puzzled, too.

"Have you come to take me back again, in the hope that I will excuse your conduct and forget the confession you made to me?" she asked him calmly, and as if with the certainty that he had done so.

He smiled, then, recovering himself, and glanced at his watch before he replied. Apparently he was merely estimating the time he could afford to spare for argument with her.

"I have come," he said, "to take you away. But not back to the clubhouse. Nor to the place you have called home. I have come back to take you—away. That is definite enough for the present."

"I will not go," she replied.

"You will have to go. If you refuse to walk to my car, which is waiting for us, you will be carried to it. Oh, *I* will not touch you— yet. But I have two men here. You have seen them both. They will perform that small service for me in case you are obstinate. Come. Are you ready to go quietly? The woman is bringing a hood and coat and motor-veil which I have provided. It is nearly half a mile to the place where the car is waiting. And—Betty is there to receive you."

"Betty?" Katherine was visibly startled. Then she was angry, for she did not doubt that he lied.

"I do not believe you," she said.

He shrugged and put out his hands deprecatingly.

"She is there, waiting for you," he said. "See, I have brought this with me to prove it."

He tossed a slip of paper upon the table between them.

"I thought you would not believe me. Betty thought so, too; so she wrote that message at my request. She approved of it, too, or she wouldn't have written it. You know her well enough for that. Read what she has said."

But Katherine did not lower her glance. She still stared at Benton Keese with that same half impersonal scrutiny that she had devoted to him ever since he came into the room; and she still doubted, not having looked upon the writing.

"Betty approved?" she repeated after him. "Of what did she approve?"

"Read what she has written. That is your answer."

So Katherine dropped her eyes, and read in silence:

Come. I am waiting for you in Benton's car. It will be better for both of us if we are together.

BETTY.

The handwriting was unmistakably Betty's. Katherine no longer doubted that she was at the car, waiting. Nevertheless she did not understand just how that could be, unless—

"Betty has made you do this, Benton? Has found a way to force you to—"

"Betty is there. It is enough," he interrupted her shortly. "And we waste time. Here is the Mexican woman with the things for you to wear."

He opened and closed the case of his watch with an impatient snap.

"Will you take me back to the club if I consent to go with you now?" Katherine asked.

"No," he said, and again snapped the watchcase. "Put on those things and come with me. My time is up."

"But I must know—"

"Will you come, or shall I call those two men to lead you—or to carry you, as the case may be?" For the briefest instant more she hesitated; and while she did so Keese spoke to the Mexican woman, who opened that inside door through which she had appeared and spoke two names into the darkness beyond it.

"Jose! Manuel!" she called; and the two ugly faced men Katherine had seen in the yard when she arrived, appeared, and stood waiting, just beyond the opening. They impressed her much as two savage dogs might have done. She felt instinctively that they would attack and perhaps bite, too, at a word from their master; and she still believed in the power within herself to control Benton Keese. She was still without actual fear of him alone.

"I will go," she said calmly, and began to adjust the things that the Mexican woman had brought.

"Hurry!" Keese ordered impatiently, and snapped his watch again.

It occurred to Katherine then for the first time that Benton had feared pursuit since the moment of his arrival. She had not asked him where he had been during the time of his absence, but she did not doubt that he had returned to the clubhouse to account there, in some manner, for her absence. Now, as she hastened to comply with his wish, it occurred to her that possibly he had been unable to account satisfactorily for her disappearance, that he had been obliged to disappear also, and that he believed he had been pursued.

She heard him giving rapid instructions to the two men and the woman who had served him there, but he spoke in Spanish, a language that she did not understand. Then she was ready. Outside the darkness seemed to her intense, coming, as she had done, from the lighted room.

She stumbled and he put out a hand and took her by the wrists.

"I told you that I would not touch you—yet," he said. "But I must lead you, or you will go astray in the darkness and fall."

She made no reply. They passed across the yard and through the gateway and into the blackness of the tree-bordered roadway. Then on with rapid steps, for Keese seemed intent upon making speed and therefore increased it as they advanced until Katherine panted with the exertion. How long she walked in that manner, how far they went while he grasped her by the wrist, Katherine did not know; but they came to a stop suddenly and she realized that they were actually beside the car.

"Betty!" she called out, startled in spite of her courage, lest her friend should not be waiting there after all.

But the reply came instantly.

"Here, Kittie," Betty called back from the darkness; and Katherine drew a swift breath of relief.

"We will have no talking now. Save that until later," Keese ordered.

Then the head-lights of the car were switched on and by the refraction from them Katherine could see that Betty was perched in the rumble seat, and that a man—the chauffeur, she decided—stood beside the car, waiting. She was assisted into one of the remaining two seats. Keese sprang into the other one, under the steering wheel. The engine was humming. The chauffeur seated himself at the side of the car, at Katherine's feet. The next moment they were plunging forward through the night at a rate of speed that was foolhardy under the circumstances, but against which Katherine made no protest.

Twice during the first few minutes she half turned in her seat to speak to Betty, but each time Benton Keese interrupted her with savage earnestness by saying:

"If you don't want me to ditch the car, sit tight and keep still." The last time he added:

"You will have plenty of opportunity to talk later."

Nevertheless after that second effort Betty managed to bend forward and to say into Katherine's ear:

"Benton forced me to come with him, dear; but I am glad he did so. Be brave, Kittie, for I won't let him harm you."

Betty meant, too, to keep her word if she could.

218

CHAPTER XL

IN PURSUIT OF THE GRAY CAR

Highways in that part of Connecticut which is among the hills just back of the Norwalks make many twists and curves. It is a locality of rocks and boulders, of hills and dales and streams—and so the flashes from the powerful headlights of Benton Keese's car shot in almost every conceivable direction at one time and another as they plunged forward through the darkness.

If you should, with a scrap of paper and a pencil, make a deeply concave loop nearly like a wide and round-bottomed letter V it would be a fairly good plan of the road that Benton Keese's car followed from the red schoolhouse when Betty first became a passenger upon it. The car stopped at the bottom of the loop. There, Keese got down and made the rest of his way to the Ghost house, on foot—nearly straight ahead; and to that point Keese returned later with Katherine, and the car went onward. Along the left side of the loop which ultimately emerged again upon another traveled highway as broad and wide and well kept as that one which passes in front of the red schoolhouse.

Rushton, seated beside Black Julius, endeavored to approximate the probable time that Keese had been gone from the schoolhouse when they discovered his escape; and he did it cleverly, as it turned out. He figured that the escape could not have been made as it was made—or would not have been—unless the man who had assisted the prisoner had also been a witness to his capture and had gone into the schoolhouse by the rear door as Rushton and Banta came out of it at the front.

Rushton and his companion had remained seated on the schoolhouse steps, talking, a long time before the darkness settled so densely that they thought it wise to go forward to the roadside in order not to miss the lights of Harvard's car when it should appear. And so, taking it all together, the ex-lieutenant believed that Keese had very nearly an hour the start of them when the actual chase began. What he did not know, and could not estimate upon, was the time that Keese lost while his car waited for him to go after Katherine. Only Rushton did figure that Keese would be obliged to make a stop somewhere, for Katherine was not then with him, and hence she was temporarily detained in the neighborhood, and Keese was undoubtedly going after her. Rushton recalled something of the character of Lady Kate, too, as he did not for a moment imagine that she would not resist with all her power a journey in Benton Keese's car, against her will. Thus he figured on delay.

He reasoned, silently of course, that the hour, and possibly a trifle more, would be very greatly lessened; that Keese would not be more than half an hour, and perhaps much less than that, in advance of them.

It was a sharp bend in the road where Keese's car had waited for him. Julius was compelled to slow down considerably; and as they were making it Rushton called out to him to stop. With his flash-light he studied the roadway, which was at a depression there; and as a consequence was sandy, made so by rainy intervals, when the water had washed miniature gutters in the ancient roadbed. Rushton was out of the car only a few moments. When he returned to it and had directed Julius to drive on, he turned in his seat and said:

"He stopped back there. He went somewhere down that branch in the road. He went on foot, because his car couldn't get through. But he did bring Lady Kate back with him. She is a passenger in his car now. Anyhow, he brought a woman back with him, and it must have been her. I found her tracks in the sand."

They shot onward after that. Several times as they advanced Rushton could see flashes of light far ahead of them that reached like fingers across the perspective, and he knew that they were made by the lights of another car. He hoped it was the car they were pursuing. It was not possible to guess the destination toward which Keese was making, only the general direction—nor did Rushton lose that when they ran out upon the highway. He stopped Julius again, and got down to make further studies with the aid of his flash-light.

"He is going to New York, all right," he announced as he reëntered the car. "Hit it up, Julius—only be careful not to hit anything else."

Bingham Harvard, in the rear, seated beside Clancy, was reminded, in spite of the strain upon him, of another wild ride he had once taken with Julius as chauffeur, in the days when he was called "The Night Wind," and at a time when he was forced to establish an *alibi* for himself in order to protect Lady Kate. That was long before she became his bride, or he had supposed she ever would be.

Harvard was strangely silent during the chase after Keese's car. At times when Tom Clancy attempted conversation or offered suggestions Harvard merely nodded; and even his best friend, as Clancy surely was, would have been amazed to know of the tempest that was raging within him.

For the "Night Wind," in all that the name implied, was aroused. All of the abnormal, unnatural strength that was bound within his muscles strained at the leashes of his self-control, eager to be free, to rend, and break, and destroy; for Bingham Harvard kept silent and motionless only because he was struggling inwardly for that self-control which he knew he must retain when they should catch up with Keese. He knew that if it failed him then Keese would be broken and torn apart and crushed and killed. Only those men who have to fight against themselves can appreciate the magnitude of that struggle of Harvard's that had been going on since the first moment of suspicion against Keese concerning what really had happened.

The outcome of the pursuit of Keese for the rescue of Lady Kate, Harvard never once doubted; but it did not lessen by one whit or jot or tittle the magnitude of the offense of the attempt.

They ran into Stamford and through it, pausing for a moment only to make inquiries for a gray roadster that had preceded them.

"Yes," a uniformed policeman told them, "a gray car, with a woman in the rumble seat and another beside the driver and a second man seated on the floor of the car, passed through twenty minutes ago."

The next definite information was received at the foot of the hill, passing through Rye. The gray car, again as graphically described, had gone past not more than fifteen minutes ahead of them. They fairly flew through Harrison and on into the border of Mamaroneck and down the hill which dips toward the railway station of the latter place, and stopped at the corner where the road branches if one wishes to take the short cut to Orient Point.

A group had collected there. A disabled taxicab, with one tire exploded and the wheel of it twisted out of shape, made the central figure of the gathering, and beside it a young woman was talking excitedly while she pointed straight ahead toward the station. Harvard and Rushton leaped from their car at the same instant, for the young woman was Betty Keese, and the man she addressed in such evident excitement was Anderson Van Cleve.

Close beside him Banta stood listening. Near by, white and frightened, was another man, cringing and cowering in the grasp of a big Mamaroneck policeman. The wrecked taxi was the one in which Van Cleve and Banta had been returning to the city.

Harvard, with the strength of a dozen men, threw the members of that group aside like straws and confronted the three persons he had recognized.

"Where is the gray car? Where is Katherine?" he demanded.

"There! They went straight on!" Betty cried out excitedly. "The taxi turned in front of us when we were trying to pass it. That man, Ben's chauffeur, was thrown off. I jumped. I was in the rumble. I saw Katherine try to jump out, but Ben held her back."

Harvard and Rushton turned and leaped into Harvard's car again. Clancy picked up Betty in his arms and put her into it after them. Then he clung to the door and clambered in after the car had started ahead. Van Cleve shouted after them:

"We'll get another car and follow." Banta called out: "Try the White Plains road!"

"Keep straight ahead, Julius," Rushton ordered. "That cop back there told me that the gray car was limping. I think they've got a puncture."

"Tell me of Katherine," Harvard demanded of Betty in a tone that was ominous in its enforced gentleness.

"She is not hurt at all, Mr. Harvard!" Betty cried out in reply. "Benton is trying to carry her off, away from you. He told me last Monday that he intended to do it. He is mad, crazy, beside himself—and desperate."

"I should have told you. I should—"

"Yes, you should have told me," Harvard replied.

CHAPTER XLI

THE NIGHT WIND'S PROMISE

The gray car had been limping, as the officer told Rushton. Moreover, Keese discovered soon after he ran into the taxi that the task of driving it and at the same time keeping a tight grasp upon Katherine's arm, so that she would not jump, was an extremely difficult one. For Katherine had made the attempt, as Betty said; and she repeated it before they had gone a dozen rods farther. When they flew past the railway station she tried it again, and Keese, in holding her, lost his control of the steering-wheel for the fraction of an instant, so that they swerved dangerously near to a big limousine they were passing, and she called out, too, to several men who stood on the platform of the station as they passed.

They flew across the main street of Mamaroneck, narrowly missing a passing trolley car, and on again past the poor huts of houses that were beyond it, and then into the darker road again. But one of the tires had collapsed, and Keese was wise enough to know that the time would be short after that before he was overtaken. He kept on as he was going for another half-mile, then turned into the road that leads toward the Sound; and there presently his headlights picked up an open gateway into a lane beside an old and deserted brown frame house that was doorless and windowless and but little better than a ruin. Keese guided the gray car into that lane.

It was a desperate chance; but there was no other way, and there was the possibility that the pursuing car might pass on. He guided the roadster with difficulty, for it was necessary still to cling to his captive. But he succeeded in taking it around behind the house, nevertheless; and there he came to a stop.

Katherine again tried to leap out, but he caught her and held her. She called aloud with all her voice-power, and he clapped one hand over her lips and held it there. Then she raised her right hand and, with the palm open, struck him squarely in the face. The blow maddened him—who was already mad. He seized her, snarling an imprecation that even he would not have used in her presence had he not been utterly crazed. He lifted her from the car. He crushed her against him so that she could not struggle. He ran with her up the rickety steps of the still more unsteady back stoop of the old house.

Katherine tried to struggle out of his grasp, but he held her firmly. But she could, and she did, call out for help—and he stopped at the top of the steps, turning his face to hers, with a savage gleam in his eyes and a snarling expression of rage upon his lips. He raised his hand as if to strike her, to compel her silence. Perhaps he intended it only as a threat; perhaps he did intend to deliver the blow. But that will never be known.

The shaky, uncertain footing of the old stoop gave way beneath them, incapable as it was of supporting their double weight. A crash, a rending of boards, a cloud of pungent dust from rotting wood, assailed them as they fell through the ruin of the old stoop. It was a short fall, and Katherine was uppermost when they struck, and the litter of debris that cluttered down upon them spared her, mercifully.

Partly dazed, but still intent upon making her escape from the madman—and by then she was wholly convinced that he was indeed mad—she sprang up and away from him instantly, nor turned to look backward as she sped away across the broken boards and through the opening where the short flight of steps had been but a moment before. Convinced that Keese would pursue her, she ran on swiftly down the lane to the ruined gate, past it into the roadway—and straight into the blinding glare of an approaching car.

Then things happened swiftly. There was a grinding and crunching of brakes. Three men and a woman sprang from the car and ran toward her. She straightened and stood white and pale, but smiling bravely notwithstanding. And then Bingham Harvard's arms encircled her, and held her, and nearly crushed her.

Rushton waited to see only that much; then he ran on past them, toward the lane and into it, flashing his light ahead of him as he ran.

Harvard slowly released his wife from that close embrace. Then he lifted her as if she had been a feather and carried her to the car. He put her inside and turned away, but Katherine reached out a detaining hand and grasped his sleeve.

"Wait, Bingham," she said softly. "Where are you going?"

"There," he replied with a quick jerk of his head. "After *him*."

"Please don't," she pleaded.

"I must," he said. "I must."

"Then promise me—promise me, dear, that you will control yourself; that you will not hurt him. Promise me, dear."

"I cannot," he said.

"I am not hurt, Bingham. I am safe. I am not worse for this experience. And, dear, he is Betty's brother—and he is mad, quite mad. Promise me, dear."

Harvard was silent an instant, struggling mightily with himself. Then he looked into the eyes of his wife, tried to smile, and replied simply:

"I promise, sweetheart."

CHAPTER XLII

SUPPLYING THE PROOFS

Harvard found Rushton standing with folded arms in the midst of the ruin of the old stoop, looking down upon a prostrate and motionless figure of a man that had been Benton Keese. For Benton Keese, otherwise Holbrook Chilton, was dead when Rushton got to him. He had been dead when Katherine sprang away from him and fled down the lane toward the road. Death had followed instantly upon his fall. A large and rusted wire nail with the point of it uppermost, part and parcel with the ruin he had wrought, fatefully awaited him when he fell upon his back beneath Katherine, whom he had still been holding tightly clasped in his arms. And by the force of his own weight, and hers, it had gone into his head almost its entire length, just at the base of the skull. The consequence had been instantaneous.

Between them, Harvard and Rushton lifted the still form and bore it outside; and for a moment after that Harvard stood quite still beside all that remained of the once handsome, if erring, Benton Keese. Rushton came up beside him and touched him on the arm.

"Come away," he said gently. "We must tell the others, Mr. Harvard."

"Shall I tell you of what I was thinking just then, Rushton?" Harvard asked soberly.

"Yes, please."

"I was thanking God, in my heart, that *I* didn't do that; for, as He has judged him, and will one day judge me, I would have done it—but for my promise to my wife. And, God only knows, I might not have had the strength to keep that promise."

226

"Well," Rushton muttered as he turned away, "if you had done it, Mr. Harvard, I'd have been willin' to help, some."

"Wait," Harvard ordered suddenly. "I had forgotten Betty. Stay here, Rushton. *I* will tell his sister. She must not see—"

He stopped as he was turning. Betty, with Tom Clancy beside her, was there. She did not speak. She uttered no sound as she went forward and bent over the still form of her brother. But, after a moment, she got down upon her knees beside him and closed down his eyelids. Then she kissed the smooth, wide forehead; and then she rose up and turned about—and went straight into the out-stretched arms of Tom Clancy. And the sobs that she could no longer control were muffled and presently stilled in his embrace.

Mr. Van Cleve and Banta arrived on the scene in a hired car a few moments later; and then—but the conventional details that followed need not be described.

* * * * * * *

The express package that Rushton had been expecting did not arrive until the middle of the week that followed. It had been greatly delayed in transit, and—

But Fate had so willed that the contents of it should not be needed. Nevertheless, during the afternoon of the day that followed upon its receipt, Rodney Rushton made his appearance at the Centropolis Bank and passed through it to the office of the president. Harvard received him with a cordial smile and handshake, and then conducted him into the directors' room where, seated around the table, were all of the members of that former conference that had been held there, save only Lady Kate.

She was not present. She had gone to Kentucky with Betty to help her, and to support her friend through the last sad duties that could be performed for Benton Keese. It was understood that Betty was to return with her and remain with her until the period of mourning was past and she could put Tom Clancy's ring on her finger for all time.

Inside of the directors' room of the bank behind closed doors Rushton addressed those present in his characteristic style, after previously placing upon the table before him some sheets of paper which bore strange and interesting marks upon them.

"I asked you to meet me here this afternoon," he said, "because this case ain't exactly closed and put away in the archives until we

227

are all satisfied with the positive proof of the fact that Benton Keese *was* Holbrook Chilton. Likewise, to announce in this official manner to all of you that all of the dough that he got away with so slick,—except a little over six thousand dollars which he spent, has been recovered. Banta an' me found most of it in a safe deposit compartment that he had hired as Keese; the rest of it was on his person when he was killed and in his rooms at the Mammoth. Also in that same safe deposit we found the two photographs that he took of himself in Mexico as Chilton and sent to Mr. Harvard for Mr. Van Cleve's pictures."

"And now, these." He bent forward and touched the papers on the table in front of him. "That evening when Keese was lying dead out there this side of Mamaroneck, while I was keeping watch while the others were makin' arrangements to bring him away, I managed to take some prints of his fingers and thumbs, unbeknown to the rest of the bunch. These, here, are *them*."

"And *these*, here, are the ones that a chap named Corona sent to me from the city of Mexico. I have had both sets down at headquarters for a private examination by the expert. Banta and the chief, here, was with me; and so, gentlemen, I wish to state to you that the finger and thumb prints of Chilton, found in Mexico, and the ones I made of Benton Keese a few moments after he was killed, are of the same man, and there isn't any doubt of it. And—that is about all, I guess."

* * * * * * *

After the others had gone from the bank, Rushton lingered behind with the man he had learned to love with all the intensity with which he had once hated him; and Harvard, leaning back in his chair with a smile on his face, nodded his head and said:

"You need not ask the question that is on your mind, Rushton. I know what it is, and I will reply to it. *You have made good.*"

"That's what I wanted to ask you, all right, all right," Rushton replied with feeling. "I can't tell you how much I thank—"

"Don't try, Rushton. You do tell me, in acts that are better than words, a hundred times a day—ever since you have been my confidential man here in the bank. But that leads me to something that I want to say, Rushton."

"Well, sir?"

"There are better things for you than remaining here with me on a salary and being confined to the mere work of this bank. You should branch out, as Redhead did once. And you could still do this work for me."

"I have thought that I would like to do that, Mr. Harvard; but, you see—" he hesitated.

"Well? What is it?"

"I'm still a convict—on parole."

"Are you? Take a look at this paper and see if you are"; and Harvard took a document from one of his pockets and gave it to Rushton. The latter accepted it, looked upon it, and his eyes bulged. Then tears of joy rushed unbidden into them.

"God!" he said, then. "Thank God! And you! Oh, I am the happiest guy that ever breathed! I'm—I'm—"

Words failed him. He dropped upon a chair and buried his face in his hands. Harvard turned to his desk and busied himself with some papers. It was a full pardon, signed by the governor of the state, that Bingham Harvard, once *alias* "The Night Wind," had given to former Lieutenant Rodney Rushton.

* * * * * * *

Just one word more.

Betty Keese was married to Tom Clancy at the end of the year. And that fact, so far as this story is concerned, brings us to the end.

ABOUT THE EDITOR

Christopher R. Yates is only called that when he is in deep, deep trouble. Otherwise, it's just "Chris." He holds a B.A. in English Literature and a Juris Doctorate. Chris has several identities, none of them secret however: Nancy's Husband, Ben & Audrey's Dad, and Assistant United States Attorney.

In 2001 he authored *The Web* for a reprint of the *Master of the Flaming Horde*, the fiftieth installment of *The Spider Magazine* originally published in 1937 (Bold Venture Press, 2001). He was a fan of hero pulps years before, but actually seeing his name in print snapped Chris' tenuous link to reality propelling him into the ranks of "disturbingly obsessive fans of hero pulps."

He is the editor of three re-releases of the original novels of the Night Wind series: *Alias "The Night Wind," The Return of "The Night Wind"*, and this title, *The Night Wind's Promise* (Wildside Press, 2007, 2008). He contributed the Foreword to *Alias "The Night Wind,"* and *The Night Wind's Promise*. Chris is also the editor for the re-release of the fourth of the original Night Wind novels; *The Lady of the Night Wind*, forthcoming from Wildside Press.

Currently, Chris is penning an all new Night Wind novel—*Behold "The Night Wind"*—for publication by Wildside Press in late 2008. Simultaneously, he and his lovely wife, Nancy, are translating and adapting the first English novelization of the French silent film *Judex* (1917) by Arthur Bernède and Louis Feuillade for publication by Black Coat Press.